Good-bye City, Hello Boonies

I pulled my hand free. "I've got to go."

"Baby, don't go away hurt. I can always tell when you're hurt. But you're going to be OK. We're both going to be fine. In a few weeks, we'll be back together. Things will be just like always."

The bus rolled out of the station and down through the gray city streets. For a few minutes, I watched the buildings and the crowds sliding by, then leaned back and closed my eyes. Good-bye city, hello boonies.

Other Scholastic books
you might enjoy:

Sheila's Dying
by Alden R. Carter

Wrestling with Honor
by David Klass

City Light
by Harry Mazer

A Band of Angels
by Julian F. Thompson

Blitzcat
by Robert Westall

Life Without Friends
by Ellen Emerson White

SCHOLASTIC INC.
New York Toronto London Auckland Sydney

point

UP COUNTRY

Alden R. Carter

SCHOLASTIC INC.
New York Toronto London Auckland Sydney

ACKNOWLEDGMENTS

Many thanks to all who helped with *Up Country*,. particularly my editor, Refna Wilkin; my mother, Hilda Carter Fletcher; and my friends Don Beyer, Dean Markwardt, Georgette Frazer, Judy Davis, Wayne Lauterbach, Tom Hayden, John Callahan, and Bob Levendoske. As always, my wife, Carol, deserves much of the credit.

ISBN 0-590-43638-4

12 11 10 9 8 7 6 5 4 3 2 1   1 2 3 4 5 6/9

Printed in the U.S.A.   01

First Scholastic printing, July 1991

For Dale, Melody, Autumn, and Casey Shadis

First Scholastic printing, July 1991

MY STOMACH TRIED TO FALL THROUGH MY shoes when I saw the cop's blue uniform through the window at the top of the basement stairs. I took a step back into the shadows and tried to stifle my fear. Take it easy, jerk, I told myself. Chances are your old lady got busted again, that's all. And if that ain't it, there's still no damn way they can pin anything on you.

I thought of checking the half dozen car stereos on my workbench. But I'd been careful to discard all the pieces of broken dashboard, and no evidence remained that I was anything but a humble repairman. My inner voice growled, Are you sure, jerk? Are you damn sure? Ya, I was sure. And, I told myself again, it was probably just something to do with Mom anyway.

I hadn't heard her come in during the night, but that wasn't unusual since I often fell asleep with my headphones on. That way, if she brought home one of her "classy guys," I slept through the noise of partying and later the squeaking of bedsprings and the other sounds that drifted into the basement from her bedroom above. I waited, hoping to hear her door open and the sound of her voice: "Ya, ya. I heard you. Keep your shorts on."

Nothing. I was alone in the house with the Law on the doorstep. I felt a slow drop of sweat slide down my side. Maybe this time it had really happened. Maybe the cop was going to tell me that they'd pulled Mom from a car wreck and laid her like a bloody rag doll on a slab in the city morgue. I'd tried to prepare myself for that news a thousand times. I'd have to go there to identify the body, following some faceless attendant down the long line of sheet-covered corpses, each with a naked foot sticking out and a dangling identification tag wired to a big toe. Would I recognize Mom from the outline of her body or the polish on her toenails? Or would I have to wait while the attendant checked tags? (What would hers say? "Veronica Staggers, age 38, no embalming necessary"? Something like that.) Then the starched sheet whipped back and the question: Is that your mother?

The cop rang the bell again and added a few loud knocks. I took a deep breath. Come on, jerk. Keep it together. Your trouble or hers, you've got to answer the door. Now be cool. Look young and innocent.

The cop's face was red with the December cold. I swung the door inward. "Hi. Sorry it took so long. You caught me in the shower." Oh, great, I thought. Start out with a lie; you're not even damp. "Or, uh, about to get in it, that is."

The cop gave me a cold stare. Typical Milwaukee cop, I thought. Give him three seconds, and he'll figure out something to pin on your ass. "Carl Staggers?"

"Yes, sir."

"May I come in?"

"Oh, ya, sure. Sorry."

He walked ahead of me into the kitchen, giving the dirty floor and the littered table a quick, appraising look. He turned, leaned against a counter, and inspected me. His mouth twitched, and I suddenly grasped that he was trying to put on a sympathetic expression. My God, maybe she really was dead! "I'm sorry to be the bearer of bad news, but your mother got in some trouble last night."

"Is she OK? I mean, was there an accident?"

"No, a fight. She's OK, but a couple of other people aren't. Do you know a Mr. Stanley Morris?"

"Never heard of him."

"A couple of people at the bar said that she'd been going out with him."

I shrugged. "Mom's got a lot of friends."

"Well, from what I saw, she tried to kill this one. Laid his head open with a bottle. Took sixty-some stitches to close his scalp, and I don't know how many to sew up his face. He's in the hospital with a concussion. Your mother's in the county jail."

I felt my knees start to go, and I leaned against the opposite counter to steady myself. I felt his eyes boring into me. "When did this happen?" I asked weakly.

"We got the call about one-fifteen, but we didn't get her until about three. She went out the back door and tried to walk home. We found her in the three-hundred block of Fifth. And she didn't do herself any good then." The cop's mouth twitched slightly. Had he almost smiled? "As a matter of fact, she kicked my partner in the nuts, then ran down an alley. But there were some rats in there, so she came out and gave up. That was about the only smart thing she did."

He paused, watching me. I could guess how he saw me—a skinny kid with zits and too much hair, hugging himself and staring at the floor. Pathetic little jerk. I felt suddenly cold and angry. I met his stare. "So why are you here?"

My unfriendly tone didn't faze him. "Your mother started yelling this morning that they couldn't keep her in jail because she had a kid at home. The dispatcher told me to come over and check on you."

"I'm OK. Nobody's got to worry about me. What's going to happen to her?"

"She'll appear before the judge at ten. He'll set a court date and bail. You can be there if you want." He straightened up to go. "Between you and me, bud, I think your mom's got a big problem with the booze.

She'd better do something about it pretty soon." He waited for a reply, but I didn't give him one. "Well, her car is still down at Gator's. Maybe you'll want to see to it."

I let him out and watched until I was sure he was actually leaving. I could imagine him turning around at the last moment: "By the way, bud, we've been meaning to ask you a few questions about a zillion dollars' worth of stolen stereo equipment. Seems your fingerprints are on every damn piece of it." He left.

My stomach had found its way back from my shoes and growled that it could use some feeding. As usual, there wasn't much food around. Well, I'd made more than one breakfast of Coke, peanut butter, and stale bread. I cleared a place at the table and sat down to think while I ate. I was still in the clear, but the old lady was in the tank again. What did this make it? Three, or was it four times? At least she'd had sense enough not to drive the car this time—one more ticket for drunk driving and she could kiss her license good-bye for the rest of the century. Would she need bail money this time? In the past, they'd always let her out on her signature, but she'd never laid open a dude's head with a bottle before. Or kicked a cop in the balls. Way to go, Mom.

I checked a second slice of bread for mold, spread peanut butter on it, and tried to remember if I'd ever met Stanley Morris. No luck. Hell, who could keep track of all Mom's classy guys? Not me—not even if I'd given a damn.

As long as I could remember, men had come and gone pretty fast in Mom's life. Back before her looks started to go, one of them might hang around for a few months, maybe a year. I'd even let myself get chummy with a couple of the more durable ones. I'd listen to how they were going to take us to the zoo or to a ball game or on a weekend in the country. Big talk, big plans, all adding up to a lot of bull. If I was real lucky, the guy might give me a couple of bucks so I'd be out of the house long enough for him to get it on with Mom. "Here, sonny, run down to the store for some ice cream." And off I'd go, thinking that this guy might be different from all the others.

But that was before I learned a couple of damn tough lessons and moved to the basement. Mom could sell herself cheap, but not me. She never quite caught on that I'd moved out of her life. If she wasn't too drunk or too horny, she'd nag me until I finally came up to meet her latest guy. In the kitchen, she'd get me ready for the big introduction. "Baby, I think this guy might really be the one. I mean, he's got money and he's got class. I mean real class. Stand up straight and be real nice. If I can swing it, this guy might be your new dad." Ya, right. I'd given up believing in new dads around the time I'd entered third grade.

Somewhere way back, I'd had an old dad. I couldn't remember the s.o.b., but Mom had shown me a snapshot once—a tall, lanky guy who looked kind of like a cowboy. My old man, the cowboy. That's how I always thought of him after that. When I was a kid, I'd think about him while I was trying to fall asleep. I'd imagine him coming to the door in a Stetson, work shirt, and jeans. He'd talk to Mom, quiet but firm. Then he'd take me with him. We'd drive west in a battered pickup truck with two horses in a trailer behind—a big gray for him and a small gentle brown for me. And I'd curl up beside him, breathing the warm smell of leather, horses, and a man who worked for an honest living. He'd put a long, muscular arm around me, and I'd let myself relax in his warmth. Just before falling asleep, I'd look up a last time to see his laughing blue eyes squinted against the glare of the setting sun. And for a little while, I really was in that pickup with my dad.

But he was never there in the morning. He'd never existed at all—or at least not the way I imagined him. Mom said my real dad had been "some loser I felt sorry for when I was a kid." He hadn't been a cowboy. As far as she could recall, he'd never been much of anything. I remember her sneering at the snapshot before shoving it back into her jumbled scrapbook. "Ya, I gave him everything I could, but that just wasn't good enough for the selfish bastard. One day he took off, and I never heard from him again. Just one more bastard added to all the others I've known."

Bastard. That's one of her favorite words. I wonder if she ever realizes that I qualify better than most of the guys who've done her dirt. She says I was "a love child." Ya, right. Pretty neat how love makes so many bastards in this world.

Well, Mr. Stanley Morris had apparently joined Mom's list of bastards, and all this thinking wasn't doing a damn thing about the fact that she was in jail for bashing him with a bottle. I washed down the last of my sandwich and zinged the Coke can at the wastebasket across the room. It bounced against the wall and rolled behind the refrigerator. To hell with it.

I was peeved at myself. I rarely let myself get sloppy about the past or all the lousy breaks I'd had in life. Just forget it, jerk, I told myself. Keep the lid screwed down tight on all the snakes because nothing matters anymore except the Plan.

I got my coat and started getting ready to face the cold. Most of my Saturday was screwed up, but maybe I could get something worthwhile done tonight. Get Ronnie out of the tank and off to work if she could make it, then try to earn a few bucks at my workbench. Every cent moved the Plan forward another tiny step.

Outside, I pulled on my stocking cap and hunched my shoulders against the wind. I didn't feel like riding the bus, so I headed for Steve's. A block from the house, I stopped for a moment to think. Maybe I should bring some money for bail. No, screw that. Let one of her classy guys bail her out; I was saving my money for a worthwhile cause.

Steve got the beat-up Chevy going.

"I hope this car's not hot," I said.

He laughed. "No, I picked it up for two hundred bucks. Beauty, huh? Got five hundred for my Dodge and figure I can make a buck on this one too."

"If it doesn't fall apart first."

"Don't worry. This thing's built like a tank."

"Sounds like one, too."

"Ya, wish it had the cannon. We could give up this petty crap and get into robbing banks." He reached out a long arm to turn on the radio, the tattooed snake on the back of his hand wriggling as he adjusted the dial. The speakers popped, hissed, then started playing something that sounded vaguely like rock and roll.

"Why don't you ever have a decent stereo? God knows, you've stolen enough of them."

"Why don't you just fix this one? I thought you could fix anything."

"I can, but it might take me a month, and you'll probably own this car about three weeks."

"Could be longer, could be shorter." He lit a cigarette. "Want one, or you still being Mr. Clean?"

"I'll join the rest of you sinners today."

We smoked slowly as the dirty, snowy streets passed. It was still early, but the Christmas shoppers were already out in force. Two weeks until Santa comes. Ho, ho, screwing ho. "How'd you guys do last night?" I asked.

"Good. Hit a parking lot in Brown Deer. Never been to that one before. Quiet, dark, no hassles. Got four there and another one on a back street."

"Good ones, I hope."

"We're following the list, professor. If it ain't one of the brands you put down, we're leaving it alone."

"You got 'em out clean?"

"Not too bad. Charlie is getting better with the pry bar. Doesn't just smash hell out of the dash and pull out what's left. I took time to pull a set of speakers out of a Caddy. Just couldn't resist screwing up that rich bastard's car as much as I could."

I grunted. Most speakers weren't worth the trouble, and I'd told him a dozen times not to take the added risk. "Well, better not drop the stuff by until I call. The old lady might not be going to work tonight. Maybe not at all if they fire her."

"Anytime. They're in the trunk."

"In the trunk!" I yelped. "Damn it, Steve. I told you not to drive around with the stuff in the trunk. Not with me in the car. You may not give a damn, but I'm not going to get hung if I can help it!"

"*Relax,* professor. Nobody's going to get busted."

I stared at him. He had a smile on his thin face. My inner voice said, Well, there you go, jerk. You've got everything riding on a bunch of real winners. One screwup, and you and the Plan are right down the tubes. How many scholarships do convicted felons get? How many companies hire electrical engineers who got their

14

early training fixing stolen stereos? Think about it, jerk. No scholarship means no degree, no job, no money, no home in the suburbs, no BMW, and no decent life. You'll end up holding some petty bullshit job and marrying someone just like your old la— I kicked my inner voice in the teeth before it could get out that last word. "Give me another cigarette."

"Sure, professor. Is that the turn up ahead?"

"Ya, then down two blocks."

Mom's maroon Ford stood at the curb half a block from Gator's, where she worked as a waitress—she preferred to call herself a hostess—and sometimes tended bar. Gator's tries to put on that it's a class place, but it never made it past garish. It attracts pro and semipro hookers, visiting businessmen looking for a fast time, and a few regulars hoping to load up on free drinks when the big spenders start throwing money around to impress the ladies. I hate the place.

"Think it'll start OK?" Steve asked when I got out.

"If nobody's ripped off the battery." I unlocked the Ford and slid in behind the wheel. The engine ground and caught. Steve waved and rumbled off.

I found the right courtroom about quarter to ten. The hall outside was already crowded with people—a lot of anger, desperation, and fear in the air. The Law was about to start kicking ass. I spotted Mom in a corner, talking with a young guy in a three-piece suit. Public defender, I thought.

Mom looked terrible: her clothes wrinkled, her hair uncombed, her eyes bloodshot and angry. I maneuvered through the crowd to her side without her seeing me. She was almost yelling. "They had me in that hole with a bunch of whores, bag ladies, and drunks. Just scum, I tell you. Where do they get off doing that to decent people? I'm going to sue them, that's what I'm going to do!"

The public defender took a deep breath. "Mrs. Staggers, please keep your voice down. None of that has anything to do with what's going to happen in the next few minutes. You have been arrested for serious offenses. We can talk about how you were treated later on. But now we have to decide how to answer some questions."

Mom noticed me. She grabbed me by the shoulder and pulled me close to her side. "This is my baby. He'll tell you I'm a decent person. That guy was trying to assault me, and I had every right to defend myself. He's the one who should be here, not me. And those cops. Christ, those cops attacked me! I oughta charge them with police brutality."

The public defender sighed. "That may be so, Mrs. Staggers, but the fact remains that you're the one who's about to see the judge. Now, if you go in there ranting and raving, they'll stick you right back in jail. When your hearing comes up, you'll have a chance to say your piece."

I pulled a comb from my pocket. "Comb your hair, Mom. It's a mess."

That got her attention. She took the comb and started pulling it angrily through her bleached hair. "Won't even let a lady keep her purse, for God's sake." The public defender opened a folder and started asking questions.

Mom stood beside the public defender while a fat court officer read the police report out loud. He finished. "Your Honor, these officers are known to me, and

I consider their reports to be highly reliable." He sat down.

The assistant district attorney started in. "Your Honor, Mrs. Staggers has a record of disorderly conduct and alcohol-related driving offenses. I request that a bail be set in the amount of one thousand dollars to ensure her appearance at the hearing."

It was the public defender's turn. "Your Honor, I submit that one thousand dollars is an unreasonable amount for a woman of limited income. Mrs. Staggers has a young son to support and care for. I request that she be released on a signature bond."

The judge shuffled papers, then gazed at Mom over the top of his glasses. "Mrs. Staggers, we have two serious charges here: aggravated battery and resisting arrest. I do not think a thousand-dollar bond is unreasonable. However, considering your parental responsibilities, I will set bond at one hundred and fifty dollars on each charge." He glanced down at his papers. "I'm going to set a hearing date of January seventeenth. Will you provide your own attorney, or will you be using the services of the public defender's office?" Mom seemed to have lost her voice on stepping before the judge. She gestured weakly at the public defender. The judge said, "Very well, the public defender's office will provide representation." He rapped the gavel. "Next case."

Mom and the public defender went out a side door. I followed, trying to look invisible. Mom was talking desperately to the public defender, while a bored female deputy watched from a few feet away. "I don't have three hundred dollars. I only had maybe twenty in my purse and—"

"Mrs. Staggers, I really can't help you with that. Perhaps your son can find some way to get the money. Here's my card. Call my office on Monday for an appointment. Now, please excuse me; I have another client to represent." He hurried off.

Mom looked at the deputy. "What do I do?" The deputy shrugged. "Are you going to put me back in jail?"

"You can wait here while your boy gets the money."

Mom turned to me. "Do you have it? I know you've made money fixing stuff in the basement. Have you got three hundred dollars?"

"Mom, do you suppose Gator could lend it to you?"

"No, no! I can't ask him. I'm afraid he's going to fire me anyway. Can you get it, baby? Please?"

I stared at her red-rimmed, pleading eyes. "Ya, I'll get it. You just take it easy. Sit down and rest."

She gave me a hug and a wet kiss. "You're my pal. My best guy. I can always count on you."

"Come on, Mom. Not here. Now just stay cool for a while."

I was fuming by the time I got home. Three hundred bucks I'd never see again—gone just as sure as if I flushed it down the crapper. God, you are a jerk, Staggers. Why the hell did you tell her you had the money? Let her spend a few days in jail. Big difference it'd make in your life. I got a beer from the refrigerator and drank half of it before going down to the basement. I reached behind the furnace and pulled the box away from the opening to the hiding place where I kept my money and all the evidence that could send me to jail for a hell of a lot longer than Mom. I hesitated. Damn it, I needed this money. If I kept letting Mom run my life, I'd never get out of this town. Might as well kiss the Plan good-bye and be a bum like most of the people I knew.

I sat at my workbench and tried to think. Maybe I ought to drop by the bar and see if I could talk Gator into coming up with her bail. My gaze fell on the box I'd pulled from behind the furnace. My old baseball glove poked through a tear in one of the flaps. Mom had given me that glove one Christmas, then spent hours outside in the cold trying to teach me how to use it. Oh, crap. Why did I have to remember that now? Why did I have to remember that, once upon a time, she'd really tried to be a good mother? She wasn't any damn good at it, but she'd tried. I lifted my beer and let the last few drops fall on the back of my tongue. OK, jerk, let's go get her out.

Back at the courthouse, I handed Mom the money, then stood around while she signed forms and got her stuff back. In the car, the first thing she said was, "God, I need a drink. Drive over to Eighth. There's a pretty good bar there."

We sat in the stale-smoke spilled-beer darkness of the bar. Mom pounded three bourbon-and-Cokes. I drank my Coke straight. I was hoping we'd get out soon, but then she spotted a friend. "Hey, Linda! Over here." Linda came over—another burned-out blonde who needed low lights to look half decent. "You remember my baby, don't you?"

"Who could forget a handsome guy like him?" She reached out to hug me.

"Hey, hands off; he's just a kid. His cherry's still on the tree and no one the likes of you is going to get it." They giggled, and I felt my face go hot, half in embarrassment, half in anger. "Hey, did you hear what that scumbag Stan Morris did to me last night? Boy, I really fixed him. Just before closing—"

"Mom, I've got a couple of things to do. Don't you want to clean up and get some rest before work?"

"Naaa, I'm OK. Take the car and go home. Play with your stereo junk. I want to talk to Linda for a while. Later, I'll walk over to Gator's and clean up a little in the ladies' room. Or maybe I'll call and say I can't work tonight. Me and Linda might go out cruisin' for some classy guys." They both started giggling again. I shrugged and started to leave. "Hey, give me ten bucks before you go." I hesitated. "Come on, come on. I'll pay you back."

I pulled the last ten out of my wallet, shoved it roughly into her hand, and left. Over my shoulder, I heard Linda say, "What's with him?" and Mom reply, "Aaah, he's just that way. Moody kid. Can't never have a good time. Now let me tell you what I did to that bastard Morris . . ."

MOM HADN'T TAUGHT ME A LOT, BUT BY GOD, she'd taught me how to bounce back. She was drinking again; I was working again.

I tackled the stereos on my bench. All but one had survived in pretty good shape; the guys were getting better. Steve, Charlie, and Dave worked fast: one holding a light, one doing the work, and the third standing lookout. They'd jimmy the door, then go at the dash with a pry bar, hammer, and a heavy screwdriver. With a little luck, they could get a stereo out in less than fifteen minutes.

I replaced the wires and connectors on the back of a Sony and checked for other damage. No problems. Now for the ownership change. I retrieved the stickers I'd made on the school's laser printer from the hiding place behind the furnace. I replaced the serial-number sticker on the Sony, wrapped the unit in plastic, and packed it carefully in a box from the gross I'd ordered. Three strips of packing tape and the package was ready for my crowning stroke of genius. I peeled an orange sticker and slapped it in place: "Reconditioned Stereo Component—S & M Electronics, Los Angeles, CA." One Sony stereo—not stolen, but reconditioned—to be sold to an unknowing customer at a cheap but extremely profitable price. I wrote a figure on the box. Steve would knock the usual five bucks off and then offer speakers at ten bucks more than we'd paid at the discount store. And, of course, Professor Carl Staggers would happily install the system in any car fast, cheap, and right. Humming, I reached for the next unit.

My life of crime had begun late one afternoon in the spring of my freshman year. I'd answered the door to find Steve standing in a chill April drizzle. "I read in the school newspaper that you fix electronic stuff cheap."

I was wary; I knew Steve had a lousy reputation. "I fix equipment at a reasonable price. That usually means cheap."

"Well, I got a cassette player here that don't work worth squat." He pulled a discount-store model from a paper bag and handed it to me.

I glanced it over. "What'd you do? Drop this from a helicopter?"

"Something like that."

"Well, let me run a couple of tests."

He followed me to the basement. "My name's Steve Sheridan."

"Ya, I've seen you around. How you doing?"

"Good." He watched me work for a few minutes, then lost interest. "Mind if I have a smoke?"

"Go ahead."

He lit up and surveyed my makeshift apartment. "You live down here or something?" I nodded. "Don't it get kinda damp?"

"Not too bad. I like the privacy."

He grunted and stared again at the stereo. "So, can you fix it?"

"Just a second." I ran another check. "OK, I know what's wrong with it. Come back tomorrow. It'll cost you five bucks."

"Sounds good." He stubbed out his cigarette. A thin trickle of blood oozed from under a large, dirty bandage on the back of his hand. He stared at it. "Oh, crap. You got any bandages, man?"

I dug in a drawer and slid a can of them across to him. "What happened?"

"Ah, I've been working on this tattoo. Damn thing's gotten infected." He stuck long fingernails under the old bandage and tore it away to reveal a crudely tattooed snake on the purplish skin of his hand.

I felt instantly nauseous, but I didn't let it show. "You better take care of that. It looks like hell."

"Ya. Hurts like hell too." He got three strip bandages awkwardly in place. He didn't ask for help, and I didn't offer any. After he left, I spent ten minutes fixing the stereo. I could have let him wait, but I needed time to think through a hunch.

By the next afternoon, I'd made a decision. I hid a heavy crescent wrench beneath a rag on the far side of my ohmmeter, then rehearsed my lines. As I'd expected, Steve showed up carrying two more broken units. "These are kind of screwed up too."

I ran a few pointless tests on them. Steve sat smoking, his gaze focused vaguely on the far corner of the basement where I had my bed, dresser, lamp, and clothes rack. "Where'd you get these?" I asked.

"From a junkyard my uncle owns."

I snapped the cover on a Realistic and tightened it down. "Well, I can't help you."

"Huh?" He stared at me. "How come? You lose the knack overnight or something?"

"Oh, I'm not saying I can't fix them. I can fix damn near anything that runs on electricity. I'm saying I won't."

His eyes narrowed. "How come?"

I leaned back, my right hand lying casually on the heavy wrench beneath the rag. "Because I could get in some very deep shit for fixing stolen property."

His voice got soft and dangerous. "Ya? And who says they're stolen?"

"I do, and any repairman with half a brain would tell you the same thing."

For a long moment our stares locked. He'd strike first with the hand that had the snake. I'd have to pivot and swing the wrench sidearm, hoping to end things quick. A hell of a lot easier said than done. My God, I must be crazy; he was going to kill me. Instead, he reached for the units, shoved them in his paper bag, and started for the stairs. "That'll be five bucks for the first one," I said. He hesitated, then pulled a crumpled five from his pocket and tossed it on the workbench. "Thanks," I said. "And, by the way, I could tell you how to get them out clean."

That stopped him. He stared at me. "What'd you say?"

"I said I could tell you how to get them out clean. There are some tricks that would save a lot of time and damage."

He sat down slowly. "What's the deal?"

"I get a cut. That's if, and only if, I figure you're running a safe operation."

He lit a cigarette, then offered the pack to me. I took one. Suddenly, he grinned. "Well, I'll be damned. Nothing goes beyond here, right?" I nodded. "OK. What do you need to know?"

I asked questions. The three of them had been at it less than two months. They hit parking lots and "targets of opportunity," as Steve called them. They took not only stereos, but batteries, wheel covers, and everything else they could get loose in a hurry. They'd started out selling the stuff to junkyards, but the profits were too low. Recently, they'd begun putting the word around school that they had stuff to sell cheap.

I shook my head. "You guys are going to get nailed."

"We're being careful."

"Oh, bull. Everybody's going to know the stuff's hot."

"Well, there's no way around that. We can't open a parts store or a junkyard."

"No, but there's got to be a safer way."

"Like what?"

"Let me work it out. I'll talk to you in a day or two." I got up. "Leave the stereos. I'll fix them tonight."

"OK. Want to come with us tonight and give some lessons?"

"Not a chance. Not tonight, not ever. All you need are some better tools and a little advice. I'll do the repair work and figure out a safe way for you to sell the stuff. I don't get involved beyond that. Don't even tell your buddies that we've got a deal."

Two days later, we founded S & M Electronics, Milwaukee Division. Steve didn't catch the joke until I suggested a whips-and-chains logo. Well, I wasn't going to be traveling in the brightest company. I taught him how to pull a stereo with minimum damage, gave him a list of the models worth stealing, and told him to leave car batteries and wheel covers alone. We'd concentrate on one line and do it as safely as possible.

Part of my strategy involved keeping my distance from Steve. In school, I barely nodded to him. Outside school, I rarely saw him except when he delivered or picked up stereos. I kept the installation side of the business separate, never admitting to a customer that I was more than casually acquainted with Steve. And, as far as I knew, Steve had kept his word about not telling anyone—not even Charlie or Dave—that I was part of the operation. My precautions seemed to amuse Steve. He thought I was a nerd—a dishonest one, but still a nerd. But I didn't give a damn what he thought of me. We were using each other, and I was getting the better half of it.

I finished the last of the stereos a little after seven. I leaned back, rubbing my eyes. My stomach grumbled, but I didn't feel like another peanut-butter sandwich. Well, it was Saturday night; maybe I could afford to splurge on some junk food.

Getting my coat from the closet, I remembered that I hadn't checked the mail yet. I got it from the box and sat down at the kitchen table to look through it. A new electronics catalogue—leave that for later. Junk. More junk. Oh, oh, a letter from the bank. I opened it and scanned the lines: mortgage past due, come in to discuss refinancing, otherwise legal action a possibility, etc. Still, it was a form letter, which meant they weren't about to send an eviction notice. I tossed it aside and picked up the last envelope in the pile. It was a Christmas card from Aunt June, Uncle Glen, and their kids. I opened it and read Aunt June's careful script:

> Dear Veronica and Carl,
>   The house is quiet this year with all our children gone except Robert, who's sixteen now and looking forward to getting out from under his mother's thumb. He's doing OK in his sophomore year, although I have to keep after him on the homework. He'd rather be outside chasing rabbits with his twenty-two or earning some money trapping. But girls are a new interest, so the twenty-two and the traps may get some rest this winter. But not his mother. Still, we've been through it with three other boys, so I guess we can do it again.

Norm writes from Sacramento, where he's working for a building contractor. He and Paula have two little ones now. Would love to see them, but Norm says they're going to visit Paula's folks in Seattle this Christmas. Well, maybe next year. Ted still likes the Navy and is thinking about signing up for another hitch when his first is over next summer. Pete joined the Marines last spring and hopes that he can get together with Ted in Hawaii for the holidays. They didn't invite us to fly over. But with the recent plane crashes, I'm not sure I'd want to go even if we could afford it. Seems they always happen in the holiday season, doesn't it?

I'm in my sixth year as head cook at the school. Can hardly believe I've been shoveling hot dish at kids for more than a decade now. Your lummox of a brother is still working for the county highway department. He keeps talking about retiring early (he's 52 now) and opening a bait shop and guiding service. And I keep telling him I'll get a divorce if he does. But it's all in good fun. We thank God that our health and our sense of humor are holding up through another long winter in the North. We remember you in our prayers and hope all is well with you too. Come and see us sometime.

Love, June, Glen, and the boys

Better start praying harder, I thought. I examined the face of the cheap card: a family of deer stood outside the glowing window of a cabin, watching Santa Claus put presents under a tree. Real classy, I thought. Well, at least we're still on their Christmas-card list. Maybe I ought to send them one. What could I write on it?

> Dear Relatives who I wouldn't recognize on the street:
>
> Pretty much the same old crap around here. Mom got busted by the cops again. I had to fork over three hundred bucks to bail her out, which really pissed me off since I worked damn hard for that money fixing stolen stereos and doing the thinking for a gang of real losers. Otherwise, things are pretty boring. Would like to get laid, but don't know any girls willing to do the laying. Still, Mom's making up for both of us on that score.
>
> Can't think of much more to write. We don't pray much around here, but hope you hicks are OK. Do us a favor and don't drop by if you're in town. You wouldn't like us or the dump we live in. And, anyway, what's the point of seeing each other once every eight years or so? Keep those once-a-year cards coming.
>
> Love, Carl and Ronnie

Well, that would really give them a charge. But nobody ever wrote stuff that honest. My stomach grumbled again, and I tossed the card on top of the bank notice. Let Mom answer both of them. Hell, she had more experience lying than I did. I wondered if she'd get her act together well enough to do it.

Driving to the nearby Mac's, I tried to picture the up-country Staggers. Maybe I'd still recognize Uncle Glen from that one visit they'd made so long ago. He was a huge guy with a big grin and a big laugh. I'd liked him.

I didn't remember much about Aunt June and the kids. She'd brought brownies, that much I remembered. And I remembered going for a walk with Bob, who was my age, and one of the older ones. Pete probably. Ya, the walk. I could remember that pretty clearly, once I tried. I'd felt inferior to those athletic country kids. To make up for it, I'd bragged about how tough the kids were in our neighborhood. Pete and Bob hadn't seemed much impressed. I think we'd just put up with each other until the afternoon ended and they'd driven away, heading toward that distant someplace politely called "up north," or otherwise, "the boonies."

I got my supper from the drive-up window and ate in the parking lot, letting my mind wander. Suddenly, I realized that I was feeling pretty good. Weird. Mom had spent part of last night in jail and was probably loaded again tonight. I had no girl, no close friends, and nowhere to go on a Saturday night. Still, I felt pretty good.

I've got this reflex about happiness. The voice in my head always says, Hey, jerk, don't set yourself up for a fall. Find something to worry about. But tonight I wanted to hold on to the good feeling a little longer. I fell back on my favorite fantasy.

I was lost in adding details to the Plan when the passenger door popped open and Steve slid in. "Hi, professor. Hey, don't get so jumpy; it's just your partner in crime."

I let out my breath. "What are you doing here?"

"For a bright guy, you ain't a great observer." He opened a carry-out bag and started wolfing down a Big Mac. "My damn Chevy wouldn't start, so I had to walk. Figured I might run into someone here. Not you, though. I thought you spent Saturday nights up to your ass in transistors and stuff." His words came fast and his foot tapped a quick rhythm on the floorboard. High on something, I thought. "So, where we goin' next?"

I hesitated, wary but tempted. I could use some fun. I didn't really like Steve, but I had to admit that I didn't have a lot of friends to pick from. A friend I didn't like. Made about as much sense as most things. "I don't know. You got any ideas?"

"Let's cruise for a while. See if we can spot some girls."

In two blocks, Steve had inhaled two Big Macs, a large order of fries, and a shake. He looked back, then chucked the bag out the window. "Hey," I said, "don't do that, damn it. You know what the fine is for littering?"

"Littering? God, the man's into felonies and he worries about littering." He grinned. "But you worry good, man. Better than anyone I know."

"If you had any damn brains, you'd worry about getting picked up with dope on you."

"Dope?" He slapped his pockets. "Hey, you're right, I do have some dope." He pulled a plastic bag from his pocket. "Want some?"

"Maybe later." What the hell was I doing with this idiot in my car? I took a side street into a quieter neighborhood.

Steve turned up the radio and began tapping his foot and humming off-key. "Hey, what'd the cops do to your old lady?"

I reached over and turned down the volume. "Let her out on bail." I told him the details.

"How'd she take it?"

"Started drinking. Probably feels OK now. Change the subject, huh?"

He shrugged. "Sure. So, tell me about yourself, professor. Hell, we've been in business going on a year, and I still don't know nothin' about you."

30

Ya, and we probably ought to keep it that way, I thought. "I sleep, eat, go to school, and get by. And I fix electronic equipment. There isn't a whole lot more to say."

"Where'd you learn all that stuff about eee-lec-tron-icks?"

I ignored the sarcasm. "Some from books, mostly from just messing around with the stuff."

"Sounds dull as hell to me." He gave an exaggerated shiver. "Brrrr. Books, science, experiments—too damn much like school, if you ask me. . . . Hey, look at that Buick sitting all alone. I bet that's got a good one. Got any tools?"

"No! And I wouldn't stop if I did."

He laughed. "Professor, we have got to get you away from that workbench. You're losing all your sense of adventure, screwing around with that boring crap."

"I don't need your kind of adventure." I thought of adding, "And electronics is not boring." But I couldn't explain that to Steve, who was probably about two-thirds brain dead already.

Not many people can tell you the day and the hour when their lives changed forever. But I can. On a bright afternoon in the October of my seventh-grade year, my science class trooped outside to see an experiment. Mr. Emmons strung a long wire from a spindly tree to the center of the basketball court, then spent a couple of minutes attaching some tiny gizmos to the end. I watched indifferently from my place near the back. We'd been studying electricity for a week, and I was only vaguely interested. Not that I wouldn't do well on the test; I almost always did, no matter what the subject.

"Carl, you can be the first victim." For some reason, he'd picked me from the crowd. I made my way to the front, uncomfortable with being the center of attention.

He handed me the headphones. "Tell us what you hear."

I don't know what I expected—maybe some popping or hissing that would explain something about electricity. Instead, I heard a radio station playing, faint but clear. My jaw must have dropped a foot. "It's a radio!" I looked at the two tiny components in the loop between the long wire and the headphones. "Is that all you need? I mean, it doesn't even have a battery!"

He grinned. "I'll explain in a minute. Give somebody else a turn." I stood back and watched. How the hell had he done it? It must be some kind of trick.

When all the kids had listened—few of them seeming much surprised—he explained: "Class, radio waves are all around us. It doesn't take much to pick them up: some wire for an antenna, a diode, an RF choke, and a pair of crystal headphones." He looked at me. "A simple radio doesn't even need a battery or household current. The power of the radio wave alone is enough to make the radio work. Now, class, what part do you suppose converts the radio wave into electricity?"

Some of the kids in the back were screwing around, and no one looked about to give an answer. "The antenna," I said.

"Right. Did everyone hear Carl? Come on, settle down. Now, you've studied about diodes in the text. What do you suppose this one does?" He waited for an answer. I could have told him, but I was already too busy working out a dozen more complicated questions. "Come on. Who can tell me about diodes?" He started calling on kids, finally getting a correct answer after four or five tries. After that, he gave up trying to conduct class outside. He sighed. "OK, kids, let's go back to the room."

"Can I listen again?" I asked.

"Sure. Bring the headphones when you're done. Let's go, kids." He herded them toward the door, leaving me standing alone, listening to the magic.

I left school that afternoon with three books on electronics and sat up long after midnight reading. The diagrams seemed to pull me in. I could almost feel the electricity flowing in the circuits—silent, invisible stuff that could work miracles. But yet it was so simple, so clean. You could change it, switch it, send it firing this way and that so easily. For the first time in my life, I'd discovered something that was completely, absolutely predictable. You only had to learn the rules.

In two weeks, I'd read every book on electricity and electronics in the school library. I was itching to try some experiments, but when I begged Mom for a little money for equipment, she wouldn't listen. "I can't afford any of that junk. Get a paper route or something."

"Earth calling the professor. Earth calling the professor." I glanced at Steve. He grinned. "You going someplace or you just in a holding pattern? We've been around this block three times."

"Sorry. Something you said got me thinking. Where do you want to go?"

"Let's go to my place and get a few tools. I want a look inside that Buick."

I drove to his house. "Let me have those stereos in your trunk," I said.

We loaded them into my car. The last one was unusually heavy, and I gave it a closer look. "Where'd you get this one?"

He glanced at it. "Oh, ya. I meant to tell you about that one. It wasn't on your list, but it was so easy I took it anyway. It was in this crazy hippie van. I figured anybody driving something painted up with all sorts of stars and rainbows and stuff probably had some dope lying around. So I popped the door and had a look. I didn't find any dope, but that stereo was just sticking out of the glove compartment with nothin' holding it but some tape. I just pulled it out, snipped the wires, and walked away." He looked at the stereo again. "Something special about it?"

"No," I lied. "I just hadn't heard of the make before."

He slammed the trunk lid. "Well, so much for this batch. Give me a second to get my screwdriver, and we'll go have a look inside that Buick."

"I'm not going with you, Steve. You know I don't get into that part of it."

"Aw, just this once."

"No. That's final."

He looked at me in exasperation. "Well, hell, let's smoke a joint, then. Maybe that'll turn you into a human being."

"Go ahead and light 'er up, but it won't change my mind."

When we'd smoked the joint, he dug a half-full bottle of wine from behind some old tires. He took a gulp and handed me the bottle. "So, what are you doing with your share of all the money we're making, professor?"

"Saving it. I've got plans."

"School, or something interesting?"

"An engineering college just as far away from here as I can get."

"Going to go straight, huh?"

"You bet."

"You plan too much. I figure, spend your money now before you lose it. Hell, they could drop the bomb tomorrow. *Baaarrooom*, we're all crispy critters." He giggled.

The dope and the wine started talking, and I couldn't shut myself up. "Look, I've worked damned hard to get this far. When I first wanted to learn about electronics, I had to get up before dawn to collect aluminum cans so I could buy equipment. The street people used to chase me off their turf, but I kept looking anyway. If you want to piss your money away, go ahead, but I've got a plan. A damn big plan."

He smirked. "What? Going to be an astronaut or something?"

"No, I'm going to be an electrical engineer."

"Wow. Big plan. Impresses me all to hell."

I felt my face get hot. "What do you want to be, huh? A two-bit thief all your life? Or are you going to give up crime and just hang around waiting for a break? Well, not me. I'm getting out!"

"Hey, steady, professor. Grass brings out the beastie in you. Relax and have another hit on the wine." He watched me take a drink that I didn't need. He smiled faintly. "You've just got to relax, professor. Live in the now."

"Screw the now. I don't like it." My inner voice was telling me to shut up, but I didn't pay attention. "You know what I've got now? Shit. You tell me your old lady is always on your ass, but that's at least something. I don't think mine would notice me if I hung myself in the basement. All she cares about is drinking and chasing her classy guys. And maybe your old man is a jerk. But at least you've got one. Mine took off fifteen years ago, and since then my old lady's had one bum after another. Our house is a dump, and this neighborhood is a dump. And you tell me to relax and spend my money? Why? So I can stick around here? That's a lot of bull, man. I'm busting my butt for good grades so I can win the biggest scholarship around. Then, bye-bye Milwaukee and everything in it. I'm gone. History."

For once I'd gotten through, and he wasn't smirking anymore. "I always kinda figured you had something like that in mind. You ain't mixed up in this just for the fast bucks, are you? You're crapping on society now, but you're going to join up later."

"You're damn right. And when you buy in, nobody cares where you got the money."

He stood watching me for a moment, then took the last swig from the bottle and turned away to hide it behind the tires. "You know why I do it?" he asked. "It ain't just the bucks. I like screwing up some bastard's car. Even if maybe he ain't really a bastard and doesn't have any more money than I got. I still like it." He looked at me. "That's why I'm going back to that Buick now. You coming or not?"

"No. It doesn't fit in my plan."

"OK. We'll see you, professor."

I drove home, my vision a little blurry. Real good, jerk. Make one mistake now, and the cops will bust you for drunken driving, transporting stolen property, and about two dozen other things. I made it OK, and sat behind the wheel for a minute with my eyes closed. Then I grinned. Now for a closer look.

In the basement, I piled the stereos on my workbench and picked up the unit Steve had taken from the hippie van. I'd been right. It was a top-of-the-line Blaupunkt, probably the finest brand of car stereo in the world. I connected power to it and, holding my breath, switched it on. Beautiful—not a grain of static or a twitch of oscillation. I could hear myself telling Steve: "Hey, that one from the van was completely burned out. But it was a cheap unit, anyway. Just stick to the list I gave you." He'd never know the difference, and someday I'd put the Blaupunkt in a car of my own. Whistling, I packed it in a box and stuck it under my workbench.

I didn't feel like tackling the others so late at night, but the voice inside me growled: Don't be stupid. Follow the rules, jerk. I lined them up and started removing the broken pieces of dashboard, dropping the chunks in a bag at my feet. It was after midnight before I had the last one cleaned up. I walked the two blocks to the Quick Stop and tossed the bag into the dumpster. Maybe I'd removed only the most obvious evidence, but it made me feel better.

I opened my eyes and listened for noises upstairs. My clock said ten to nine, but I still hadn't heard Mom popping the top on her breakfast beer or cursing because she couldn't find the aspirin. Well, maybe she'd stayed with one of her guys. Or maybe . . . I pushed the other possibilities from my head. The police could tell me later.

Getting dressed, I replayed my conversation with Steve. The voice inside me said, You talk too stinking much, jerk. You can't let *anybody* know so damn much—especially a reckless ass like Sheridan. The voice was right. But at least Steve knew now that I was one damn serious guy. Maybe he'd lay off the smirking hints that I was a nerd. Oh, hell, who cared what he thought? My stomach growled, Feed me. I headed for the kitchen.

Mom sat at the kitchen table, slowly stirring a cup of coffee. She looked up at me. A leech could have eaten itself to death on the blood veins showing in her eyes. "Hi, baby."

"Mom. I, uh, didn't know you were home." I glanced into the next room.

"It's OK. Nobody's with me." She added another teaspoon of sugar to her cup and stirred.

"What time did you get in?" She shrugged. "Everything OK at Gator's?"

"Ya, everything's OK. Gator ain't going to fire me."

I checked in the cupboards and refrigerator, hoping I'd missed something the last time. Not even bread or chips left. Well, we still had Coke, peanut butter, and crackers. And beer too. So why wasn't she killing her hangover with it? I brought my food to the table. "We're going to have to do some shopping."

She nodded. "We'll do that today. We've got to get a lot of things done today." Uh-oh, I thought; we haven't had one of these in months. Maybe I should suggest she have a couple of beers. Get her leveled out before she can start. But it was too late. "I've been doing a lot of thinking, baby. A whole lot. I haven't been treating you right. Been just boozing and chasing all the time recently. Gotta get straightened out."

"Don't worry about me; I'm doing OK." Mom, just don't get into this, I thought. It won't do any good. And, by the way, what's this "recently" crap. It's been a hell of a lot longer than that.

"I know you are. You're a good kid. But you still need a mother." She sighed and lit a cigarette. "And now I've got this damn thing with the cops. I don't know what the world's coming to. Can't even defend yourself without ending up in court with some old bastard in a black gown staring down at you like you was some kinda garbage." Her lower lip started to quiver, and she put her face in her hands. Oh, just have a beer, I thought. We don't need this.

She went on. "I know I shouldn't have slugged him. But he was grabbing at me, baby! Pinching my butt and trying to feel my boobs. I slapped his hand and told him not to get fresh in public, but every time I came by he'd do it again. And the guys at the bar were laughing. You know, egging him on like I was some kind of whore anybody could paw. And I just lost my head. But I didn't mean to hit him hard. I didn't think that bottle was going to break." She was getting desperate. "Look, he even left a bruise." She started pulling up her sweater.

"It's OK, Mom. You don't have to show me."

She let it fall back in place. There were tears on her cheeks. "You believe me, don't you, baby?"

"Sure I believe you, Mom. Do you want another cup of coffee?"

She snuffled. "There ain't any. I made all I could find."

"I'll go buy some. Why don't you take a nap while I do some shopping?"

"No, I've got to clean up this pigsty."

"OK. You get started, and I'll help when I get back." I got up from the table. "Do you have any money?"

"Ya, I got Gator to pay me early. My purse is on the counter."

Standing with my back to her, I counted the money in her wallet. I'd shortchange her on the groceries today. Little by little, I'd get my three hundred and ten bucks back. "We've got to pay the mortgage one of these days," I said. "We got another notice from the bank yesterday. That's three, I think."

"I know, I know. Just don't bug me about it right now."

I am not bugging you, bitch. I'd just like to keep a roof over our heads. "OK. I'll be back soon."

I drove to the supermarket. It could go either way now. She could start drinking beer and get almost nothing done, or she could have one of her cleaning frenzies and start drinking later. Sixty-forty on the former, I decided.

I lost the bet. When I got home, she was on her hands and knees scrubbing the kitchen floor. "Give me the frozen stuff," she said. "Leave the rest on the porch. What do you want to do? Clothes or the bathroom?"

I dragged four baskets of dirty clothes to the laundromat and read my latest *Popular Electronics* while the washers churned. Not a bad way to spend an afternoon.

She was drinking a beer when I came in our back door. She grinned at me. "Look at the shine on this floor. You can damn near see yourself in it. Why, it's almost as clean as my conscience today. What do you think?"

"Floor's clean. Grab this basket, huh?"

She finished her beer while we put away clothes. Back in the kitchen, she opened another. "I've earned it," she said. "Boy, did I make the dirt fly. I'll finish the bathroom in the morning if you'll finish dusting the living room."

"Sure." I reached into the refrigerator for a beer.

"Naughty, naughty. You're not of age."

"Ya, right. But I earned it." I popped the top and sat on a chair at the table. I lit one of her cigarettes.

"Baby, I don't mind if you drink a beer now and then, but I wish you wouldn't smoke. It's a real bad habit."

"One won't kill me."

"I guess not, but please don't smoke too much."

"I won't."

"Well, I've just got time for one more brew before work." She went to the refrigerator. "Did you buy something good for your supper?"

"Pizza."

"Carl, I wish you wouldn't always buy junk food.

You're a growing boy. You ought to eat wholesome things."

"I do. Don't worry."

"Well, I do, baby. I mean, working all these late hours, I can't look after you like I should."

"I do OK."

She ruffled my hair. "I know you do. You're a good kid."

3

MOM'S REFORM LASTED LONGER THAN USUAL. For the next couple of weeks, she stayed more or less sober and got home every night not long after Gator's closed. Alone, too. I wondered how her guys were doing, having to get it at home or actually paying for it. Mom would probably get a thank-you note from the local hookers' union.

I went to school, sitting through classes with my usual lack of outward attention. I'd learned the trick years before. As long as I listened, I rarely needed to take notes or ask questions. The teachers never caught on that I was more than the average dirtball until I aced the first test. Then it would get touchy for a while. They'd start calling on me in class, but I'd never give more than the minimum answer. Now and then, one of them would try to "reach" me outside of class. A cold stare and a politely worded invitation to bug off usually cured them.

Of course, most of the kids had long since figured out my act. But since I didn't suck up to teachers or give a damn about school rules, they didn't lay any crap on me about my four-point average. In return, they could always depend on the ol' professor to let them copy a few test answers or give them enough bullshit for a quick book report. As far as real friendship . . . well, there was little of that. The ol' professor didn't make friends easily—or try very hard, either. In time, I told myself. Just wait until you're away from here.

Steve came over on the evening of the last day of school before Christmas vacation. "We are making a killing, professor. I started upping prices ten bucks and still didn't have enough to sell."

"I figured as much. The installation business is real good." I went to get the accounts book from behind the furnace. We settled up.

Steve counted out a stack of tens and twenties. "There you go, professor. Another semester's college tuition."

"Not quite, but it'll help." I made a last entry in the book, then took it back to the hiding place.

"You know, I hope no one ever finds that," he said.

"Since when have you started worrying?"

He shrugged. "It's just that we're getting pretty big time. Before, they could just nail us for petty theft. But with that book they could prove a hell of a lot more."

I'd never seen him so serious before. I took a cigarette from his pack. "Something got you worried?"

"I'm not sure. It's just kind of a feeling. Last week, we had to get out of a parking lot pretty fast. Maybe it was just Dave's imagination, but he swore he saw someone ducking between some cars. Like they were spying on us."

"Probably just a street person."

"Ya, maybe. But, the other day, this real straight-looking senior—Bill somebody—bought a stereo, then wanted to ask a whole bunch of questions."

"Like what?"

"Oh, I don't know. Just things like if S & M Electronics gave any guarantees and could he order parts from them and what did I really know about the company. Stuff like that."

"I hope to hell you didn't send him over here for an installation."

"No. I got rid of him as fast as I could."

"But he did buy a stereo?"

"Ya, that expensive Alpine."

I thought. The parking lot thing didn't bother me, but the other . . . Damn. We'd better find out something about the kid. "Look, after vacation, we'll just lie low for a few days. See if anything is coming down. . . . Say, wait a second, it wasn't Bill Hoyt, was it? Blond, glasses, about my height."

"Sounds right. Got a big gap in his front teeth."

"That's him. He's into ham radio. Probably just wanted to know if he could get ham equipment from S & M."

"You think he's OK, then? Not doing any narc work?"

"We sell stereos, not dope." I thought for another second. "Ya, I think he's probably OK. We'll still lie a little low, just to be sure."

"Sounds good to me. Well, Merry Christmas, professor. I'll bring by some stuff in a few days."

"Right. Merry Christmas." He left. I sat considering the wad of bills that represented my share of the last month's take. Hell, why not? I could afford it this year.

I rode the bus out to one of the big shopping malls, ate supper at the Mexican restaurant, then wandered around, enjoying the crowds and the holiday bustle. At the Radio Shack, I bought a few parts I needed and a digital ohmmeter—my big Christmas present to myself. What should I buy Mom? Hell, I'd already stood her bail. But her reform had begun to impress me. Maybe this time she really was going to stay straight. I priced blenders and finally bought one at Sears. Ya, she'd like it, and I could get some use out of it too.

Walking home from the bus stop through a light snow, I could see Christmas trees in the windows along our street. For once, I felt positively in tune with the season. If Mom really had reformed, this might be a Christmas to remember. The voice inside me growled,

Don't kid yourself, jerk. She's just taking a breather. Ain't nothing going to be different for long. Ya, probably, but just suppose . . .

I listened to Christmas music while I set up our artificial tree. It had seen better times, but once I had the lights strung, it began to look fairly decent. I made the best use of the couple dozen ornaments that had survived the years, then sat down with a cup of cocoa to admire my work. Maybe I'd leave the lights on the tree lit when I went to bed. It might give Mom a good feeling—make our home seem a warmer, happier place. I let my mind wander back to some of those Christmases when we'd been OK. Maybe I just hadn't noticed stuff when I was younger. Maybe she'd been drinking just as much and going to bed with just as many guys the year she'd given me the baseball glove—or even way back when we'd played together on the floor with trucks and blocks. But somehow I was sure that things really had been better once. And if she could just stay straight now, maybe—

There was a ruckus at the back door. I heard Mom's laughter and an unfamiliar voice—a guy's voice. "Hold the door. . . . OK. Got it? Now grab the other end. . . . Ouch. Damn, you almost got me in the jewels, lady. . . . OK. Here we go." There was a sliding, rustling sound and a thump. "Whew. Made it. Where's the pissoir; I'm about to burst."

"Give me a kiss first," Mom said.

I sat for a long moment with my eyes closed, then took a long breath and got up. I raised my cup in a toast to my tree. Nice while it lasted, tree. Merry Christmas. Ho, ho, screwing ho.

They still had their arms around each other. "Hi, baby," Mom said. "This classy guy with the very big Christmas tree is Charlie Wyden."

"Hi," I said.

He nearly stumbled getting over the big spruce to shake my hand. "Hi, fella, Merry Christmas. Hey, tell me where to find the pissoir. Your mom ain't letting on, and I'm about to get a rupture."

"Through the living room and take a right."

"Thanks, buddy." He slapped me on the shoulder and left in a haze of whiskey vapor.

"Come here," Mom whispered. She took me by the shoulders, her fingers a little too urgent. "Baby, this guy's got real class. I mean it this time; he's different from the others."

"Because he knows the French word for pisser?"

"Baby, don't be like that. Look at this beautiful tree he bought us. He could have bought something cheaper. But, no, he wanted the best. And I didn't even ask him to. We were just talking at the bar, and I told him how bad I felt that you were home all alone, and here it was almost Christmas and I hadn't even had time to put up a tree. And he says, 'Well, let's go buy the kid a tree.' And when I say I have to work until closing, he talks to Gator. Gave him twenty bucks to let me off early." We heard the toilet flush and the sound of the sink running. Mom leaned closer, almost knocking me over with her breath. "Please, baby, give him a chance. Don't go running off to the basement. Stay with us and help put up the tree. This guy might be the one we've been waiting for all these years. A new dad for you, a new hubby for me."

"Who says I want a new dad?"

"Baby, don't! Just don't be like that! Now you at least want a Christmas tree, don't you?"

"We've got a Christmas tree."

She looked confused for a second, then pushed by me

to the door. She spun. "Damn it. Why'd you go and do that? What's he going to think? You've gone and spoiled everything!" She was so mad that I thought she was going to slap me.

"You guys still in the kitchen?"

"Just a minute, Charlie," Mom called. She glared at me. "OK, I'll make up some excuse about the tree. But, damn it, you stay up here and be friendly! Hear?"

"I hear you."

"Hey, I thought you said you didn't have a tree, Ronnie."

Mom hurried into the living room. "Oh, that old thing. The kid put it up while I was at work. Hell, I thought we'd thrown it out last Christmas. But I guess he hid it away. You know how kids are."

I stepped over the spruce and got a beer from the refrigerator. I lit one of Mom's cigarettes and stood leaning against the counter, watching the clumps of snow on the tree slowly melting into dirty puddles.

I got hammered that night. It was the only way I could stand the long process of taking down the artificial tree and putting up the spruce. I did about ninety percent of the work, since Mom and Charlie were too busy groping each other, getting another drink, or draining off the last one in the pissoir. They didn't object when I excused myself to go to the basement. I went to bed with my headphones on, the music wailing in my ears. On the edge of sleep, I thought I heard a voice whisper deep in my head: *How does it feel to be on your own, son? Lousy, Dad, but it's made me damn tough.*

Charlie Wyden stayed with us until late Christmas day. In two days, he and Mom drank enough beer, eggnog, and whiskey to flood half the pissoirs in France. By the middle of Christmas afternoon, I couldn't take it anymore. I got my coat and went for a walk.

Why the hell was I still here? Mom wasn't going to change—not as long as her liver held out. My God, I had over two years left in high school. Twenty-nine months of watching Mom and her endless parade of classy guys marching through the kitchen on their way to the bedroom. How many more nights would I have to go to sleep with my headphones on? How many more mornings would I have to wash my face in the kitchen sink because some guy I didn't even know was puking his guts out in the bathroom? Ya, and how many more times would I find a cop at the door? Would one of them finally say, "Hey, bud, hate to tell you this, but your old lady's lying down at the morgue with her brains dangling halfway to the floor. Real nasty accident, but I told you that she should cut down on the booze."

I had to get the hell out! I'd tried all my life to love her. Maybe I'd done a lousy job of it, but—damn it—I'd tried. And it hadn't been enough. Now it was get out or die with her. I stopped and looked around me. I'd covered ten blocks since I'd last been aware of my surroundings. Not far away, I could hear the traffic on the interstate. A few more blocks, and I could be standing by the road with my thumb out. Going where? Chicago to the south, or Oshkosh, Appleton, or Green Bay to the north. Ya, but going where really? Nowhere. A kid with only a few bucks in his pocket, hitchhiking toward some dead end on the other side of a gray horizon.

But did running away have to be like that? Hell, I was no dope-crazed dropout. I was smart. I had talent. If I waited until the bank opened in the morning, I could even take a fair stake to live on. Traveler's checks. Ya, I could take the money in traveler's checks. But how about my bench equipment? How about my new ohm-meter, still lying unopened in its box because I'd promised myself that I'd wait until Christmas before using it? Well, I could carry some of my stuff. Or sell it and buy new stuff later.

Reality began trickling back. But how was I going to earn enough money for college? And how about my grade-point and my chances for a scholarship? Could I ever make the Plan work if I ran away? I stood, listening to the hiss of passing cars on the interstate. No, I had to stay, had to see it through, no matter what my mother could do to me—or to herself. But, by God, I'd have my bags packed on the night of graduation.

I started back. I had stereos to fix, money to earn, a future to plan. I'd get my calculations down fine. Work out just how many weeks, days, and hours remained before I could get free. I'd count them off, each one another link snapped from the chain holding me to her.

Mom sat at the kitchen table, an ice pack against her cheek, a drink in front of her. She looked up, her eyes red with anger and tears. "See what the bastard done to me?" She pulled the ice pack away to show a large red bruise.

I glanced quickly toward the living room. "Where is he?"

"Gone home to his wife in Chicago. I caught him talking to her on the phone. 'Yes, dear. Yes, dear. I'm sorry, dear. The car's fixed now and I'll be home by nine.' And then the lousy bastard sees me, grins, and has the damn nerve to blow me a kiss. That did it. I went for that phone, but she'd already hung up. And good old Charlie says, 'Hey, Ronnie. Settle down. I never told you I didn't have a wife.' Well, no one treats Veronica Staggers like a whore. I hauled off and slapped him." She paused to wipe away tears.

"And he slapped you back."

"Ya, and he's going to pay for it. Just wait until I get his number from the phone bill. I'm going to call his wife and tell her where he really was and what he was doing. I'm going to give her every damn detail. I'd call her now, but the damn operator said his phone number is unlisted. Stupid bitch." She drained her drink. "God, can you believe that bastard? Didn't even tell me he was married."

I felt like saying: Well, what do you expect from a guy whose only class is knowing the French word for pisser? Instead, I said, "Did he hurt you bad?" I moved closer to have a better look.

"Na. He just cuffed me the one time." She shoved the glass toward me. "Make me another drink, baby."

What was the use of telling her that she didn't need another? Hell, let her be mad at Charlie, not me. I went to the bottle on the counter and made her one.

"Well, that's it," she said. "I ain't falling for no more guys just because they got a good line. From now on, I'm waiting for class. Real class."

I can't listen to any more of this, I thought. But when I put the drink in front of her, she reached for my arm. "Sit down, baby. Stay with me a while." I sat. After a long minute, she said, "Thanks for the blender, baby. Charlie and me whipped up a bunch of daiquiris in it last night. It works real good." I didn't say anything. "The sweater. Does it fit OK, baby?"

"It fits fine, Mom." We sat in silence. Mom stared into her drink and I stared at nothing as the room turned gray in the dusk. Twenty-nine months, I thought. Eight hundred eighty-five days, give or take a few. The phone rang, and I got up to answer it. "It's Gator, Mom. He wants you to work at five."

"Tell him I can't—" She put her face in her hands, as if she was going to cry again. But then she looked up, her eyes hot. "No, wait. OK. Tell him I'll be in."

I was in the kitchen making a sandwich when she came through dressed for work. She pulled a compact from her purse and studied the makeup on her cheek. "Damn, it still shows."

"Tell them I hit you with a snowball."

She snapped the compact shut and glanced at her watch. "Crap, not even time for a brew before work. I'll tell you one thing. That bastard Charlie better never show his face around Gator's again. I won't let him off easy like I did Stan Morris." The door slammed behind her.

I ate my sandwich, then started washing all the dirty glasses and plates from the last three days. Suddenly, my eyes stung with tears. Damn it, Mom. You could have made it! Our artificial tree looked fine. You didn't need Charlie Wyden and his tree. You never needed any of them. My God, don't you have me?

That night I went to sleep thinking of Jennifer, of her long dark hair and trim figure, of her big smile and gentle laugh. Jennifer, who was cool and graceful with everybody else but warm and playful when we were alone. At the country-club parties, I'd see other men watching her, trying to imagine how it would feel to be in my place in her life. But they'd never have a chance to watch her slip out of the long dress in our bedroom, her skin smooth and dark from the hours she'd spent in the summer sun. I'd wait in bed, smiling at the funny stories she told about the people at the party until, at last, she'd turn off the light and slide between the sheets to purr like a cat in my arms.

Like me, she'd grown up keeping the world at a distance. But she'd done it with laughter, not bitterness, and she'd taught me how to do the same. She had a serious side, too—a questioning, uneasy side that kept her close to me. Sometimes, when she didn't think I'd notice, she'd study me with her big brown eyes. Then, a little later, she'd find an excuse to touch me, to put her arms around me, to tell me without words that she loved me.

During the week, she drove our red minivan to her part-time job at the local radio station. On my way to work in the black BMW, I'd hear her clear musical voice come on the air, predicting clear skies and warm temperatures on another perfect summer day. And I'd know that she was promising them to me. I spent my working hours designing electronic equipment at a big international corporation—a job that not only paid gigabucks but kept me always interested. I'd drive home tired and satisfied to find her waiting for me in our large, efficient home in one of those clean, new suburbs, where young professionals lived orderly, peaceful lives.

After supper, we'd sit out back in lawn chairs, protected from prying eyes by the tall hedge that walled the yard. We'd talk quietly about starting a family. Yes, it would be a good thing, but not just yet. Now was the time to sit contented with each other, listening to the sleepy birds, the warm breeze, and the distant sound of children playing down the block.

It had taken me a while to get the picture right, to imagine Jennifer, our home, and our lives. When I'd first designed the Plan, I'd tried to picture some of the girls at school in that place in my future. But none of them had ever seemed quite right. So, I'd invented Jennifer, and she'd become real in my dreams. Inside my head, I talked to her, brought her presents, took her on trips, and made love to her.

I was jealous of her, protected her from the reality of my life with Mom. I tried not to think of her every night, but kept her safe in the future most of the time. There were things she must never know about how I lived now. But tonight I needed her, needed to drift off to sleep dreaming of her in my arms on a summer night with a soft breeze stirring the leaves beyond our bedroom window.

I awakened to the sound of Mom popping the top on her breakfast beer. We were back to life as usual. Ya, same old shit.

I worked all the rest of the vacation. I fixed the stereos on my bench and told Steve to bring more. Screw the lying-low crap; we had money to make. If we couldn't sell the stuff safe and fast at our school, we'd look for a contact at another. We'd expand the operation, work harder and longer. Steve shrugged. "Why not? I could use the money. That new little girl of mine's got expensive tastes."

"Who is she?"

"Donna Grissom. Know her?"

"*Donna Grissom.* Ain't her old man a cop?"

He laughed. "Ya. Ironical, huh? I'm sticking it to her and the law at the same time."

"Well, for God's sake, don't say anything to her."

"Not even, 'I love you, baby'?"

"Damn it. You know what I mean. Look, not one damn hint to her about the operation. I mean it. Don't even joke about it."

He grinned. "Relax, professor. Everything's cool."

On New Year's Day, he brought me a dozen units.

The cops came at two-thirty the next morning. Mom beat them home by less than five minutes. I heard her slam the door and fumble for the lock. "Carl! Carl, baby! Get up here!"

I made it to the top of the stairs, trying to shake sleep from my foggy brain. She grabbed me by the front of my pajama top. "They're after me!"

"Who, Mom?"

"The cops! The cops, for God's sake. You've got to tell them you were driving, baby. They can't hurt you; you're just a kid."

"Mom, what happened?"

"I don't know. I don't know. I was turning a corner, and this other car pulled out in front of me and I hit him. And then I got scared. I mean, it was a bad neighborhood. So I didn't stop. But then a cop saw me." A car rounded the corner and came slowly down the street, its searchlight playing on the parked cars and house numbers. My God, they really were after her! "They're here, baby. You've got to help me!" She ran through the kitchen into the living room.

I took the stairs three at a time. I'd just buckled the belt on my jeans when I heard heavy knocking at the door. I climbed the stairs, trying to get my act together. A tall, tough-looking cop stood outside. "Yes, sir?" I said.

"Does that car belong to someone in this house?"

"Yes, sir."

"We want to talk to the driver."

"Uh, I drove it last."

"When?"

"I just got home."

His partner, a shorter, heavier guy, finished talking on the squad's radio and started for the house, pausing to examine the crushed fender on Mom's car. "What'd you find out, Frank?" the tall cop called.

"She's got several priors. A drunk driving and some others."

The tall cop turned to me again. "Where is she?"

"Who?"

"Don't play stupid. Veronica Staggers."

"I, uh, don't know where she is."

He stared at me. "May we come in?"

"Uh, sure, I suppose so."

They took up a lot of space in the kitchen. The tall cop looked down at me. "Why don't you go get her?"

"I told you, I was driving."

"Bull. You've got sleep in your eyes and your pajama tops are hanging out."

"Well, I, uh, hurried and—"

"You go get her, or we'll find her." The other cop shined his flashlight down the basement stairs.

"She's not down there," I yelped. "I mean, she's not home."

The tall cop looked at me in disgust, then started into the living room, a hand on his nightstick. We followed him. "Mrs. Staggers, this is the police. Come out here and let us talk to you."

Mom came out of her bedroom in a bathrobe. She yawned into a fist—it was a lousy act. "Is that boy in trouble again?"

"I think you're the one in trouble, Mrs. Staggers. Let's just drop the acting. The officer in the other unit got a pretty fair ID on you before he stopped to check on the victim."

"The victim?" She stared.

"The old man in that car you hit. I'm putting you under arrest for operating while intoxicated and hit and run with an injury involved. Frank, read Mrs. Staggers her rights."

Mom backed into the corner by the table she calls her desk. "It wasn't me! The kid had the car tonight."

The tall cop took a step toward her. "Come on, Mrs. Staggers, none of this is doing—"

Mom panicked. She grabbed the lump of quartz she uses as a paperweight and held it high over her head. "Get away from me, you bastard."

Both cops had their nightsticks out in a flash. The shorter cop snapped at me, "Sit down over there and be quiet."

I sat. The tall cop said very carefully, "Mrs. Staggers, put that down. You're in enough trouble already. Put it down, and we won't add resisting arrest."

For a second, time seemed frozen. Light glinted on the quartz, and I could hear Mom's ragged breathing. Then she screamed and hurled the rock at the cop. He ducked, but not fast enough. It ricocheted off his shoulder and crashed into the far corner of the room. Mom was pulling at the table drawer. What she hoped to find there I've never figured out, but the shorter cop jerked his revolver free and leveled it at her. "Freeze, lady!" I lunged for him. He tried to block me with his nightstick, but I got his other arm, the revolver cold under my hand. A roar shook the room, and my hand blazed with pain. The cop swore and kicked my legs out from under me. He came down hard on my back, his nightstick across the side of my neck. "Don't you *move*, stupid."

Across the room, the tall cop had spun Mom against the wall, one big hand twisting her right arm up behind her. She let out a yelp of pain. He fumbled for cuffs.

"Give me your other arm! *Now*." He twisted harder, and she screamed. He snapped the cuffs on her wrists. "On the floor!" She went down, whining with the pain. He pinned her there with a knee. "You OK, Frank?"

The shorter cop shifted his weight, the nightstick grinding my face against the carpet. "Ya. The stupid kid grabbed my gun. His thumb must have hit the trigger. Burned the hell out of his hand on the cylinder."

They paused, both breathing heavily. "God, I hate this domestic crap," the tall cop muttered. "Where'd the bullet go?"

They looked around. "Over there in the wall," the shorter cop said. "Wouldn't have gone through at that angle."

"Would you please get off her?" I croaked.

"You shut up," the shorter cop said, pushing down with the nightstick so hard that my cheekbone screamed with pain. But the tall cop took his knee from Mom's back. She was sobbing "It wasn't me" over and over again.

The shorter cop nudged me hard. "You going to do anything dumb if I let you up?"

"No," I whispered.

"OK. Get up." He stood behind me with a hand bending my wrist down just to the point of pain. I knew he could drive me howling to my knees with a tiny movement.

The tall cop checked the pockets of Mom's bathrobe. "OK, Mrs. Staggers, it's over. Let's get going." He hauled her to her feet. The bathrobe flapped around her bare legs and feet. "Crap. We can't take her like this. She'll freeze her ass off." He looked at me. "You're going to help her on with her clothes, kid. You got it?" I nodded.

Mom sat on the bed, the tall cop holding on to her handcuffs from behind, the shorter one watching me as I slid her slacks over her ankles. She stared down at me, then whispered, "You let them in. You let them in so they could take me away."

WE RODE IN THE CAGE BEHIND THE TWO cops. For a few minutes, I thought Mom had passed out, but then she bounced back. She started softly, trying to make her pleading sound reasonable. But when the cops ignored her, she came apart. In a few blocks, she was yelling, sobbing, begging, and threatening. I leaned forward, trying to shut out the sounds. Stop it, Mom. For God's sake, stop it.

The shorter cop slashed his nightstick against the cage. "Shut up, lady! Shut up, or we'll find something else to pin on you." Mom started to say something, but he slammed the nightstick against the cage again. "I said, *shut up!*"

"Jeez, Frank. Take it easy," the tall cop said.

"Stupid bitch . . . Do you know I'll probably have to go through that damn safety course again? All because I didn't watch that stupid kid closer. Shit."

The tall cop shrugged. "Ya, well, things happen."

Mom turned to me, whispering frantically. "Baby, they don't got nothing on us. We can say—" I pressed my forehead hard against the cold glass of the window, trying not to hear. "Baby, don't turn away from me!" She sobbed, and I felt my face scrunch up. I fought back the tears. God, don't let me start crying. Let me keep something for myself. She collapsed into the opposite corner.

The black desk sergeant pushed his glasses up on his nose and surveyed us. "What do ya got, Jim?"

"Veronica Staggers," the tall cop said. "Hit and run with injury, DWI, resisting arrest. Kid tried to interfere with the arrest."

Mom tried to get closer. "Sergeant, they've got it all wrong. It wasn't me—"

"Stick her in a holding cell. Put the kid over there." The sergeant looked down at his paperwork.

"Listen to me, you black bas—" The tall cop gave Mom's cuffs a twist and she gave a gasp of pain. He propelled her down the hall and through a door.

The shorter cop led me to a long wooden bench, already half filled with dozing derelicts and sullen toughs. He looked at me for a long few seconds, then said, "Hell, even you ain't dumb enough to try anything here." He unfastened my cuffs. "Sit down and wait your turn." He left through the door where the tall cop had taken Mom.

My fingers shook uncontrollably, and the powder burn on my palm throbbed. I pressed my hands between my knees and stared at the dirty floor. My God, we were finished. This time they'd lock up both of us. Hell, I was in worse trouble than Mom. One quick look in our basement, and they'd nail me for a dozen felonies. And the charge of attacking a cop would prove I was dangerous. They'd put me away, far and deep away.

It took an almost physical effort to slam my brain into gear. Shut up, jerk. Lose your cool now, and you'll lose everything. And I mean every goddamn single thing. I tried to think things through. Was my alibi of being just a humble repairman good enough? No, I'd been kidding myself all along. Somehow I had to get all those stereos out of the basement. I'd call Steve. Hell, they gave you a phone call, right? But suppose a cop overheard me? They might even have the phone tapped.

Maybe Steve could catch a hint the cops would miss. Bright he wasn't, but—

"Come on, kid." The shorter cop was back. Too late even for a phone call. I followed him to a desk. "Sit down." He rummaged in a drawer, then tossed a tube of burn salve across to me. "Don't use it all." He rolled a form into a typewriter and started asking questions— name, age, phone number, and so on. He didn't tell me what had happened to Mom, and I didn't ask.

Across the room, I saw a tall, thin guy with a graying beard talking to the tall cop. The bearded guy came over a few minutes later. "Patrolman Trezewski, I'm Rich Mullan, intake worker."

They shook hands. The cop handed him the form. "He's all yours."

Mullan read the form, then looked at me with tired blue eyes. "Carl, I'm from social services. Patrolman Schmidt gave me a rundown on what happened tonight. He also told me that the police aren't going to press charges on your involvement."

My stomach jolted with surprise. My God, was I going to get out of this after all? I glanced at the shorter cop. "Uh, thanks." He gave me a look that let me know it hadn't been his decision.

The social worker went on. "Your mother is being taken to DePaul Rehabilitation Center for an alcohol-dependency evaluation. She'll be there until her court appearance on Tuesday. So, we have to make arrangements for your care until the court decides whether to release her or to hold her in custody."

"I'm all right. You don't have to worry about me."

"I'm afraid I do. Now here are your rights." He handed me a different form. I read it. Basically, I had the right to a lawyer and the right to keep my mouth shut. "If you understand, sign at the bottom."

"Uh, I don't see what the deal is here. If they're not going to charge me, why can't I just go home?"

"The law says that a minor has the right to protection, supervision, and care. That's what I'm here to arrange."

"Ya, but I've taken care of myself for years. I mean, Mom works at night, so I've had lots of practice. I'll be OK on my own."

"That might be so, but the present circumstances don't allow me to release you into your own custody." He held up a bony hand to stop my protest. "Now, if you disagree with my placement decision, you have the right to see a judge within twenty-four hours. But, for the moment, just sign that you understand your rights."

The voice inside me said, Go easy, jerk. The cops could change their minds and lock you up. I shrugged and signed the form.

He started adding to the form the cop had typed. "Do you have any relatives you can stay with?" I shook my head. "Do you have a minister or anyone who could arrange for you to stay with a family?" I shook my head. He sighed. "Do you have any relatives in another town?"

"An aunt and uncle in Blind River."

"That's way up north, isn't it?" I nodded. "Would one of them drive down here?"

I shrugged. "I doubt it. We haven't seen them in maybe eight years."

"Well, I'd better get their names anyway."

"June and Glen Staggers."

He wrote that down, then checked over the form. "OK, we'll have to put you in an emergency foster home for now." I started to say something, then stopped myself. Easy now. Wait. He handed a copy of the form to the cop and stood. "We're done here. My car's out back."

Inside his aging Volvo, he said, "Want a smoke?"

"Thanks."

"We're going to take a run by your house. You'll need some clothes."

I gave it my best shot. "Look, really, this is all a lot of trouble for nothing. You don't have to take me to a foster home. I'll be fine at my own house."

He sighed again, sounding about a million years old. "Friend, I suggest you just relax and ride this out. You're going to be in a foster home until the court makes a determination about your mother. Now, as I said, you have the right to request a hearing." He glanced at me. "But I wouldn't be telling you the truth if I didn't say that it's not going to do much good. I'm an officer of the court, and the judge usually listens to me."

I felt my anger rising. Who the hell did this turkey think he was? "Look, I don't want to go to a foster home. I'm sixteen, and I'll be fine by myself. Can't you get that straight?"

The s.o.b. just yawned and lit another cigarette. "Yes, I've got it straight. I've heard it a thousand times before, and the answer is no soap. My professional responsibility is to see that you are safe, fed, and supervised during the time your guardian is unavailable. And that is just exactly what's going to happen."

"Supervised, crap. I haven't been supervised in years."

"Then I guess things are going to change."

I was screwed, and he was about to get close to some very incriminating shit. Somehow I had to keep him out of the basement. When we pulled up at the house, I said, "I'll just run in and get my stuff. Back in a minute."

"Nope, I'm coming in with you."

"You've got a right to do that?"

"It's either that or you go without fresh underwear this weekend."

Damn. "OK. Let's go."

Inside the house, he said, "Where's your room?"

"I live in the basement."

He raised his eyebrows. "Oh? That's unusual."

"It's private," I said. He nodded and started for the stairs. "Uh, look. The place is kind of a mess. And, I've got some kind of private stuff down there. Why don't you wait here?"

He hesitated. "Well, OK. But hurry up."

"Ya, sure."

In the basement, I looked around at all the stuff that could get me put away until a day or two after the year 3000. Would the police come poking around for something more about Mom? No, that was paranoia. But how about that damn gun going off? Maybe they'd have to shoot pictures of the scene or dig the bullet out of the wall. Damn. Could I hide any of this stuff? Where, for God's sake?

Mullan called from the top of the stairs, "Let's not pack any drugs, booze, guns, knives, or lead pipes, my friend. And bring a bathrobe if you've got one."

"Uh, right. Just about done." The accounts book. Should I at least take that with me? Oh, real bright idea, jerk. It's a hell of a lot safer where it is. Now just calm down; nobody's going to come looking around. I threw some clothes in a paper sack and headed for the stairs.

I'm not short, but the foster mother had me by a good four inches. Mullan closed the door. "Mrs. Bergstrom, this is Carl Staggers. His mother will be undergoing an alcohol-dependency evaluation until Tuesday. He doesn't want to be here."

"Hello, Carl. I hope you'll change your mind about that." She shook my hand with a grip like a brick ma-

64

son's. "Come in and sit down." Mullan and I took chairs at the table in the brightly decorated kitchen. Mrs. Bergstrom handed me a long list with the title "Bergstrom Receiving Home Rules." "Read this while I make some coffee."

She clanked around while I read, and Mullan sat with his eyes closed. Most of the rules weren't any hassle: no booze, drugs, swearing, stealing, or refusing to take a shower; no smoking except in the dining room; no long-distance phone calls or local calls longer than five minutes; no radio or TV after 10 P.M.; and so on. Then I hit the clinkers at the bottom: "#16. It is important for you to become part of family activities. Hence, you may not spend daytime hours isolated in your room. #17. On admission, you will be restricted to the house—with the exception of school attendance and family activities—for the first 72 hours. This will give you time to adjust to your new surroundings and for your house parents to get to know you."

"Uh, I haven't really done anything. It's my mother who's in trouble. So maybe these last two don't apply to me, huh?"

"All rules apply to everyone we take in, Carl. Do you want some coffee?"

"No, thanks. You see, I've got some kind of important things to do at home."

She put a cup of coffee in front of Mullan and sat down. "Seventy-two hours isn't very long. I think those things can wait that long." Mullan opened his eyes and stretched. She smiled at him. "Long night, Rich?"

"Ya, three calls between nine and four, and I've got to work a full day tomorrow." He picked up the coffee cup.

"Well, let's get you out of here then. What else do we have to cover?"

He pulled a form from his folder and pushed it across to me. "This is a waiver of your right to a hearing. If I were you, I'd sign it and just relax until your mother goes to court. If the judge decides to hold her in custody beyond Tuesday, you can withdraw the waiver and ask for a hearing." He fixed me with a tired but not unsympathetic gaze. What the hell could I do? I signed. He seemed to consider me for a moment, then looked at Mrs. Bergstrom. "I'm not sure. I don't think so, but he could have."

She nodded. "Carl, I want you to take some underwear and your robe to the bathroom." She pointed at a door. "Toss your old clothes outside the door. If you flush the toilet a couple of times, we'll just figure you answered nature's call." I got the point—they thought I might have drugs on me. I blushed angrily. She smiled. "I've been at this a long time, Carl. There aren't many tricks that I don't know and not much that'll shock me. And there's no reason for you to be embarrassed, either. Now go on."

I did as I was told, making a point of not using the toilet, even though nature could have been answered.

I half expected her to lock the bedroom door behind me, but she didn't. I stood looking at the two vacant beds in the faint light from the window. She'd said I could sleep late. But, hell, who could sleep after a night like this? Suddenly, I was shivering hard. I kicked off my shoes and slid under the covers. Where did they have Mom now? Visions of cold showers, padded rooms, and straitjackets. They didn't really do that anymore, did they? Maybe just coffee, cookies, and understanding. Was that all she really needed? Just a little understanding? I curled myself in a ball and tried to stop shaking. God, why'd I turned away from her in the cop car? I should have helped her. Somehow there must have been a way.

To my surprise, I fell asleep trying to figure out that somehow. The next thing I knew, someone was hammering on the door. "Time to get up, Carl. We're going shopping in half an hour. There's just time for you to take a shower and grab a bite to eat." Who the hell was that, and where the hell was I? "Did you hear me, Carl?"

Mrs. Bergstrom. The foster home. "Uh, ya. Right. In a minute."

"Don't fall asleep again, or you won't have time to eat."

"Yes, ma'am."

I sat on the side of the bed, trying to get everything straight in my head. My other voice was awake. OK, jerk. You dodged about twenty bullets last night, including a real one. Now, get your act together. Remember something called the Plan? Well, get it back in focus. Just play the game until you can figure a way out of this dump.

At the top of the stairs, I paused to put on my ol' professor look of complete indifference. OK, be cool. I started down, expecting to find maybe a dozen skull-bashing thugs and drug-crazed psychos draped over the furniture in the living room. Sort of a meeting of apprentice Hell's Angels and future serial killers waiting to inspect the fresh meat. Instead, a boy about three and a girl maybe five were playing on the floor with blocks and toy cars. Mrs. Bergstrom came in from the kitchen. "These are my kids, Nancy and Joe. Say hello to Carl, kids." They chorused a hello. "Things are pretty quiet around here. You're our only guest at the moment, and my husband is working for the Navy in Guam for six months. How do you like your eggs?"

"Uh, sunny-side up, I guess."

"Sunny-side it is. There's juice and toast on the table." The kids went back to playing without paying me another moment's notice. I sat down at the table and buttered some toast.

About thirty seconds after my plate went into the dishwasher, we were all in Mrs. Bergstrom's station wagon and rolling toward the supermarket. I was assigned a shopping cart, Joe, and orders to bring up the rear. Mrs. Bergstrom pushed ahead through the busy aisles, while Nancy held calculator and coupon folder at the ready. Joe babbled about something that I couldn't follow, but he didn't seem to mind that I only grunted now and then. In forty-five minutes, we were waiting in the checkout line with both carts overflowing with food. "Are you expecting an army tonight?" I asked.

"No, just a few hardcore punks. You know the type— purple and orange hair, safety pins through their noses, spiked bracelets, sharpened teeth. The fun crowd." She winked at me. "You'll have seniority by then, and I'll make you a trustee."

"No, thanks."

She laughed. "No, I'm not expecting anyone. I just shop this way. Less time in the damn store. Oops, got to remember rule number three: no cussing. Let's start unloading. How'd you like spaghetti tonight?"

I had to admit that I almost liked her, especially when she didn't hassle me with questions during the next two days. And the food was good. But I wasn't used to obeying someone else's rules, and I wanted out.

———————————

I hadn't even thought about school. Somehow, I'd figured that no one would expect me to go until after Mom's hearing. But at six-thirty Monday morning, Mrs. Bergstrom was pounding on the door. "Up and at 'em, Carl. We leave for school in forty-five minutes."

At the table downstairs, I said, "I think I'd better go downtown and see what I can find out about Mom."

"Nope. You go to school unless I hear different. Rich Mullan is a good social worker; he'll call when there's news." I opened my mouth, but she said, "Save yourself the effort. Finish eating and get your coat."

I flushed. Hey, hold on a second, lady; I ain't some punk you can shove around. The voice inside me said, Steady, jerk. Play the game. I spoke evenly. "I'm a straight-A student. I can miss a day for my mother's sake."

"You're wasting my time and yours. Rich knows where to find you." She froze my reply with a look that could have driven nails through a wall. I got my coat. In the car, she said, "I'll be waiting in the parking lot at three-thirty."

"I can get a ride with a friend."

"Nope. That's my job."

The story was on the grapevine. I heard whispers and felt stares all day, but I ignored them. The ol' professor didn't stoop to gossip—not even when he knew all the intimate details. I didn't bother paying attention in class. Screw it. I had more important things to figure out— like what the hell to do about all the evidence in the basement.

I took a chance on talking to Steve in the afternoon. "Did you hear?"

"Just the basic stuff, no details." He took a quick glance behind him.

"Look, I'm not sure how long it'll be before I can get back to my workbench. So—"

"Uh, things are a little spooky around here today, man. Call me tonight." He strode off. What the hell was the matter with him?

I stood waiting in the cold. I ought to get my butt downtown and find out what was happening to Mom. To hell with the foster-home rules. I mean, what could they do to me? Toss me in jail for checking on my mother? Mrs. Bergstrom's blue station wagon rolled into the parking lot.

"Rich Mullan is coming over at four," she said when I climbed in.

"What's happening?"

"You'll have to ask him."

He was already waiting. In the kitchen, Mrs. Bergstrom made coffee. "Well," Mullan said, "I heard from the public defender about an hour ago. He's cut a deal with the D.A. If your mother agrees to forty-five days of alcohol-abuse treatment and a month or two in a halfway house, the D.A. will ask the judge to postpone her case. If she does well in treatment, they'll probably let her off easy."

"Mom agreed to this?"

"She didn't have a lot of choice. It was that or the county jail for a few months. She doesn't think she needs treatment, but it could still do her a lot of good." He paused. "So, I think we'll send you up north to your aunt and uncle's until she's released from the halfway house."

"Huh?" I looked at him, dumbfounded. "Wait a second, I don't even know those people. I mean, I haven't seen them in years."

"I talked to them on the phone, and they're willing to take you. Seemed like nice folks."

"I don't need nice folks telling me what to do."

"I'm afraid the state feels you do." He raised his palm to stop my objection. "Now just hold on, and I'll explain it to you. The state sets rules for juveniles in your situation. My job is to put you in what is called the 'least-restrictive setting' that still ensures your welfare. That means I look first at possible guardians within the family. If you can't get along with them, I consider a foster home. But if you still can't get along, things start getting heavier: a group home where you'd be sharing a room with seven other guys, or a residential treatment facility where you'd have to earn the right to make a phone call, buy a candy bar, or smoke a cigarette. And, if nothing else works, there's always Lincoln Hills School. That's the state juvenile reformatory, and—believe me—you don't want to end up there. At Lincoln Hills, things get very heavy."

"But I haven't done anything! I just want to go on with my life. It is my life, isn't it?"

"Yep, but that doesn't mean the state is going to let you be on your own for three months. So, following the policy of making the least-restrictive placement, we're sending you to your aunt and uncle's."

"Then I want that hearing."

"That's your right. But if you've got a better plan, why don't you just tell me now and save everybody a lot of time?"

Whatever the cost, I had to stay in the city. "I'll stay here. It's not so bad." I glanced at Mrs. Bergstrom. "I kind of like it, I guess."

She smiled. "I'd love to have you, Carl, but this is a receiving home—just a temporary shelter for kids until they can go home or are placed somewhere else."

Mullan said, "And temporary means a maximum of thirty days. So, I'm afraid Mrs. Bergstrom's is not an option."

They waited, watching me. Suddenly, my eyes blurred with tears. The Plan. They were tearing it down brick by brick. "Excuse me." I got up and stumbled blindly into the bathroom.

I splashed my face with cold water, then stared at myself in the mirror. You pathetic little jerk. Did you ever think you could really beat them? They've won. They're sending you up country—into the boonies where the hicks and the grizzly bears roam. And there isn't a damn thing you can do about it, except dive through a window and run like hell. That too seemed like a lousy option.

Mullan and Mrs. Bergstrom were talking state politics when I took my seat at the table. "So," Mullan said, "come up with any ideas?" I shook my head. "Do you still want a hearing?"

"Not if you've already got it wired."

He sighed. "It's not wired, Carl. I've told you what's likely to happen, but if you want to find out for yourself, that's OK. It's your right; go ahead and take it."

I hesitated. Maybe I could delay things. Maybe I could even win. But suppose the judge sent cops and social workers to dig around in my affairs. If they took one look in the basement, I'd really be screwed. Proceed directly to Lincoln Hills. Do not pass Go for scholarship, degree, or future. "No," I said. "I'll go along with your plan."

"Good enough." He unbent his long frame—a bearded praying mantis finished devouring the fly. "Your mother will have a brief court appearance tomorrow afternoon. You can attend and say good-bye afterward. Or I'll talk to her and tell her that you're doing fine."

"I want to see her."

"OK. Meet me in the school office at eleven-thirty. We'll arrange to have your records sent up north, then stop by your house for your things on the way to the courthouse. Your mother's case is scheduled for two, and your bus leaves at three-twenty."

"Tomorrow?"

"Yep, tomorrow."

I stared at the tabletop. "You don't give a guy a lot of breaks, do you?"

He hesitated, then stood. "Carl, I'm genuinely sorry that you don't feel better about this. Believe it or not, I've tried my best to keep both your feelings and your welfare in mind. This is the best solution I could find." I didn't reply or look at him. "Well, thanks for the coffee, Marge."

I heard him leave. Mrs. Bergstrom watched me for a long moment, then got up and opened the refrigerator. She scooped up a double handful of potatoes and dumped them in front of me. "I need some potatoes peeled. If you feel like talking, go ahead." She started making supper. Talk? How could she possibly understand all I'd lost in the last three days? I picked up the peeler and began slowly carving away long brown ribbons of potato skin. I had nothing to say.

I had to get those damn stereos out of the basement. At supper, I said, "My seventy-two hours are nearly up. Can I go do a few things tonight?"

She looked at me quizzically. "Do you want to guess?"

"Uh, I guess yes."

"Want to guess again?" She smiled. "Don't get hostile. I know that you didn't really expect a yes, so why fight about it?" I returned her level gaze for a moment, then went back to eating. There was no damn sense arguing with her—like trying to dent a brick wall with a Ping-Pong ball.

After supper, I asked to use the phone. "Sure. Remember, only five minutes, and don't call Brazil or anything."

"Wish I knew somebody there. I'd go." She smiled, set the kitchen timer for five minutes, and left the room.

Steve answered on the fourth ring. "Steve, listen close; I've only got a couple of minutes." I explained what was happening. "Now you've got to get those stereos out of my basement. The spare key is above the window to the right of the back door. Go in and get them the hell out of there."

"I don't have any place to put 'em, professor."

"Well, you're going to have to find a place. Get the accounts book too. You know where I keep it. Burn it. I've got the latest figures in my head, and we don't need the rest. And, one more thing, don't use my house for any wild parties, man. I've got enough problems right now." There was silence on the other end of the line. "Have you got it, Steve?"

"Ya, I've got it, but . . . I don't know, man, those units might be safer there than anywhere else. That damn Bill Hoyt keeps watching me. It's spooky."

"You're paranoid. Look, just figure out something to do with the stereos. Sell them at a discount or something. Now, I'm going to give you my aunt and uncle's address, but don't write me about anything confidential until I'm sure they're not the type who open other people's mail." I told him the address in Blind River.

"Sounds out in the sticks, professor. Rural route, huh?"

"Ya, I think they live on a farm or something." I glanced at the timer—nearly five minutes gone, and I didn't think I could reset it without ringing the bell. "OK, you got any questions?"

"I guess not. . . . Well, it's been nice doing business with you, professor. Take 'er light."

"Don't make it sound like I'm going on an expedition to the Arctic. I'll be back in a couple of months. We'll make up for lost time." The timer rang. "And stay cool. Don't take any chances."

"I am cool, professor. You just worry about all those bears and the other sharp-toothed critters."

"Right. I'll buy an elephant gun or something. I'll see you."

Mrs. Bergstrom came into the kitchen. "Bring me your dirty underwear. I'm going to do a load of wash, and you might as well go north with clean clothes."

Mrs. Bergstrom wished me luck when I got out of her car with my paper sack of clean underwear and socks. I walked into the school and down the long hall to my locker. I'd never given a damn about the school or the people in it, but I was homesick already. I tossed my bag in the bottom of the locker and stood staring at my books. What was the point of going to class? But what was the point of doing anything else?

At eleven-thirty, I pulled open the office door, caught it with my foot, and edged through with my stack of books. Mullan glanced up from reading my transcript. "You've got a heck of a record. Straight A's and then some."

I dropped the books on the counter. "Doesn't make a lot of difference to you guys, does it?"

"Not in terms of what needs to happen, if that's what you mean."

A secretary checked off the books against a list. "OK,

that's all of them. His library fines are paid, and he's got no other obligations. We'll send his records to the school in Blind River this afternoon."

No one said good-bye or good luck. Outside the main door, I said to Mullan, "You know, I might have been valedictorian in a couple of years. Now they'll probably find an excuse to give it to somebody else just because I'm leaving for a couple of months."

"I doubt that'll matter," Mullan said. He glanced at me. "Why don't you try to put the best light on this? Enjoy the change of scenery and hope your mother gets well."

Did he really think there was any hope of that? Hell, she had to put in her time, and I had to put in mine. But neither of us would enjoy the change of scenery.

All that I had worth taking fit in one suitcase and a garbage bag. I finished packing, then went to the hiding place behind the furnace. I put the two hundred bucks I had on hand in my wallet, then hesitated. There was just no way around it. I opened the checkbook for S & M Electronics and scrawled a check to cover the mortgage payment. More money I'd have to beg or steal from Mom. I took a reassuring look at the bottom line in my savings book, then shoved it and the checkbook back in with the accounts book and the stickers for S & M. Well, at least the bank wouldn't take the place while I was gone. I surveyed my cave a last time, then turned off the light over the workbench and climbed the stairs.

Mullan was leaning back in a kitchen chair, his eyes closed. Was he always tired? He opened his eyes and stretched. "Put 'em right here, champ." He'd already warned me that he'd check for "contraband," and I set the garbage bag and suitcase on the table without objecting. He pawed through the contents while I found an envelope for the mortgage payment. "OK, you're all set for a clean, wholesome vacation in the north woods."

"Do me a favor and skip the jokes," I said.

"No problem. Let's go."

The public defender stood. "Your Honor, I request a postponement of my client's case until she has completed treatment for alcohol abuse at the DePaul Rehabilitation Center and one of its halfway houses."

"Does the district attorney's office have any objections?"

"No, Your Honor," the assistant D.A. said.

The judge studied the papers in front of him. "I see that Mrs. Staggers has a minor child. Have arrangements been made for his care?"

The assistant D.A. spoke. "Yes, Your Honor. Social services has arranged for him to stay with relatives."

"Very well. I will accept counsel's motion for a postponement until such time as Mrs. Staggers completes treatment." He stared over his glasses at her. "That does not mean that you can go in and out of treatment whenever you want to, Mrs. Staggers. If you drop out of the program, you'll be brought back here immediately. Do you understand?" Mom nodded. "All right, Mrs. Staggers is released on her own recognizance on the condition that she return to the DePaul Rehabilitation Center directly." He banged the gavel. "Next case."

Mom and the public defender waited for us in a small room off the corridor outside the courtroom. A guy who must have been from the hospital stood near the door, looking bored. Mullan put forms on the table in front of Mom. "Mrs. Staggers, these are the papers giving your brother and his wife temporary custody of Carl. Please sign at the bottom." She signed.

The public defender said, "Mrs. Staggers, I don't think I can do anything more for you right now. Good luck. I'll check to see how you're doing in a couple of weeks." He left.

Mullan dated the form, then glanced at his watch. "I think you'd better hold the good-byes to about five minutes. The court was running late, and your son has a bus to catch." He closed the door behind him.

I stood watching Mom. How long had it been since I'd seen her completely sober? She wiped away a couple of tears and looked up, trying to smile. "Well, I guess they got us, baby. But don't worry. Glen and June will treat you nice." She reached out to take my hand. "And when I get out, we'll have some fun."

I pulled my hand free. "I've got to go."

"Baby, don't go away hurt. I can always tell when you're hurt. But you're going to be OK. We're both going to be fine. In a few weeks, we'll be back together. Things will be just like always."

I hadn't expected it, but suddenly my anger surged to the surface. "Ya, just like always. I'll hide in the basement while you come home drunk with more of your classy guys, or stay out all night kicking cops in the nuts. But no problem, I can handle—"

She came out of her chair, swinging an open palm at my face. I didn't duck. "You little bastard!"

"Hooker." I spat the word at her with every ounce of the hatred I felt. Then I spun and walked out. "Let's go," I snapped at Mullan, and kept walking down the long courthouse hall toward the door and the cold gray afternoon.

We rode in silence. At the bus station, he bought a

ticket for me, then said, "Do you want a Coke or something while we wait?"

"I don't want anything from you."

He shrugged and bought one for himself. We waited on one of the hard benches in the dirty, drafty station. Just before they called my bus, he said, "I want you to understand that you're going to your aunt and uncle's on a trial basis. If you end up back here for any reason, I'll have to worry about other options. And none of them are going to be very pleasant, because we're burning up all the easy ones today." He gave me a long look. "Now you're a bright kid, and you can figure out the score. On the ride north, I suggest you take a real hard look at your attitude. Comprende?"

"Ya, I got it."

At the bus, he handed me a brochure. "I thought you'd like to have this. It's put out by the treatment center and tells something about their program. For example, your mother isn't going to be allowed any phone calls for a couple of weeks. That's for her own good; she's got to concentrate on her problem." I shoved the brochure in my coat pocket without a glance. He offered his hand to me. "Well, good luck."

I hesitated, then gave him a halfhearted shake. Just to make sure he'd really gotten rid of me, the s.o.b. stood outside the bus until the door swung shut. He waved a bony hand. The bus rolled out of the station and down through the gray city streets. For a few minutes, I watched the buildings and the crowds sliding by, then leaned back and closed my eyes. Good-bye city, hello boonies.

5

I HAD TO WAIT AN HOUR IN GREEN BAY FOR the bus that would take me west, then north, then back a few miles east again, before finally dumping me in Blind River. I'd never heard of most of the small towns along the route laid out on the station's big wall map. Blind River was shown with a dot so small that it almost disappeared in a surrounding wilderness of lakes, rivers, and federal forest.

This was ridiculous; I couldn't go there. I slumped on a bench and considered my options. Maybe I should just walk out of the station and let fate take over. I might get lucky and find some beautiful divorcée just looking for a horny young stud like me. Ya, right. And I was going to win the state lottery, too. Face it, jerk; you don't have any options worth a damn.

They called my bus, and I went out to stand in line behind a half dozen other fools headed for the boonies. I settled into a seat near the back and lit a cigarette as the bus engine rumbled to life. In a few minutes, the lights of the last city I'd see for a long time faded behind us.

The deeper the bus got into the country, the rougher and narrower the roads became. In the afternoon, I'd ridden a smooth interstate through long stretches of open farmland. Now trees crept close to the road, and our headlights seemed the only sign of life in a thousand miles. Snow started falling, and I had images of the bus overturned in the ditch and the survivors being eaten by wolves before another car passed. I switched on the light above my seat and started paging through *Popular Electronics*.

I had to keep things in focus. My future wasn't ruined, only delayed. For three months, I'd have to put up with my hick relatives. But they wouldn't be real thrilled to have me around either. They'd leave me alone to find my own ways of killing the time until I could get back to the city. Hell, there must be lots of possibilities for a slick city boy in Hicksville. Maybe even a girl for the ol' professor. Hadn't there been some movie about a city boy going to the boonies and getting chased by every girl in ten counties? And all the girls in Blind River couldn't look, smell, and act like grizzly bears.

No, they'd be healthy, outdoor girls. And I wasn't any slick city stud. I was a skinny nerd, a pale slug who hid in a basement playing with electronic junk and dreaming of scholarships, BMWs, and a life in the suburbs. I had about as much chance of scoring with one of those country girls as I'd had of finding that divorcée in Green Bay. The image of Jennifer, my dream girl, came into my mind. Look at what they're doing to your guy, Jenny. Just look. I flipped off the overhead light and let the tears come.

I'd rewired my act by the time the bus pulled into Blind River almost an hour late. Or at least the sign up the road had said Blind River. But there wasn't anything there! Just a lonely crossroads and a darkened gas station standing under a single streetlight. The driver swung in and parked near the pay phone. I moved hesitantly to the front. "Is this where I get off for Blind River?"

"This is it," the driver said.

"Uh, where's the town?"

"Up there." He gestured at the road running to the north. I squinted. Through the blowing snow, I could make out a few more streetlights.

"Not much to it, is there?"

"Nope." He swung the door open. "Come on, son. I'm running late. How many bags do you have?"

Outside, I looked around while he got my stuff from under the bus. That's when I spotted the old Ford parked close to the station. The streetlight outlined a dark hulk in the driver's seat. My uncle? Well, why didn't he move, then? Maybe he was asleep. Or maybe it was just a big box that looked a little like a person. I couldn't be certain, but I sure as hell wasn't going to start poking around and maybe wake the wrong person. I could see the headline already: "Crazed Lumberjack Kills Milwaukee Native." I'd call the house and find out the score. I took a step closer to the pay phone. "Out of order" read the sign taped to the dial. Oh, great.

"Is that all of them?"

I looked at the driver. "Huh? Oh, ya. Just those two."

"OK. Thanks for riding Greyhound."

The door shut behind him, the gears ground, and the bus disappeared down the dark highway. I stood alone in the swirling snow. Never in my wildest dreams had I imagined anything this bad. My God, I was going to freeze to death or get eaten by a bear if I didn't do something. Either I had to find another pay phone or take a closer look at that object in the front of the Ford.

I became aware that my ears were about to fall off. I dug for my stocking cap. Damn. I must have left it on the bus. Well, take a chance on the Ford or probably die trying to find a working pay phone. I walked cautiously to the passenger side of the car. It was a man, all right. He was asleep with his hands over his big stomach and his mouth open. And there was a second person curled up under a coat beside him. I leaned close to the window. Ya, it was Uncle Glen at the wheel and probably my hick cousin Bob under the coat.

I hesitated, then tapped lightly on the window. Nothing happened. I rapped louder. The figure behind the wheel stirred, rubbed its eyes, looked at me, and grinned. "Hi, Carl." Uncle Glen nudged the sleeping form beside him. "Wake up, Bob. Your cousin's here."

Bob came awake instantly and sat up. He grinned at me idiotically. "When'd the bus get here?" He swung open the door, almost clipping me in the shins, and wrung my hand. "Welcome to the country, city coz. Jeez, we didn't think you'd ever get here."

"Neither did I."

Uncle Glen crawled out of his side of the car and came over to shake my hand. "Sorry we fell asleep on you, Carl. We thought we'd hear the bus pull in. Didn't end up hitchhiking here, did you?"

"No."

"Well, must have been a quiet bus then. Those your things?"

"I'll get 'em," Bob said, and trotted over to my suitcase and garbage bag.

"Your aunt wanted to come, but she's got to be up early. She cooks at the school, you know. She said she'd see you tomorrow. Climb in front. Bob can ride in the back."

We drove through town—two bars, a grocery store, a café, and perhaps a half dozen other businesses. Bob pointed out every one for me: ". . . And that's Hammond's Drug Store. The bowling alley next door has four lanes and a pretty good bunch of games. And over there's the school." I looked and saw a three-story brick building. My God, it must be a hundred years old.

"We've got thirty-eight kids in my class and about a hundred and twenty in the school. That's not counting the junior high school on the first floor or the grade school in the new addition. There are a lot of kids there."

This is ridiculous, I thought. Just find me a pay phone, huh? I'm going to call Mullan and tell him I'll take Lincoln Hills School, but not Blind River High. Not with this idiot babbling from now until spring. We cleared the edge of town and speeded up. Uncle Glen said, "Bob, you don't give your cousin a chance to say anything. How was your trip, Carl?"

"Long," I said.

He hesitated, then asked, "And how's my sister doing?"

I bit my lip and stared out the side window. What was I supposed to say to this stranger? "I think she'll survive OK."

"Well, we were real sorry to hear about her trouble. I guess we haven't kept in touch like we should. We figured out the other night that it's been six or seven years since we saw you folks."

"Eight," I said.

"I couldn't believe it. Time just goes by too darn fast. Seems people are busy all the time." Ya, I'll bet it's a real rat race here in the boonies, I thought. "Anyway, she's going to get some help now, and we'll do our best to make you comfortable here. Say, that social worker of yours seems like a real nice fellow."

Get to know him a little better, I thought. "He's OK."

"Deer on the left, Pa," Bob said.

"I see 'em." He stepped on the brakes. Three deer looked up from where they'd been pawing at the snow in the ditch. Their eyes shone in the headlights for an instant, then they bolted across the road and into the woods.

Five miles farther on, we turned off the blacktop onto a gravel road. We bumped along for half a mile, then turned left into a driveway. Ahead I saw a frame house, two or three outbuildings, and a tumbledown barn. "Home sweat home," Uncle Glen said.

I glanced at him. "That's one of Pa's jokes," Bob said. "He says no farm is sweet because you've got to put too much sweat into it. Right, Pa?"

"That's right. And that's why I didn't want to be a farmer when it came my turn to take it over from your ma's pa. I said, nope. I'll live on it, maybe raise a few chickens or a beef or two, but no dairy cows. He didn't like it much. To him farming was the only life. Me, I drive a grader or a dump truck or anything the county wants me to, just as long as I'm sitting on my butt most of the time."

"And that's why he's got me to do the work around here," Bob said.

"And that's why he's so happy you've come," Uncle Glen said. "Bob here feels put upon now that his three brothers are gone."

"Put upon, hell. You're working me to death. How come I had to be the last kid? You run out of gas, Pa?"

"Got more than you'll ever have, boy. I just got smarter. Three mistakes was enough."

"Only three? Which one of us wasn't?"

"Ha. You guess."

We hung our coats in the kitchen. Uncle Glen wasn't as huge as I remembered, but he was still a big dude. Bob, on the other hand, was two or three inches shorter than I was. But I could see the outline of powerful muscles under his shirt. He'd worked all right—probably strangling grizzlies with his bare hands. "I'm going to check the fire, then turn in," Uncle Glen said. "Bob, see if Carl wants something to eat, but don't keep him up all night. He's got a big day tomorrow." I looked at him questioningly. "That social worker of yours said you're supposed to start school right away." He grinned. "I think his exact words were, 'Don't give him any time to get in trouble.'"

Bob interrupted. "I told Ma and Pa that you ought to have some time to look around first. I could miss a couple of days of school, no sweat. We could do some trapping and ice fishing."

"Ya, and that went over real big with your ma," Uncle Glen said. "You're lucky she doesn't hobble you like a mule to keep you at the books. Maybe your cousin can teach you how to study, so I won't have to listen to her yelling at you all the time. Now you boys get a snack. I'm going to bed."

I ate a ham sandwich and a piece of pie. Bob had two sandwiches and dumped a couple of scoops of ice cream on his pie. "Want some?"

"No, thanks." I leaned back and reached for a cigarette.

"Uh, Ma isn't going to like that."

I looked at the cigarette. Since when had I started smoking so damn much? "Ya, OK. No problem. . . . Do you smoke?"

"Na. Tried it once and got sick. I like air better. Come on, I'll show you your room."

We climbed steep, narrow stairs. The walls needed paint. "You're lucky," Bob said. "I didn't get my own room until a couple of years ago. I had to sleep with one of my brothers. They took turns giving me a corner." He swung open the door of a tiny room. It was freezing inside. "It'll warm up in a few minutes," Bob said, and wrestled with the lever on a heat vent. A cloud of soot came out. "Jeez, why didn't Ma do this?"

I set my suitcase and garbage bag on the bed. Above the ceiling there was a squeak, then a rustle. "My God, have you got mice up here?"

"No, bats. The mice are in the basement."

"Oh, great."

"Don't worry, the bats sleep most of the winter. When it warms up, they go in and out through cracks in the roof. I don't think more than two or three got into the house all last summer. Ma kind of hypes out, but they don't hurt nothin'. They're neat creatures. Ever see one up close?"

"No, and I don't want to."

He had an inspiration. "Hey, if you're still here next summer, you can help me fix the roof. Ma's been after Pa for a couple of years about the bats, and I think he's going to give in this summer. With the two of us, it'd go real fast."

I took a deep breath. "I'm going to be long gone by summer. Look, I'm really beat, man."

"Oh, ya. Sure. I'll see you in the morning."

"What time do we have to get up?"

"Pa usually starts yelling about quarter to six, but he doesn't get serious until six, maybe even six-fifteen. The school bus comes at seven-twenty."

I grunted and glanced at my watch. It was nearly midnight. "OK if I use the shower?"

"Sure. It worked a week or two ago." I glanced at him sharply. He laughed. "Just kidding. Go ahead. There should be towels under the sink."

I unpacked my stuff. Bob was moving around in the next room. A radio clicked on, and I heard soft country music. What else? I took my shower, then climbed into bed. For a few minutes, I tried to take stock of my life, but I was too numbed with fatigue to stick with it.

Uncle Glen set a platter of pancakes, sausage, and eggs in the middle of the table. "Hey, not just cold cereal this morning," Bob yelped, and started shoveling his plate full.

"Save some for others. You've got the manners of a hog, boy."

"Oink, oink," Bob said, and grinned at me.

"You want coffee or cocoa, Carl?"

"Cocoa, thanks."

"Cocoa, too? Boy, we ought to have guests more often."

"Shut up and eat," Uncle Glen said. "You ain't never left this house in the winter without a hot meal." He sat down and reached for pancakes. "Almost twenty below this morning. You get up to the chicken house right after breakfast and gather the eggs, or else we'll have egg popsicles."

"How do you get the sticks in, Pa?"

Mullan, you son of a bitch, I thought. These people are going to drive me crazy.

Bob wanted me to go to the chicken house with him, but I said I had to find something in my stuff. Uncle Glen had left for work by the time I got back to the kitchen. Bob came in, his face red with the cold. He packed a dozen eggs in a carton with quick efficiency. "We've still got half an hour before the bus comes. Want to go have a look around?"

"Uh, let's wait on that. It looks damn cold out there."

"It's cold all right. You got the right clothes for it?"

"I doubt it."

"Ma will find you some."

We sat at the table. Bob babbled about his trapping, hunting, and fishing like I should be excited about the prospects of joining him. "Is it really a bummer to smoke in here?" I asked.

He paused. "Ya, I think so. Nobody smokes in the family. Ma just won't have it. She isn't going to be real happy to find out that you smoke, either."

"That's kind of up to me, isn't it?"

"You don't know Ma. She isn't likely to see it that way."

I got up. "Well, I'm going to go burn one."

Cold. God, it was cold. My toes were numb in seconds, but I stubbornly smoked the cigarette down to the filter. Bob didn't seem to notice the cold. "Not a bit of wind," he said. "Look at that smoke go straight up from the chimney. Be a good day to go rabbit hunting. You could get right on top of 'em before they smelled you. Want to go shoot a couple after school?"

You have got to be kidding, I thought. "I'll think about it."

"Oops, I hear the bus. I've got to grab my books."

The bus ride lasted forty-five minutes. We took every side road, digging kids out of the most godforsaken places. Not that most of the houses were all that bad; I just couldn't figure out why the hell they were built in the middle of nowhere. Most of the kids who got on were younger than us. They seemed to think Bob was some kind of hero, and he seemed to like talking and kidding with them too. Strange dude this. They asked about me, of course, and Bob introduced me as "my cousin from the big city who knows all about that stuff you see on TV. Like he knows some real cops and robbers." Little do you know how well, I thought. The kids asked me a lot of stupid questions.

Near the end of the trip, we pulled up to a house that looked like it was built of oversized Lincoln logs. A cute dark-haired girl hopped aboard and took a seat near the front. Bob grinned. "Back in a few minutes."

He went forward and plopped down beside her. I couldn't hear what he was saying, but he had her laughing in seconds. He came back when we got into town. He winked at me. "I figured I could talk her into going with me. There's a dance Saturday, and she's one fine dancer. Almost as good as me."

"What do you do? Polka or square dance?"

He looked puzzled, then laughed. "Hey, you can make a joke, after all. Why, we rrrrock an' rolllll, son. How about you?"

"Now and then," I lied. (I didn't dance a step, but I'd be damned if I'd let this hick know.) The bus pulled into the school parking lot.

Bob led me to the school office. "Mrs. Carson, this is my cousin Carl from Milwaukee. He's going to be going to school here for a while."

The secretary looked up from her desk. "Oh, yes. Welcome to Blind River, Carl. Your school counselor called about you yesterday." Naiman, I thought. I'd iced him a couple of times when he'd tried the reaching-out crap, but he didn't know anything bad about me. The secretary punched a button on her phone. "Mr. Dowdy, Bob Staggers is here with his cousin from Milwaukee." She listened a moment, then hung up. "He'll be with you in a few minutes, boys."

We sat waiting. "Howdy-Dowdy is the principal," Bob whispered. "He's not your brightest bear, but he's harmless." He glanced at the clock. "Looks like I'm going to miss half of Old Lady Baxter's English class. Just breaks my heart." He grinned.

The principal—a balding, potbellied guy—didn't invite us to sit. "We don't have your records yet, but I spoke with a Mr. Naiman from your school. Sounds like you're a good student. We could use more of them and fewer of Bob's type. Right, Bob?"

"You bet, Mr. Dowdy. I'm ready to leave any time you can convince Ma."

"Don't tempt me." He turned back to me. "We can't offer all the things a big-city school can, but I've done my best." He pushed a sheet across the desk to me. "I've put you in the same classes with Bob except for chemistry—"

"I'm taking general science," Bob said. "That's where they put the dummies."

Dowdy gave him an irritated look. "We don't have French, only German, so I decided you might as well take woodworking with Bob."

"Uh, that isn't really my thing. Do you have something with electronics, maybe?"

"No, sorry." He checked a list. "I don't see any other classes that would fit in your schedule. It's kind of late in the year for you to start in typing or German."

Bob nudged me and whispered, "Come on, take woodworking. It's a gas."

I ignored him and asked, "How about drafting?"

"Well, we do have a drafting class, but it's usually reserved for seniors."

"I can handle it. I've done a lot on my own."

"Drafting it is then." He made a change on my schedule. "Bob, why don't you wait outside for a minute?" Bob looked puzzled, then left. Dowdy was rechecking my schedule. "Mr. Naiman said you're a good student but not very friendly. That you don't like talking to teachers or counselors or even spending much time with your peers." He looked up at me. "Is that true?"

I shrugged. Careful, the voice inside me said, this guy

could cause you some real trouble. "I guess I'm just quiet."

"He also said you've got a couple of pretty tough friends."

What the hell was going on? "Uh, it's a little hard not to know a few pretty tough kids where I come from, but I wouldn't say any of them were my friends."

His eyes probed me. "Well, I just want you to know that things are different in a small school. We all know each other, and we try to keep things relaxed and friendly while still getting the work done." He paused, trying to make me squirm. "We'll expect you to try your hardest to fit in here."

"I'm not going to cause anybody any trouble."

"Good. I'll look forward to seeing you in the halls." He handed me the schedule.

Outside, Bob asked, "Everything OK?"

"Ya, everything's OK." But was it? Had Naiman told him some dirt about me? But he couldn't know any— not unless I'd slipped up and let my association with Steve become obvious. "Uh, Bob, is Dowdy into mind games? You know, testing somebody with a little b.s.?"

"Howdy? Heck, he ain't smart enough." We climbed the stairs to the floors reserved for the high school.

A tall, rawboned woman turned from the chalkboard when we came in. Bob introduced me to Mrs. Baxter. I felt a whole classroom of stares while she dug around on a shelf for grammar and literature texts for me, recorded their numbers, and finally told me to sit next to Bob in the back. Bob was whispering to a knot of other kids, looking very pleased to have the major excitement of the day in his care. "All right, class. Let's get back to work," Old Lady Baxter boomed. "Turn to page one-thirty-five, transitive and intransitive verbs." There was a groan, but the kids started turning pages.

I found the page, but my mind was still on my interview with Dowdy. Maybe Mullan had told Naiman about Mom's trouble, and Naiman had passed everything on to Howdy-Dowdy. And, hell, any kid with a barfly for a mom must be a tough customer. Ya, that was it. Mullan, you son of a bitch, somehow I'm going to get you for this. I surveyed the kids in the class. Hicks. Just ignorant hicks. It wasn't them I had to worry about, but some very real and some very ugly people in Milwaukee—some bastards who planned to do me in.

Bob was developing into a royal pain in the ass. Between classes, he introduced me to everyone we saw. That made me damned uncomfortable. I didn't want to know everyone. As a matter of fact, the fewer the better. I'd always worked that way—let people come to the ol' professor if they needed something. Otherwise, bug off. Between history and geometry, I told Bob to knock it off. "Look, I know you're trying to be a good host, but give me a break, huh? Not so much on the first day."

"Oh, OK. But maybe I ought to introduce you to a few more girls. Get you a date for Saturday night."

I glared at him. "I'll take care of my own love life, thanks."

"Well, sure. Just trying to help."

At least classes didn't look tough so far. English would be a bit of a drag with all the grammar, but history and geometry would be a snap. Maybe too much so. I wanted to keep my four-point, but I didn't want to be bored to death in the process.

The little kids got fed first, while we waited out the last hour of the morning in a study hall held in the small basement auditorium. "God, I hate this," Bob said.

"Give me gym days. At least you're doing something then."

I glanced up from the geometry text. "Why don't you read or do your geometry?"

"Aw, too much like work."

I shifted my position. "Aren't you worried about flunking?"

"Me? Na. I get B's and C's without working very hard. Ma just thinks they ought to be A's and B's like my brothers got." He snapped a rubber band at a kid a few seats in front of us. "Damn, missed him. You got any rubber bands?"

"Nope. Sorry." I went back to the geometry.

I slid my tray down the metal rails of the lunch counter. I wasn't sure which of the cooks was Aunt June. Ahead of me, Bob said, "Hi, Ma. Meet Carl."

A short, plumpish woman with iron-gray hair stuck a hand over the counter. "I've met Carl, but it's been a long time. How are you, Carl?"

"Fine, thanks."

"Good. Lift up your tray." She reached over with a ladle of runny hot dish.

"Not too much, please."

"Looks like you could use a full one." She dumped it on my plate. "Sorry I couldn't meet the bus last night. I imagine the guys fell asleep waiting."

"Uh, ya, they did."

"Typical. Well, I'll see you after school. We've got to get these kids fed. Maggie, hold your tray higher or I'm liable to miss and you'll have hot dish all down your front." The girl behind me lifted her tray obediently.

At the table, Bob said, "Well, that was Ma. She's got our number and she'll probably get yours." I grunted, staring at the small mountain of hot dish on my plate. "Hey, Signa," Bob yelled. "Where were you this morning?"

A big blonde girl with a broad face turned. "Had a dentist's appointment. Look, no braces!" She opened her mouth to show him.

"Allll righttt!"

"I'm going downtown after school and buy a bushel of taffy, then spend the whole night eating it. I'll give you a piece at milking."

"Save a piece for my cousin here. Signa Amundsen, this is my city cousin, Carl."

I said "Hi" and she said the same back to me. Another girl called to her from a few tables away. Signa waved. "I gotta run, guys. We'll see you later."

She hurried away, her long ponytail sweeping across her broad back. She didn't cradle her books across her chest, but swung them at arm's length like a boy. "Signa's our neighbor," Bob said. "Maybe you ought to ask her to the dance. She's a lot of fun."

"She's not my type. Hell, she's taller than I am and probably outweighs me by twenty pounds."

Bob turned and studied her for a second. "No, she's a little shorter. Maybe the same weight. But she is really good people." I ignored him and took an experimental forkful of the hot dish. "So, uh, did you have anything particular going in Milwaukee?"

"I did pretty good fixing stereos."

"I meant with a girl."

I set down my fork and stared at him. "Bob, I know what you meant. I was trying to let you know I didn't want to talk about it. The answer is: nothing steady. Let's just leave it at that, huh?"

"Oh, I get it. Sorry, I didn't mean to pry." He put on his hillbilly drawl again. "You city boys are kinda subtle for us country types." More likely you country boys are a little dense, I thought.

Bob devoured his food, even wiping his plate clean with a slice of bread. I ate a little of my hot dish but left most of it. That was a mistake I didn't make again. Aunt June was supervising the student dishwashers. She froze the kid ahead of me in line with her flint-gray eyes. "Brad, your mother would have your hide if she saw you dumping all that good food in the garbage can." The kid apologized sheepishly.

When it was my turn, I managed a rueful smile. "It was good, but I wasn't very hungry. Kind of nervous, I guess."

"Well, I can understand that today. Have a good afternoon. I'll see you at home."

Bob showed me the door of the chemistry room, and I was on my own for a couple of hours. I signed in with the teacher, got a text and a course outline, and took a seat at a vacant lab table in the back. I started reading the course outline. Oh, crap, the whole damn approach was different. I opened the text, leafed through a few pages, then closed it in disgust. Stone Age. And the lab looked even older. I leaned back and watched the teacher flop around for the entire hour, trying to explain a simple concept. It was going to be a long three months in chemistry.

Drafting was my last chance for something interesting. I got lucky. The teacher found out what I could do and seemed impressed. "We'll make it kind of independent study for you. Have a look at the text, then tell me what you want to do." Good. The name of the game, my friend, is electronic circuitry.

The class got out a few minutes early—apparently a privilege given seniors and now me by default. I waited at Bob's locker, paging through the drafting text. "Hi." I looked up from the book. A perky blonde girl was spinning the combination dial on the locker next to Bob's. "I'm Ginger. You must be Bob's cousin. I think half the school met you, but I got left out."

"Uh, ya. I'm Carl."

"How do you like it here? Must be a change from the big city." She opened the locker.

"Uh, it's OK so far, I guess." Come on, jerk. Don't clutch up now. My God, this girl is a walking damn dream! "So, uh, what do you do for excitement around here?"

She shrugged. "Oh, we party a little. Have a dance now and then." She looked into my eyes, laughing. "And try to keep each other warm."

"Oh. Well, maybe—" A very large hand attached to an arm the size of a gorged python appeared between me and her. She put a couple of books in the hand like she'd been expecting it to arrive at that exact moment. I looked up to see a guy about ten feet tall staring down at me. He didn't look friendly.

Bob hurried up, and I thought I caught a hint of worry in his expression. "Hi, Ginger. Hi, Cliff. I see you met Carl, huh?"

"Yes, we were *just* talking," Ginger said. She gave me a smile. Cliff gave a bull-moose grunt. They left hand in hand. Ginger came to about the height of his belly button.

Bob stuck some books in his locker and handed me my coat. "Better stay clear of Ginger. Cliff's a jealous guy, and she likes teasing him. She's a bitch, one of the few we've got."

"Like she said, we were just talking."

"Right. But Cliff doesn't need much of an excuse to get ornery."

I was shaken. God, that guy was big. And ugly. But I

didn't want Bob to see that I'd gotten the crap scared out of me. I shrugged. "Ya, well, we got a few like him in Milwaukee."

Bob was antsy on the ride home. "I hate this stupid bus. Jeez, it'll be after four when we get home. If I had a car, I could be home in fifteen minutes." I nodded and continued paging through the drafting text. This might be kind of fun.

Bob hopped out of the bus and jogged toward the house. "Come on."

"What's the rush?"

"Lots to do and not much light to do it in."

Aunt June was standing at the stove, making supper. "Hi, Ma." Bob started digging in some containers on the counter.

"Did you get the eggs this morning?"

"Yep. Pa said we'd have egg popsicles if I didn't."

"Ugh. How'd your day go, Carl?"

"OK."

"Help yourself to some milk and whatever else you can find. It's certain Bob won't offer you any. Bob! Stay out of that."

"Aw, Ma. I'm a growing boy."

"You'll be a dead one if you eat any of that cheese-cake. That's for the church women's meeting." Bob trotted upstairs with a cookie in his mouth and a glass of milk in his hand. "Well, you'd better hurry. He gets changed in about thirty seconds. It didn't look like you brought much for warm clothes, so I dug out some boots, wool pants, and a coat one of my older boys left behind. They're on your bed."

I felt my face flush. "How did you know what I brought?"

She turned to me, a little surprised at my tone. "Well,

98

I looked, naturally. How else was I going to know?"

I was about to say, "You might have asked," but I stopped myself. Steady. Let's not get into anything with her. I shrugged. "Well, uh, thanks for finding me some clothes."

"I'll look around for some more this evening. I think there are a few things I can alter for you. Supper's at six."

The boots fit OK, but they weighed a ton. I clumped after Bob to the chicken house. A cold wind bit my face and the wool pants made my legs itch. Why the hell hadn't I thought of an excuse to get out of the chores? If I let myself get caught up in their routine, I'd be taking orders all the time. "Chickens ain't bright," Bob said. "They'll try to run through your legs, just so they can freeze to death or get eaten by a fox." He swung the door open. "Here, chickie, chickie, chickie. Big bad Bob's here to steal your eggs."

The smell of chicken crap almost knocked me back through the door. I tried to block it by breathing through my mouth until I thought of all the shit vapor that would be coating my tongue. Bob was expertly rifling the chicken nests. One big hen kept pecking at him. He swatted her, then lifted her tail to get the egg beneath. Suddenly, a sharp pain hit the back of my leg. "Holy shit," I yelped.

Bob spun. "Get out of here, you stupid cluck." He charged the rooster that had sneaked up behind me. It scurried away. "Sorry. I should have told you to watch him." Bob got a couple more eggs, and we started back for the house. "You OK?" he asked. "I was afraid you were going to hit your head on the ceiling."

"I'll live, I think. I just hope my tetanus shots are up to date."

He laughed, and handed me the bucket of eggs. "You take these inside, and I'll open the cellar doors. We've got to get wood for the furnace next." Joy, oh joy, I thought.

I was frozen by the time we had the third wheelbarrow load into the basement. "How many more do we have to do?"

"Three or four more, and we won't have to do any tomorrow."

"Maybe it'll be warmer tomorrow."

"Ya, but then we won't want to waste time on wood. Hey, if you're cold, go on in. I'll finish up."

Not a chance, you hick. You're not going to make me look like a wimp. "No, I'm OK," I said. I grabbed the handles of the wheelbarrow and started pushing it toward the cellar door, hoping I wouldn't get a hernia in the process.

"Milk next," Bob said, when we'd stacked the last of the wood in the basement. "We've got to walk over to the Amundsens' for it. Just a second, I'm going to get my twenty-two and my knapsack."

The light was fading fast as we trudged along a snow-packed path running over the ridge behind the house. Bob gestured at the rolling fields ringed by woods. "Grandpa and his pa before him used to grow hay and corn out there. Now we just sell what hay still grows. Pa says someday he's going to plant it all in Christmas trees. I ain't holding my breath."

He shifted the rifle to his other hand. "What's the gun for?" I asked. "Just in case we run into a bear or something?"

He laughed. "Another joke, right?"

"Well, not really."

He gave me an odd look. "All the bears are hibernating. Besides, if you shot one with a twenty-two, it'd just piss him off. I'm hoping for a rabbit."

"Oh," I said. "Uh, I don't mean to sound stupid, man, but how about wolves?"

"Timber wolves? God, I wish. They say there are a few around, but they stay real clear of people. Pa saw a pair of 'em years ago. I think maybe I spotted one once, but I'm not sure. But if you do see one, you'd better not shoot it. The game wardens will string you up by the thumbs and leave you for the crows."

I surveyed the snow-drifted fields and the dark woods beyond. Somehow, I wasn't completely convinced. "No wolves, then," I said.

"Well, we've got quite a few coyotes, but they ain't going to bother you none. As a matter of fact, there ain't nothin' up here that can hurt you. We don't even have poisonous snakes. You're the guy who comes from a place where you can get hurt."

"What do you mean?"

"I mean the city, man. All that crime. You know, muggers and burglars and drug dealers and so on."

"It's not that bad. Not where I come from, anyway. You shouldn't believe everything you see on TV."

"Well, maybe not, but—" He stopped short, putting a hand on my arm. "There's a snowshoe," he whispered. I watched him kneel slowly and brace the rifle on his knee. A snowshoe? What the hell was he talking about now? I looked but couldn't see a damn thing. The rifle cracked. I saw a puff of snow, then a big white rabbit bounded away, losing itself almost immediately in the whiteness. "Damn," Bob said. "Missed. Not enough light for a good shot. Have a good life, bunny," he shouted. "Watch out for the owls. Hoot, hoot."

Well, he wasn't Davy Crockett, and I was just as glad

that I wasn't going to be eating wild rabbit. Ya, have a good life, I thought. But watch out for big bad Bob; he might get lucky next time.

We crossed the fields on the far side of the ridge toward the lights of the Amundsens' farm. Bob leaned the rifle against the wall of the barn and swung open the door. For the second time that afternoon, the smell of animal crap almost knocked me over. If I hadn't been so damn cold, I would have waited outside. Signa turned from where she was attaching a milking machine to a giant black and white cow.

"Hi, guys."

"Hi, Signa. Hi, Mr. Amundsen." Bob waved to a tall, wiry farmer working at the far end of the line of cows. The man waved back. "Where's my taffy, Signa?"

"You know, they didn't have any of the good stuff. How's that for a gyp? A girl waits years for a good sticky hunk of taffy, and all they've got is this brittle strawberry stuff for kids. I'm going to make some of the real thing after supper. Come over and help me pull it."

"Sounds like fun," Bob said. Wow, big thrill, I thought.

"I'll get your milk," Signa said. She straightened and walked to a far corner, one of the rubber boots she wore over her jeans making a sploosh when it hit a stray cow pie. She didn't seem to notice. She returned with two half-gallon bottles. Bob turned his back to her, and she stuck them in the knapsack, fastened the straps, and gave him a swat on the butt. "There you go."

Bob staggered. "God, Signa. Take it easy, huh? You don't know your own strength."

"Flattery, flattery," she said. "I'm going to get back at this milking. We'll see you later, guys. Come by around seven-thirty. Mom and Dad are going out, and we can tell dirty jokes while we're pulling the taffy."

"I don't know any dirty jokes, but I'll listen to yours," Bob said.

Bob was wrestling the door open when she called, "Be sure to bring your city cousin. I wanta see if I can make him smile."

It was dark now, but we could see our way by the starlight on the snow. At the top of the ridge, I was startled by a brilliant white light just above the tree line on the far side of the fields. It was the rising moon, brighter and closer than I'd ever seen it before. "God, is that beautiful!" I heard myself say.

"Ya, ain't it?" Bob said. "Full moon. Time to howl." And, of course, he let go a wolf howl. It wasn't a bad imitation, or at least it sounded pretty damn real to me. I jumped when an answering howl drifted up from behind us. "Signa." Bob laughed. "She must have come out for a second and heard me. God, she's fun." He howled again and, sure enough, there was an answering howl with a distinctly female quality.

A hundred feet on, he said, "You know, you really ought to take her to the dance. You'd have a great time."

"If you think she's so neat, you take her, and I'll take that little brunette you were talking to on the bus."

"No deal. Debbie and I got some serious dancing to do. Besides, Signa really is taller than me."

Aunt June told Bob to say grace. He bent his head. "Good food, good meat. Good God, let's eat!" He lunged for a pork chop. She caught him hard across the knuckles with a spoon. He yelped. "Ouch, Ma. That hurt."

"You'd better hope the Almighty has a sense of humor; you've just about exhausted mine. Now stop showing off for your cousin and say it right." Bob grinned at me, then bowed his head and ran through a blessing.

A couple of minutes later, I reached for my glass of milk, then hesitated. "Uh, aren't you supposed to pasteurize this or something?"

Uncle Glen said, "Raw milk never killed me. Tastes a heck of a lot better than anything you can buy in the store." I took an uncertain sip. It tasted rich and sweet. Too much so. Uncle Glen looked at Bob. "I heard you take a shot when I was getting out of the car. Hit anything?"

"Ya, I got some really good snow, Pa. Had to shoot around this stupid rabbit to get it too."

Aunt June said, "Maybe we should buy some rabbits come spring. It's been a couple of years."

"Ma!" Bob whined. "I don't want to spend my summer raising a herd of stupid rabbits. I've got enough to do around here."

They went on eating and talking. I just ate. I was about to excuse myself when Aunt June said, "I see some pretty shaggy heads around here. I'm going to sharpen up my scissors right after supper."

"Aw, Ma," Bob said. "We were going over to Signa's and help her make some taffy."

She glared at him. "It's a school night; you've got homework."

"I did it in study hall."

"Oh, let them go," Uncle Glen said. "Carl's only been here a day."

She didn't like it, but after glancing at me, she grumbled, "Oh, all right. You boys clear the dishes. I'll wash them later—*after* I shorten a few ears."

I didn't expect to be included in the haircutting, but as soon as Bob got off the high stool, Aunt June patted the seat. "You're next, Carl."

I looked up from the chemistry text. "Huh?"

"I said, 'You're next.' Come on, bring those curly locks over here."

"Uh, they're not curly, and I like them the way they are."

"Just let me take off a couple of inches. You'll fit in better at school."

"I fit in fine back where I belong."

"Well, you're not—" She stopped herself. "Just let me even up the back a little. I won't take any more than you want me to." I stared at her stubbornly. "Look," she said, "if you don't trust me, you can watch in the hand mirror and stop me any time you want."

It wasn't worth fighting about. I moved to the stool and let her put a sheet around me. But I watched every move she made with the scissors. A couple of times she hesitated, the scissors poised to hack away a sizable hunk. "It's short enough already," I told her.

When she finally let me go, I went to my room and lay on the bed with the chemistry text. Bob leaned in the door. "You ready to go pull some taffy?"

"You go ahead. I'm going to stay here and figure out what I've missed in chemistry."

"Jeez, you can't do that, man. Ma's only letting me go because she thinks it'll be fun for you. Come on. I don't want to stay here and study."

I had between zero and zip interest in going to Signa's to pull taffy, but Bob's eyes were pleading. "Oh, hell. OK, but you owe me one." He grinned.

Signa was standing over a steaming kettle, watching a thermometer. "Hi, guys. You're just in time." She brushed back a wisp of blond hair and studied the thermometer. "Riiight aboutt . . . now!" She whisked the heavy kettle off the burner and made for the table. "Gangway, this stuff is hotter than blazes." She poured a dark, syrupy liquid onto three greased cookie sheets. "Beautiful. I ain't lost the touch." She stood back and wiped steam and sweat from her hairline. "So, make yourselves comfortable. We've got a few minutes to rest while it cools. Then we go to work."

She dug three cans of pop out of the refrigerator, and we sat around the table in the hot little kitchen. A big golden retriever padded into the room, paused to sniff me and wag his tail, then flopped down at Signa's feet with a loud grunt. She reached down to scratch his ears. "Real graceful, Bullion. Impresses the heck out of guests. So, what do you think of Blind River High, Carl?"

You wouldn't want to know, I thought. "It's OK, I guess. I think I met just about everybody there, thanks to Bob."

I'd meant that to be a little pointed, but Bob missed it. "Including first Ginger, then Cliff," he said.

Signa winced. "Oh? And what did you think of our little Ginger-sweetums and the Beast?"

I shrugged. "They look pretty tight."

"Ya," she said. "They deserve each other." She stuck out a finger to test the temperature of the taffy. "Just about ready. Wash your hands and roll up your sleeves, guys."

We did. I felt embarrassed to show my skinny forearms, but there didn't seem an option. "Hold out a hand," Signa said. I did, and she slapped a gob of shortening on my palm. "You've got to keep your hands really greased or you'll end up having to eat yourself free." She sat and greased her big hands. "OK, guys, watch me." She gathered the contents of one of the pans into a huge blob, dug her fingers in, and pulled until the

106

blob became a heavy rope a couple of feet long. "You just keep folding it over and pulling until it starts getting stiff. Twist it a little, too."

I did as she'd shown us. Holy shit, the stuff was hotter than hell. I gritted my teeth and tried to ignore the pain. After my third or fourth pull, my fingers started getting stuck. I pulled the mass another time and had the sudden realization that the damn blob had grabbed control of my hands like some kind of alien creature in a low-budget horror movie. I tried to get free but only made things worse. "Uh, I think I'm stuck."

"You don't have enough grease on your hands," Signa said. She reached over with a lump of shortening and worked the taffy off my right wrist, then down the back of my hand. In a minute, I was able to get the hand free and take over the job. "How you doing, Bob?" she asked.

"Damn sticky crud. Give me some more grease."

The pulling took over twenty minutes, and my wrists and forearms were sore by the time she told us to start making thinner ropes. She cut the ropes into bite-size candies, her strong hands fast and sure with the kitchen shears. One of the middle buttons on her blouse had popped open, and I had a disconcertingly good side view of a cupped breast moving as she worked.

She glanced my way. "Well, did you like learning how to make taffy? Or did you just come for the dirty jokes?"

"Uh, I came because Aunt June was going to keep Bob home if I didn't."

She raised her thick, unplucked eyebrows. "She on you again, Bob?"

"Ya. Hell, I don't know what she expects. I've already told her that I just want to work in the woods. I don't need any super high-school record for that. City coz here is going to be a doctor or a lawyer or something."

"An engineer," I said.

"Oh?" she said. "What kind?"

"Electrical." For a second, I was tempted to start babbling about it. It seemed like a year since I'd had my fingers on circuitry or even had a chance to think much about electronics. Instead, I said, "I've been interested in electronics for a long time."

We finished a few minutes later and got ready to leave. Signa handed a tin of taffy to Bob. "Well, thanks, guys." She looked at me. Maybe she was a fraction of an inch shorter than I was, after all. "I didn't get around to my dirty jokes, and I still haven't made you smile."

"I guess I just don't smile a lot."

"You should. It's good exercise for the face." She winked at me. "See you in school."

On the drive back, Bob said, "Hey, did you get a look when she had that button open? Pretty nice, huh?"

"Bob, will you just drop it," I snapped. "I am not interested in Signa Amundsen, and I'm not going to be."

"Well, sure. I just thought you might have enjoyed the view."

When we got out of the car, I said, "Sorry, I'm just tired. On edge, you know."

"No problem. Hell, you've only been here twenty-four hours."

Amazing as it seemed, it hadn't even been that. In bed, I tried reading a page of the chemistry text, but couldn't. I pulled the string on the light above the bed and lay in the darkness, thinking. Only five days since the cops had busted Mom. It seemed a year ago. And ever since, strangers had been telling me what to do.

Suddenly, I missed Mom very much. Missed her more than I could ever remember missing her. Once upon a time, we'd been a team. It'd been us against the world. And we'd had a lot of good times before everything started going to hell. God, what had happened to us? Maybe it was my fault. A thousand times she'd called me her pal, her best guy, her only friend. But I'd never measured up. Instead, I'd picked on her, made a big deal out of every little thing that went wrong. And now she was alone in that hospital, where God only knew what they were doing to her. If I'd only loved her a little more, loved her instead of being such a selfish little bastard . . .

I lunged for the light. Damn it! I couldn't let myself drown in those thoughts! One of these days, I wouldn't make it back on my own. I'd float to the surface, my eyes blank and blood running from my ears—a vegetable they'd prop in a corner of the mental hospital. "Damnedest case I've ever seen, Doc. Looks like his brain just blew up. The X-ray boys say there ain't nothing left but mush." "Well, there's not much we can do for him. Hook him to an IV and hose him down once a week." "Sure, Doc. No problem."

I took a long, deep breath. Not yet. No, I wasn't quite finished yet. I used a corner of the sheet to wipe the sweat from my face. OK, I was a bastard. I'd turned away from my mother in the cop car and called her a hooker in the courthouse. Evidence enough. But I was going to be one hell of a smart bastard. I reached for the chemistry book under my bed.

At two o'clock, I closed the book and sat for a moment, resting my burning eyes. Maybe I could sleep now. I turned off the light and lay in the dark, trying to relax with thoughts of Jennifer and the life we'd have together when the Plan came true. But the images wouldn't come. Instead, my cowboy-dad appeared—tall, smiling, and sunburned. Hey, I see they sent you up country, son. Don't sound like a bad deal to me. Lots of fresh air and the chance to do a man's work. Have fun and worry about your mom and your big ol' plan later. And, hey, that country girl down the road don't look so bad to me.

I turned over. Screw you, I thought. A hell of a lot you ever did for me. Besides, you're not even real, just a dream I made up a long time ago. How about Jennifer, then? a voice whispered. No, damn it, she was real. Not exactly as I pictured her, but still real. Somewhere out there she existed. And I'd find her. But I fell asleep thinking of Signa's strong hands pulling the taffy as she talked and laughed, of the down of golden hair on her forearms, and what I'd seen when that blouse button came open.

AUNT JUNE HAD LEFT A SET OF GYM CLOTHES
for me on the kitchen table. Oh, hell. I'd planned to
delay my entrance into the wonderful world of physical
education at Hillbilly High as long as possible. Back in
Milwaukee, the gym classes were so large that I got by
without doing much. But here it was going to be different, and I didn't look forward to making a fool of
myself in front of a bunch of hicks. Maybe I could still
get out of it: "Uh, Aunt June, I wasn't real excited about
wearing somebody else's jock. I mean, I'm sure all your
boys are real nice guys and didn't have cooties or anything, but . . ." No, it'd never work.

Bob grabbed us two lockers and started changing. He
was fired up, ready for some action after sitting bored
through English, geometry, and history. "I think we're
going to play volleyball. You like volleyball?" He pulled
on his gym shirt over bulging muscles.

I shrugged. "I haven't played much. I've never given
a damn about sports."

"Me neither. Not unless it's hunting or fishing. But
anything beats sitting in class. Come on, I'll get you on
my team."

I took the position next to Bob's and hoped nothing
would come my way. To my surprise, no one was very
good. On the other side, Cliff got in a couple of lethal
spikes, but screwed up twice as many. Nobody on our
team seemed able to serve worth a damn. Time and
again, the ball got whacked so hard that it sailed over
the end line. When it came my turn, we were behind,
8–2.

I had it calculated. I probably couldn't knock the ball over the end line, even if I hit it as hard as I could. That left getting it over the net. I did a safe underhand serve. The ball dropped untouched on the far side. Three more of my serves made easy points, and I began to see why—Cliff was slow and the guy behind him was a first-class klutz. As long as I hit the ball their way, we had a good chance to score without a return. We chalked up two more easy points and tied the game at eight.

I'd already done enough to keep from being labeled a complete wimp. But, suddenly, I wanted more. I wanted to win this damn game. I could feel my heart pick up speed. Steady, jerk. Just move like a machine. Use the same motion every time. Four more of my serves dropped neatly into their weakest area: 12–8. The guys on my team were pumped up, cheering and yelling insults at the other team with every point. I could see faces on the other side getting grim. I cradled the ball for the next serve. I'd done little except put the ball in play, but I could feel the sweat streaming from my armpits. Stay calm, damn it. Just three more points. I served again, then again: 14–8, one to go. And I was going to blow it. After twelve straight points, I was going to slap the winning serve into the net. I took a deep breath, ignoring Bob, who yelled, "Come on, city coz. We're going to lick 'em." Shut up, I thought. This is between me and this damn ball.

In my fantasies, I'd seen myself with Jennifer on the country-club tennis courts: Carl and Jennifer Staggers, mixed-doubles champions. She'd be quick and fiery, while I'd be smooth and relaxed. Confident of my mastery, at ease with the flow of the game, I'd deftly place the long shots while she patrolled the net. And even though I'd never even held a tennis racket, I more than half-believed that someday I'd be that tanned, muscular, confident Carl of my fantasies. With the Plan, anything seemed possible.

But the volleyball in my hand was solid reality—a reality with the specific gravity of a bowling ball. I bounced it once on the court, cradled it in shaking fingers, and hit it. I felt the air explode from my lungs as it cleared the net by an inch. Cliff reached out a huge paw and smacked it back. The kid in front of me—Jim somebody—picked it off his shoe tops, setting it up for me. And I froze. I'd never thought beyond making that serve, and now, for an agonizing split second, I couldn't remember what to do. Somehow, I managed to punch feebly at the ball, but it didn't even reach the net. Jim glared at me, and all the guys on my team groaned. I made my face expressionless. In the far court, Cliff started serving overhand. Seven times, the ball came screaming our way. We lost every point and the game.

In the locker room, Jim snapped at me, "We could have beat them except for you."

I gave him a cold stare. "And I really don't give a shit."

Bob said, "Hey, come on, guys. It was just a stupid game."

Jim stomped off. I couldn't help muttering, "He seems to forget that I served twelve straight points."

"Was it that many?" Bob said. "I knew it was quite a few. But, heck, I never pay much attention to the score. What difference does it really make? Jeez, I'm hungry. I hope Ma Staggers and her cooks got something good."

I steamed about the game all through lunch. I knew Bob was right, but I was still pissed—especially at myself. Why the hell had I blown that shot? Crap. I could have been a hero, if only for a moment.

In chemistry, I settled into my seat at the lab table, wearing my ol' professor expression. Come on, jerk. Just forget the damn volleyball game. Phy. ed. ain't required for an engineering degree. Signa came in and took a seat near the front. Had she been there the day before? I hadn't noticed. She turned and waved a piece of taffy at me. "Here, catch."

I barely had time to react before she fired it my way. By some miracle, I caught it. God, you could lose an eye around this woman. "Uh, thanks," I said. She grinned and started passing out hunks of taffy to the kids around her. When Mr. Pankratz came in from his office, she popped a last piece in her mouth and sat back, chewing contentedly. Just like a cow, I thought.

Pankratz announced that the class would have a unit test on electricity the next Monday. There were some groans. "Look, I could give it to you tomorrow, but I thought you'd like the weekend to study. Does anybody have any objections to that?" He waited a moment. "All right, let's begin our review."

I leaned back and gave him half my attention. Well, no sweat with this. Hell, I could teach it myself. I caught myself staring dreamily at Signa's long blond hair. Let's not space out completely here, jerk. I shifted my eyes to watch Pankratz trying to explain the speed of electron flow. "Now electricity—the flow of electrons—moves at the speed of light." He wrote figures on the board. "But an electron moving in a wire travels very slowly." He checked a book and wrote more figures on the board. God, he was making a mess of it; the figures didn't explain a thing.

The kids didn't get it and started shooting questions at him. He sidestepped, flopped, and wriggled. Hell, he didn't understand it himself. His face got red, and he started snapping at kids. I don't know why I didn't let the whole class go to hell on him, but suddenly I felt my hand go up. He pointed to me with an irritated "Yes."

"Look," I said, "just think of the wire as a tube filled with electrons. Like a paper-towel tube jammed with red marbles. Now stick a marble in one end. An identical marble pops out the other end instantly. That's electricity: electrons nudging electrons." Almost without thinking, I started demonstrating with my hands. "Now pick a marble of a different color—say, green—to represent the individual electron you want to watch. Stick it in one end and start shoving red marbles after it. It's going to take a long time for that green marble to travel the length of the tube, right? But for every marble you shove in, another will pop out the other end. So, the movement of the individual electron—the green marble—is slow, but the total flow of electrons is constant and very rapid. Almost instantaneous."

My hands stopped moving, and I became conscious of all the kids watching me. Instantaneous? God, would these hicks have the vaguest idea of what that meant? A guy sitting near Signa said, "Run that by again, huh?"

I did, slowly and in more detail. Another kid asked, "Well, how slow does that individual electron move?"

"An average snail could beat it easy."

Everyone seemed satisfied and turned back to where Pankratz stood looking helpless. "Uh, thank you for the example," he said. "Now, class, I want you to take another look at these figures." They've got it, I thought. Just don't screw it up.

I glanced at the clock. My God, I'd been running the class for fifteen minutes. That realization exploded my sense of satisfaction. I'd blown my cover. The word would get out that I was some kind of super student. Damn. I didn't want these hillbillies to know that too soon. Maybe not at all.

Signa caught up with me in the hall after class. "Hey, that was really good. I never understood any of that before. Pankratz is such a dope. Maybe you can teach us something."

"No, thanks."

"Why not?"

"Nobody's paying me to teach chemistry to a bunch of—" I almost said "hicks," but then I looked into her smiling face and said "kids."

"Well, it's going to be fun having you around anyway. Here, have another piece of taffy. This is my next class. See you later."

I kept on toward the drafting room. She'd been close enough for me to smell her perfume. And, to my surprise, it hadn't been a mixture of tractor oil and manure. She'd smelled pretty darn nice. My inner voice growled, Hey, cut that out, jerk. I mean, just think about that woman for a second. Can you imagine arm wrestling her? Hell, she'd rip your arm off. I almost smiled. Ya, I could hear her now. "Oops, I'm sorry. Here, maybe I can stick it back on with some taffy." Still, she had smelled nice.

"Do you want to get the eggs or chop kindling?" Bob asked.

"Kindling, I guess." I sure as hell wasn't going to risk getting maimed by that rooster again.

"OK. The kindling and the chopping block are in the shed over there."

The shed was musty and dim. I pulled the hatchet from the chopping block and examined it. No moving parts, anyway. I picked up a piece of old board from a pile, balanced it on the block, and gave it a good whack. It split neatly and the hatchet blade continued on to within an inch of my thigh. Whoa. OK, figure this out before you lose something important. I sat down on another block and started again, but carefully this time.

"Why are you working in the dark, son?" Uncle Glen stood at the door. "You need some light on the subject." He flipped a switch.

A bulb above me blazed. "Uh, ya. Thanks." Well, jerk, maybe you'd better wait a few days before telling him how you plan to be a hotshot electrical engineer, I thought.

"Watch your fingers, son. I damn near took one off when I was a kid." He left. I looked at my fingers. Maybe I should have asked him for a lesson. But up country you were apparently expected to learn on your own.

I heard Bob outside. "Hi, Pa. You're home early."

"Yep. I want to clean that chimney today. Put away the eggs, then get the ladder."

"Aw, Pa. Carl and me were going out to check some traps."

"That'll have to wait. We don't want a chimney fire burning down the house."

I finished what I thought was a pretty impressive stack of kindling without shortening any of my fingers. When I carried an armload to the house, Bob was tilting a long extension ladder against the roof. Well, at least I wouldn't have to see how many animals he'd slaughtered in his traps.

Aunt June was sitting at the kitchen table in a heavy sweater, peeling potatoes. "Chilly in here," she said. "I hope the men hurry with the chimney cleaning." Overhead, I could hear boots moving on the roof. Was I expected to join them? I'd never been on a roof, not even a flat one, and I didn't like the thought of testing my fear of heights. Aunt June thunked another potato into a saucepan. "After you get the kindling in, you can walk over to the Amundsens' for milk." I stared at her. *Alone?* Hey, there are bears out there, lady! Or wolves. Or at least some very pissed-off rabbits. She glanced at me with her sharp, gray eyes. "That's if you think you can find the way."

"I can find the way."

"Good. And get an extra gallon; I'm going to make yogurt."

I brought in the rest of the kindling, then shrugged into Bob's pack. His rifle leaned in a corner of the porch. Should I take it just in case? No, it'd be a dead giveaway that I was scared. Besides, I'd probably trip and shoot myself in the foot. (Headline: "Milwaukee Native Bleeds to Death in Hunting Accident.") I crossed the yard to the path leading to the ridge. From the roof, Bob shouted, "Watch out for the snipe, city coz. Snipe are real mean this time of year."

What was he babbling about now? Probably just making another stupid, hillbilly joke. I waved without looking back. Snipe? What the hell were snipe?

The light was already fading on the fields, and the woods beyond looked dark and threatening. I walked fast, not even wanting to think about making my way back in the dark. I was breathing hard by the time I reached the top of the ridge and turned to look back at the farm. Bob and Uncle Glen were tiny figures against the gray roof of the house. Even the farm itself seemed small against all the loneliness of trees and snow. Why the hell did anyone want to live here? Give me the city.

A different voice spoke inside my head. Oh, ya? And what's the city done so special for you? Give me the country. It was my cowboy-dad again. He hadn't intruded in years—not since I'd come up with the Plan and Jennifer—but here he was for the second time in twenty-four hours. Oh, screw you, old man, I thought. I started down the far side of the ridge. And, by the way, I added, this ain't cowboy country. Hell, I haven't even seen a horse, except that girl down the road you think is so damn neat.

Signa was sitting on a stool beside a cow, her big hands jerking on the udders or teats or whatever you called them. "Hi. They send you over by yourself tonight?"

"Ya," I said. "Uh, we need an extra gallon this time."

"No problem. Milk we got. Just let me finish stripping the last from this bossy, and I'll get your bottles."

"OK," I said. But hurry, for God's sake. The smell in here is choking me.

She picked up a cup of red-brown liquid and dunked each nipple in it. "Iodine," she said. "Kills the germs." She slapped the cow on the flank. "There, you're done." She crossed the barn to get the milk. "Hey, you really impressed the heck out of the kids in chemistry. I heard your name mentioned half a dozen times after class. From what I hear, Howdy-Dowdy's going to fire Pankratz and give you the job."

"Well, I only know about electricity," I said. "Not much about the other stuff."

She came back with the milk. "You don't have to be modest with me. I know a brain when I meet one. Turn around." She shoved the milk bottles into the knapsack. *Do not slap me on the ass*, I thought. "There you go. See you tomorrow."

"Ya, sure. Thanks." I glanced after her as she walked back to the long line of cows. A big, strong, confident girl. Everything I couldn't handle. Not now. Not for a while yet—if ever.

I made it over the ridge a few minutes after dark and trudged across the fields toward the warm square of light shining from Aunt June's kitchen. With a little luck, I'd make it without getting eaten by snipe or any other varmints.

I made toast while Bob fried bacon. He grinned at me. "As Mom says, 'Thank *goodness* it's Friday.'"

"I guess. Where's Uncle Glen?"

"He always leaves early on Friday so he can get off at two. Me, I think it's a big waste of time working at all on Friday. Someday I'm going to own me a pulp truck. I'll work like hell four days a week and take off three. Nothing like being your own boss, I figure."

"I thought you wanted to be some kind of mountain man. Run around strangling grizzlies with your bare hands."

That was my third sarcastic crack of the morning. Like the others, it missed. The guy was immune. "I would, but I was born a couple of hundred years too late. Scrambled OK? I broke the darn yolks."

"Fine," I said. Maybe good ol' Bob was just too damn stupid for sarcasm.

I'd gotten up in a lousy mood after a bad night. The dreams had come nonstop. Just crazy stuff. In the one I remembered best, Steve and I got busted for having a mountain of dope in my basement. Mullan and the cops came in through a pair of outside cellar doors that I knew damn well didn't exist. And Mullan wanted a cup of coffee, for God's sake. So I went upstairs to get him one and found Mom sitting at the kitchen table drinking beer, which wasn't too unusual, except that she was topless and seemed to be having a great conversation with Signa, who wasn't topless, unfortunately. I think they were talking about going into the taffy business. And, then . . . Oh, hell, it was just too damn weird to figure

120

out. Leave that to the shrinks and the other people who believed dreams meant something.

Still, I knew that my dreams did add up to one thing—I was worried about those stereos in my basement. By now, Steve should have them out of the house, but maybe his new girl and his doping had distracted him. I'd better call him soon. If I could just get a little privacy around this house . . .

"Tomorrow's Saturday," Bob said. No shit, I thought. "I sure wish you'd let me set you up with Signa. We could double."

"Bob, don't start on me."

"OK, OK. Maybe I could find you somebody else." I just glared at him. He shrugged. "All right, pardner. But if you're still alone when the dance gets over, I'm going to dump you at home and head for the woods with Debbie."

"You don't have to worry, *pardner*. I'm going to skip the big dance at Hillbilly High."

That time I got through. He pouted until we got on the bus. But in five minutes, he was good ol' Bob again. God, he was resilient.

The morning passed uneventfully, and I had some time to get my head straight. Damn dreams, anyway. Maybe I'd try calling Steve tonight. At lunch, I cleaned my plate like a good little boy and got an approving smile from Aunt June. I headed for chemistry. Rounding a corner, I nearly got run over by Cliff. He ignored me and boomed, "Hey, Ginger."

"I don't want to talk to you, Cliff. Just leave me alone." She ducked into a classroom.

I kept going. How tall was that guy, anyway? Ten feet, maybe twelve. OK, maybe he was only six-four—just six and a half inches taller than I was. But I couldn't keep that straight when I thought of him or anyone else who intimidated me. Like Signa. I knew she was shorter than I was by at least an inch, but . . .

Pankratz took roll. I leaned my stool back and stared at the ceiling. "All right, kids. Today, you can study for the test by yourselves or in small groups. No more than four to a group, and keep them quiet."

Instant chaos. Signa and about six other kids dashed for my lab table. *Wham, thunk!* Signa's books hit the table and her butt hit the seat across from me. Two other girls hurled themselves on the remaining stools. The kids who'd moved too slow stood staring at them. "Come on, Signa," a guy whined. "You guys are already getting good grades. Give some of the rest of us a break."

"Not a chance, slowpoke. This guy's ours. Only four to a group. Now beat it." They left, grumbling. Signa looked at the other two girls. "Didn't I tell you we'd have to move fast? Great job. Here, have a piece of taffy." She looked at me for the first time. "Smile, darn it. You're popular. At least close your mouth; you look like you're trying to catch flies."

I closed my mouth and let the front legs of my stool drop to the floor. I stared into her blue eyes, then managed, "Got another piece of taffy?"

"Sure. Now where do we start?" She thumped her text open. "Oh, by the way, these two are Sonia and Marcia. They're identical twins and always try to telepath answers to each other during tests. But it never works. They're almost as dumb as I am. Come on, brain, let's get going."

I stared at her for another long second. "Well, OK. Let's start with the different types of electricity. . . ."

Again that afternoon, the drafting teacher let us out early. I waited for Bob, a book open in my hands so I wouldn't have to acknowledge any of the kids in the hall. Ginger came up and started getting her locker open. "I just can't believe that guy," she said. "I mean, you met Cliff the other day, didn't you?"

She was talking to me, and I glanced quickly around to see if the Beast was in sight. "Uh, ya. I did."

"He just thinks he owns me. And he doesn't. I've got a right to do anything I darn well please." This was dangerous as hell; I could get squashed just for talking to her. I grunted and made like I was reading. "We've got this dance tomorrow night, and I told him maybe I'd like to dance with some other guys. I mean, I get a little sick of getting my feet stepped on by that moose. And he told me—"

I closed the book. "Excuse me. I've got to find Bob."

I started down the hall. Behind me, I heard her mutter, "Chicken." Better yellow than dead, lady.

"How's it going, young man?" Howdy-Dowdy stood in a corner by the water fountain.

"Uh, fine, Mr. Dowdy. Just fine."

He fixed me with a long stare. "Good. Let's hope it keeps going that way."

"Yes, sir."

"Hi, Mr. Dowdy." Good ol' Bob, I thought—and meant it.

"Hello, Bob. Staying out of trouble?"

"Ya, it's weird, Mr. Dowdy. No matter how hard I try, I just can't seem to find any."

Howdy-Dowdy gave him a twisted smile. "Well, keep looking." He walked off.

On the bus, I said, "Dowdy's got something against you, doesn't he? I mean, all those digs aren't just for fun."

Bob shrugged. "Aw, he just enjoys riding me because Ma's got him scared shitless. They get into it a couple of times a year over the lunch program. He always loses."

"I can believe that."

"Ya, Ma don't take no crap. And *nobody* messes with her kitchen. Anyway, since he never wins against her, I guess he figures he might as well try to get something on me. But, heck, I don't worry about it none; I am much too slick for Howdy-Dowdy." He glanced at me. "Maybe you'll get included in his little game too."

"Maybe, but I am also much too slick for Howdy-Dowdy."

He smiled. "Ya, I'll bet you are. Hey, I'm going to talk to Debbie for a few minutes."

I leaned back, feeling a little better. Probably Naiman hadn't told Dowdy any real dirt about me, after all. Dowdy just gave me that probing stare every time we met because he had it in for the whole Staggers clan. Or maybe Dowdy stared at every new kid that way. To hell with it; he wasn't going to get anything on me.

We did the chores. Bob volunteered to do the milk run by himself, since I'd had to go alone the night before. I almost said, "I'll go along. I feel like a walk." But I didn't. Too obvious. And stupid, too.

I was freezing to death on the windy pond. Bob finished chipping the ice from one of his trapping holes. He handed me the pointed steel bar and pulled on rubber gloves that stretched to his armpits. Lying on the snow, he felt around gingerly in the water. "I don't want to lose a hand if that trap is still set," he said.

"Can that really happen?" I had a vision of Bob flopping on the ice with his hand caught somewhere deep below. I might have to slug him a couple of times with the bar just to stop his screaming.

"No, but you'll sure as hell feel it if it snaps on you."

He pulled his arm out of the water. "It's still set. Damn it, where are the beaver in this pond? Well, let's try the last hole." I followed him nervously. The ice groaned again. "Just stay in my tracks," he said. "If one of us has to get wet, it might as well be me."

"Thanks," I said. "By the way, I ain't much of a swimmer, so you'll have to save yourself."

"No problem. The water's only three or four feet deep." He stopped at the last hole. "Boy, I hope there's one in here. I need the money." Try stealing stereos, I thought, it's a hell of a lot safer and warmer than this. The trap was empty. Bob shook his head in disgust. "If I don't get anything by next Tuesday or Wednesday, I'm going to find a different pond."

We walked back to the car. Bob seemed different out here—all business, with even his hillbilly way of talking forgotten. In the Ford, he poured cocoa from a Thermos, handed me a cup, then sat brooding, his stare on the sliver of pond showing through the trees. "You know, I like the critters out here. I never set a trap that lets 'em suffer. But, doggone it, they make me mad sometimes. I'm sure there are beaver in that pond, but I can't catch a single one."

My mind was on something besides killing animals. Was I really going to ask about Signa? I might have to eat some pretty serious words. I lit a cigarette and blew smoke at the windshield. Well, here goes, but find out one thing first. "Bob, what did you tell Signa about why I'm living here?"

He looked at me in surprise. "Signa? Why, nothing. Hell, I don't even know for sure. All Ma said was that Aunt Veronica was in the hospital and that I shouldn't ask you for details. That it was personal."

I was stunned. All the time I'd thought Bob knew. Wasn't half his good humor aimed at cheering me up?

Hey, sorry your mother's a drunken floozy, but never mind, things are just a barrel of laughs in the boonies. "Well, you must have guessed," I said.

He shrugged. "I don't know. I guess I figured she was having an operation. Something to do with female plumbing or something else Ma wouldn't want to talk about. It's not cancer or anything, is it?" I stared at him, then started laughing. For some reason, that was the funniest thing I'd heard in months. He looked at me curiously, then grinned. "Hey, it's good to hear you laugh. Jeez, I didn't think you knew how."

I caught my breath. "No, it's not cancer. And it's nothing to do with female organs." I hesitated; I'd never told anyone before. "She's a real heavy drinker. An alcoholic, I guess. She's had some run-ins with the law, and now they've put her in hospital to dry out."

"Oh. . . . Hey, I'm sorry. That must be tough on you."

"Sometimes," I said. And suddenly, looking at my hick cousin's face, I felt like smiling again. "Hell," I said, "I just thought you knew. . . . Is there any more cocoa?"

"Sure," he said, and reached for the Thermos.

On the way back, I finished what I'd started out to say. "OK, you win. I'll take Signa to the dance. That's unless you think it's too late to ask."

"Hey, I knew you'd come around. She is real good people. I mean it."

"Ya, you've said that before. But, listen, I'm not real thrilled about getting shut down. So if you think she's already got a date—"

"She didn't as of last night's milking." He grinned at me. "She told me I'd better get her a date with you, or she was going to come over and take you by force."

"Oh," I said. "That's charming."

"Yep. Signa usually gets what she wants, and right now I figure it's you, brain."

"Don't start with the 'brain' crap. And, uh, don't mention anything about Mom to her, OK?"

"No problem." He whistled a few bars off-key as he steered the car from the bumpy forest road onto the blacktop. Well, you self-satisfied turkey, I thought. You wired it up, after all. Still, I couldn't help feeling pretty good that any girl would want a date with me that bad. I mean, Signa wasn't exactly the girl of my dreams, but she was at least real.

"I was beginning to give up hope on you." Signa laughed. "The answer is: you bet I do. When do you want to pick me up?"

We settled that. "I'll have to warn you that I'm not much of a dancer," I said. My palm was sweating, and I shifted the phone to the other hand.

"Then I'll have to teach you. But call me a little earlier next time, huh? It takes me two or three hours to clean the cowshit off my dancing boots." She laughed again, and I attempted to join her. "I've got to do some chores. I'll see you soon," she said.

I'd done it. Now how was I going to kill the hours until evening? Bob had wandered off across the fields looking for rabbits, and Uncle Glen and Aunt June had gone to town. For the first time since Mom's bust, I was really alone. Maybe I should call Steve. But I hadn't asked anybody's permission to make long-distance calls. To hell with it; calling Steve could wait a while longer.

I was sitting at the kitchen table, messing around with some ideas for a drafting project, when it hit me. What the hell was I doing? I'd been up country less than four days, and already I'd started to fit in. I was running around like a good little boy, doing all sorts of chores. I was the star of the chemistry class. And now I'd asked the neighbor girl to a dance. And all this time Mom was sweating it out in a padded cell, maybe seeing snakes and spiders, and beating her head on the walls because they wouldn't give her a drink.

The point of the pencil broke under the pressure of my hand. For a long moment, I stared at the heavy, jagged lines I'd carved in the pad. What kind of a selfish bastard was I? I couldn't run around having a good time while she was in that place. Not without betraying her! That fact seared through my brain like a ten-billion-watt laser beam. I shoved back my chair so hard it toppled to the floor. It took my shaking fingers two minutes to find Signa's number in the phone book again. Calm down, damn it. Now keep it clean and simple. Just tell her you can't go out tonight and leave it at that.

But my finger hesitated on the dial. No, wait a few minutes. Give yourself a chance to calm down, or you'll make a complete ass of yourself. I hung up the phone slowly and went outside to smoke a cigarette.

I never did make the call. I kept procrastinating until people started coming home and it was too late. While I was changing into the best of my shabby clothes, I tried to talk myself into having a good time. Hell, it was only a dance, and Mom would never have to know that I'd gone. Starting tomorrow, I'd get serious about life again. Monday, I'd get some books from the library and read up on juvenile rights. Somehow, I'd beat that least-restrictive bull and get back home. They wouldn't let Mom have visitors for a few more days anyway, so I still had a little time.

Bob came to the door. "You about ready?"

"Ya, I'll be down in a minute."

I combed my hair, then stared at myself in the mirror for a long minute. OK, jerk, try to look like you're having a good time. You can't do anything for Mom tonight. And she's all right. They've got her in a hospital, not some lunatic asylum. Just remember that. Now put on a smile and try not to make a fool of yourself in front of the hicks.

A hot, stuffy din enveloped us when we stepped through the doors of the gym. "Let's boogie!" Signa yelled, her voice hardly penetrating the noise around us.

"Uh, hold on," I said. "Let's try a few slow songs first. I want to get back in practice."

"Anything you say, brain."

"And make that Carl, huh?"

"OK. Here's a slow one starting now." She put her arms around me, and I clumsily followed suit. We danced. Or at least she danced, and I tried not to break her feet. Maybe she wasn't quite as big as I'd first thought, but she was still one very substantial girl, and I was sure everyone in the place was staring at us.

Midway through the third slow number, I figured the band was about to rev up again. I started looking for a place to sit in the bleachers. I could see Bob and Debbie through the crowd, doing their best to "rrrrock an' rolllll" to the slow tempo. "You know, you've really got me worried," Signa said. "I mean, don't you ever smile?"

I looked at her. She looked OK in new jeans and a gray sweater. No, she looked a lot better than OK—and a hell of a lot better than I did. "I'm smiling," I said. "I'm just not very obvious about it, I guess."

She leaned close, studying my mouth. "Well, maybe you're trying, but . . . Well, I don't know. It's like you're seasick and trying to hide it." She dug strong fingers into my ribs. "Come on. Give me a real smile."

I pushed her hands away more roughly than I'd intended. "Knock that off!"

"Well, sure." She looked hurt.

"Uh, hey, I'm sorry. I'm just kind of ticklish, that's all. . . . Let's go get a Coke or something."

"OK," she said, for the first time not looking at me with those big blue eyes.

The evening didn't exactly collapse, it just slowly deflated. Sitting in the bleachers, we couldn't seem to keep a conversation going. We tried one subject, then another, but couldn't find a single common interest. Finally, Signa spotted some of her girlfriends talking near one of the exits. "Come on," she said, "I'll introduce you to some kids."

"Uh, I've had enough introductions for one week. You go ahead."

"Well, OK. Back in a few minutes."

I sat by myself, watching the other kids dance. Ya, I wanted to be part of it, to be comfortable with all the noise and laughter and confident movement. But it wasn't for me. Hadn't been before and wasn't now. I was still sitting alone when Bob and Debbie danced through the crowd. They timed it so they reached the foot of the bleachers just as the song ended. Bob wiped sweat from his forehead. "Where's Signa?"

"Uh, I saw her a second ago. There she is." I pointed to where Signa was giggling with a knot of other girls.

"We've about worn our feet off, and we're hungry. Let's find out if she's ready to go to the bowling alley for pizza."

She was. I felt conspicuous as hell when we left her group of friends. Had she been telling them what a nerd I was? At the bowling alley, the three of them did all the talking, almost like they'd forgotten me. Maybe they had.

When we dropped Signa off, I said, "Thanks for tonight. I had a good time."

She gave me a grin. "Me too. Good night, now."

Well, she could lie even better than I could. Bob dumped me off. He winked at me when I got out. "See you later, coz."

The house was quiet. I got ready for bed, so depressed I felt like crying. What a stupid, sour, boring nerd I'd been. I lay in the dark, thinking of Jennifer. Who was I kidding? Even if I found my dream girl, how could I ever win her? Somehow I'd have to change. I'd start trying as soon as I got back to the city. Until then, I'd have to depend on my dreams. Signa was just too damned real. And I couldn't handle that.

THE SOUND OF THE GUNSHOT TRIED TO FIND
a place in my dream. My eyes came open when I heard
Bob's feet hit the floor in the next room. His door
banged against the wall, and he went pounding down
the stairs. What now? I heard voices in the kitchen.
"Ma," Bob whined, "why didn't you call me?"

"Because that skunk would've eaten half my eggs and
been home telling the story by the time you got down
here."

"But, Ma, I've been trying to get him for months."

"Oh, stop bellyaching. Go get some clothes on before
you freeze. And get your cousin up. You two can go out
and bury that creature after breakfast."

"Well, you shot him."

"Right. And it's up to you to bury him. That's unless
you want to do your own cooking and washing around
here."

Bob came grumbling up the stairs. "Time to get up,
coz. We gotta go bury a skunk." I put my head under
the pillow. This was too much. God, what the hell was I
doing here? Memories of the dance and Signa started
creeping into my brain. I pulled the pillow away and
swung my feet to the cold floor.

Bob spent most of breakfast complaining to Uncle
Glen about Aunt June blasting the skunk. Uncle Glen
brushed back his uncombed gray hair and grinned.
"You've got to get up pretty early in the morning to
keep her from shooting the meat for you, boy. I learned
that a long time ago. That's why I sleep in on Sunday
mornings."

Aunt June turned from the griddle. "You'd sleep in every morning if I didn't keep a fire burning under you."

"That's why I married you, sweetheart. To keep me warm."

"That's probably about it, too," she said.

Bob used a stick to push the body of the skunk into the shovel I held. "Well," he said, "at least she hit him in the head so he didn't have time to stink much. North-country perfume, that's what I call it. Hit a skunk on a hot summer day and your car smells for a month." The skunk was smaller and lighter than I'd expected. Bob tossed the stick away and took the shovel. "I ain't gonna dig any holes in this hard ground. Come on, we'll throw him in the swamp."

I followed. Maybe Bob didn't think the skunk stunk much, but I was getting a definite whiff of something very bad in the cold air. On the far side of the hill beyond the tumbledown barn, we came to an old barbed-wire fence bordering a wide tangle of swamp. Bob reached the shovel back and, with a grunt, swung it forward to catapult the skunk into the brush. Bad move. The skunk's body left the shovel much too early and shot straight into the sky above us. I looked up just in time to see gravity take over. The skunk corpse plummeted straight for my nose, its striped body getting very large very fast. I dove for a nearby snowdrift.

The skunk's fall and my dive intersected neatly. I felt a furry whack across the back of my neck a split second before I plunged headfirst into the drift. I could feel the skunk clinging to my back. The damn thing was still alive! I leaped to my feet, trying to twist away from it. The skunk swung over my left shoulder, the claw of a

133

back foot caught in the collar of my sweater. I yelled and batted at the grinning features. The body swung clear around to slap my right ear. In about two seconds, I'd go completely out of my mind. Desperately, I reached over my shoulder, ripped the paw loose, and flung the skunk away from me. It landed just as dead as it had been before.

I should have tried to hit good ol' Bob with it. He was doubled over, laughing. "Bob, you son of a bitch, I'm going to kill you! Give me that shovel. I'm going to wrap it around your damn head."

That made him laugh even harder. I stood glaring at him, my hands balled into fists. Finally, he was able to choke out, "Oh, God. I'm sorry. But you—" He started giggling.

"Bob, I'm warning you—"

He waved a hand. "I know. I know. I'm sorry." Still chuckling, he kicked the skunk back into the shovel and heaved the body into the swamp.

On the walk back, I snarled at him, "Look, you idiot. Don't you tell anybody about this. Not your mom or dad or Signa or anybody. Nobody! You got it?"

"Sure, coz." He tried to hide a smile.

"I mean it, Bob. If you say anything, so help me, I'll get you."

"My Lord, which one of you stinks?" Aunt June didn't wait for a reply. "Out of my house." She waved a big spoon threateningly. "Get those clothes off outside."

I stripped to my underwear in the subzero cold. Uncle Glen came to the door. "Bob, catch." He tossed a blanket over the porch rail. "This is a story I've got to hear." He went back inside.

I glared at Bob. "You'd better leave out a lot of details."

He was gazing at the sky. "Sure, coz. You know, I can't figure out how Ma knows how to shoot so good. I mean, pow, right through the head. Just one shot. I wonder if—"

"Bob, just shut up. Or I swear one of these days you're going to wake up with a dead skunk shoved down your throat." He grinned.

Aunt June sniffed the air when I came shivering into the kitchen. "That's better. Now take a good shower. I laid out some clothes that'll be good enough for church. Bob, get a garbage bag and take his other clothes down to the washing machine. Then help me get the food for the church dinner into the car. Come on, get moving, boys."

I snapped, "You can count me out on the church thing."

She stared at me coldly. Uncle Glen was standing in the doorway, knotting a tie over a white shirt. "He's had a big week and a rough morning, Mother. Let him off this time."

For a moment she gazed at him stubbornly. "Well, all right. *This* week. But you wear one of those new ties I bought. That one looks like you spilled breakfast on it." He glanced down at his tie, shrugged, and went back to their bedroom.

In the shower, I reduced half a cake of soap to a sliver before I was satisfied I no longer smelled of skunk. Screw this country living. I'd gotten hit by a skunk, for God's sake. Bob would probably tell the whole story on the way into town. Well, to hell with him; I was getting out of here!

I pulled on the clothes I'd worn on the trip from Mil-

135

waukee, then started emptying drawers into my battered suitcase. I'd leave a note on the table and head for the highway. One good hitch and I'd be far down the road by the time they got back. I was struggling to get the lid fastened when my ol' professor side started fighting the idea. Hold it right there, jerk. Your aunt will have the cops after you the second she sees you're gone. And if they don't catch you, that s.o.b. Mullan will be waiting at the other end: Off to Lincoln Hills, champ. And take a hard look at your attitude on the way. Comprende?

I slumped on the bed. Deep inside me, another voice was crying: Just do it! For once in your life, just do something because you feel like it! I lunged for the suitcase. With one foot on the lid, I got the catches fastened. I took one last frantic look around the room and ran for the stairs. My foot slipped on the top step. I caught my balance but lost my grip on the suitcase. It shot into the void, recognized the aerodynamic impossibility of flight, tumbled once, and hit. The lid blew on impact, scattering clothes half the length of the stairs.

I should have quit right then, but something had hold of me. I plunged down the steps, swept my clothes into a pile, then ran upstairs to throw the broken suitcase under the bed. I'd come with a garbage bag; I'd leave with one. Five minutes later, I was out the door and running down the driveway toward the gravel road and the highway that would take me home. I hadn't left a note; the more time before they knew the better. The cold burned my lungs, and my city shoes slipped on the icy road. But I was moving; I was free.

Like hell. To avoid going through town, I had to walk three miles of back roads to the highway. I never made it. The ol' professor saw to that. You're crazy! he screamed. They're going to bring you back or send you someplace worse. And how about those damn stereos, jerk? How do you know that idiot Sheridan got them out of the basement? What happens if Mullan or the cops go looking for you and find them instead? Then you're dog meat, jerk. They'll stick you in with the real criminals. You'll lose your virginity to a five-hundred-pound ax murderer.

That other voice—the one that had pleaded with me to run—tried to argue, but it got fainter and fainter until it fell silent altogether. I stopped and stood for a long time with my garbage bag at my freezing feet and the wind from the gray woods freezing the sweat under my thin clothes. Not far beyond the next turn of the road, a truck geared down to take a hill on the highway. I had to go back. Mullan had told it straight: living up country was the least painful of my options. Tears welled in my eyes. Mom, why did you do this to us? How could you ever let things get this bad?

I started back, my pace quickening as my sanity started returning. God, life was tough enough with my aunt and uncle already. If they found out about this idiocy— I looked at my watch. Could I beat them home? It'd be close. I started jogging.

A light snow was falling by the time I got to the driveway. Fresh tire tracks ran up the hill toward the farm; they'd beaten me back. I had one chance left, and that was to find Bob. He owed me one, damn it.

Getting through the woods unseen was twenty times harder than I'd imagined. I wallowed through deep snow, tore my jeans on brush, and nearly lost an eye when a branch hit me in the face. Finally, I leaned gasping against the back of the garage. God, I was cold. I had snow down my neck and the back of my pants and up my shirt sleeves and pants cuffs. Somewhere below my ankles, there were feet, but I'd long ago lost any nerve contact with them. I took one more breath and peeked through the window into the garage. For the first time that day, I got a break. Good ol' Bob was sitting next to the barrel stove, happily doing something to a beaver corpse. Thank God. I slipped around the corner and ducked in the door. He looked up. "Hi, coz. I thought you were in your room studying."

The barrel stove was cold. "God, why don't you have a fire in here?"

"It's not that cold, and I'm not staying long. Hey, you look bad, coz. What the heck you been doin'? You oughta—" He caught sight of the garbage bag and stopped.

"Ya, I started to run away, Bob. But I changed my mind and came back. Now you could do me one hell of a favor if you'd help me keep your parents from finding out." He looked uncertain. "Look, I'm not going to do it again. And, damn it, you owe me."

He shrugged. "OK. What do we need me to do?"

"To begin with, get my boots from under my bed before my feet fall off. Then help me think of a way to get this bag to my room."

He was back in a couple of minutes, my boots under his coat. I pulled them on with blue shaking fingers. "I got it figured out, coz. I'll drop a rope from my window. You tie the bag to it, and I'll pull it up. Then you can walk in and say that you just went for a walk."

"There must be a simpler way, but I'm too cold to care."

I crouched just to the right of the living-room window. The end of the rope dropped at my feet, and I looked up to see Bob leaning out the upstairs window, a big grin on his face. Stay serious, you hick. I tied the bag to the rope and pumped my arm. He started pulling. Halfway up, my knot let go and the bag dropped, sending clothes cascading about me. Bob almost passed out trying to stifle his laughter, as I scrambled around in the snow getting everything back in the bag. This time I made about six knots in the rope. He pulled it up a lot slower than I thought necessary. I let out a long breath when the garbage bag disappeared inside Bob's window. I ran as fast as I could on frozen feet to the back door and warmth.

I was standing under a hot shower when Bob called through the door. "Hey, coz, I'm going into town to pick up the folks. Ma stayed behind to clean the church, and Pa decided to bowl a few lines. See you later."

"Bob, you son of a bitch," I screamed. I could hear him laughing all the way out the door.

Later, when I was finally warm enough to think straight about the afternoon, it scared the crap out of me. What the hell had sent me running out the door and down the road with my ridiculous garbage bag of jumbled clothes and dreams? I'd risked everything on a crazy impulse. I hadn't behaved like the ol' professor; I'd behaved like Mom. And not Mom when she was sober, either, but Mom when she was drunk—somebody gives you a hard time, bash him with a bottle; a cop shows up, kick him in the nuts or brain him with a rock. My God, that wasn't me. I was a planner; I never did anything on impulse. Well, almost never. The cop and the gun, that'd been different. A little, anyway.

I lay on my bed and thought most of the evening. I had to get back in control. I was the ol' professor, damn it. And I had a plan. The Plan, and it was all that really made any difference. I went downstairs to use the phone. Steve answered on the third ring. "Hey, professor. How are things in the sticks?"

"Don't ask. How are things down there?"

"Real good. We've got a whole bunch of good units for you. When are you getting back?"

"As soon as I can find a way. Did you get the stuff out of my basement?"

"Don't worry, man. Everything's cool."

"How about Bill Hoyt? Is he still following you around?"

"Na, he's given up. I think it was something to do with my new girl. Seems she went out with him a few times. I ain't worried."

"Good. I'll be in touch."

Signa waved to me when she came into chemistry on Monday, but I made like I was engrossed in the textbook. Pankratz started handing out the test. When he got to me, he said, "You don't have to take this, you know."

"I don't have anything better to do."

"Suit yourself."

Easy? God, it was almost embarrassing. I finished in twenty minutes and picked up my drafting book.

Signa caught up to me in the hall. "Hey, why didn't you telepath me some answers? I could have used them."

"On that? Hell, that was kid stuff."

"We aren't all brains, you know. But I guess I did OK. So, how are things going? You didn't come for the milk last night."

"Bob and I made a deal. I do chickens, he goes for the milk. Gives him a chance to blast rabbits on the way. The walk just bores me."

"Oh."

"This is your next class, right?" I gestured at the door without slowing my pace. I didn't look back.

I'd iced her, and that's what I was going to do to all of them. From now on, straight ice. The ol' professor was back, his stainless-steel heart pumping frozen methane—a creature designed for one of those distant outer planets where nothing lived but the wind and the cold. That's where I belonged, standing on a planet a billion miles from earth. I wanted to look up and see the sun no bigger than a pea, a sun so small that I could pinch out the light between thumb and forefinger and imagine I heard the pop.

That night at supper, Aunt June fixed me with a hard stare. "I saw you across the street at noon smoking a cigarette."

I shrugged. "So? That's where you're supposed to go, right?"

"Not if you care what teachers and other people think of you."

Oh, for God's sake. "Aunt June, where I come from, teachers are happy if you just show up for school. A lot of kids don't bother."

"Well, you're not back in the city. You're here, and I care what people think of this family." On the far end of the table, Uncle Glen sighed and rubbed the back of his neck, while Bob suddenly got very interested in a far corner of the room.

I kept my temper. "Look, Mom smokes, and she knows I smoke sometimes. But I don't smoke a lot, and I don't smoke in your house. Isn't that enough?"

"I don't think you should smoke at all. It's dirty and it's unhealthy."

We stared at each other for a long moment. "I'm sorry, Aunt June. But at this point I really don't give a damn."

Uncle Glen jumped in before she could go for my throat. "Mother, he's got other worries now. A little thing like smoking just isn't worth a big fight."

She glared at him. "Smoking is not a little thing. It's a killer." She got up and started noisily clearing the table. "And your hair's still too long." She turned away. Uncle Glen shot me a wry look.

Later that evening, Bob told me, "You got off easy. She would've horsewhipped me. Pa's gonna take some heat for butting in."

"That's his problem. I didn't marry her."

Bob studied me. "Well, I'll guarantee you one thing, she's not gonna forget about the cigarettes or the hair. Or church, either." He was right. She didn't give me— or either of them—any slack the rest of the week. Twice I had to fish my cigarettes out of the wastebasket in my room. After that, I always kept my extra pack above the door in the shed where I split kindling.

Mom called Friday evening. Bob was out with Debbie, and Uncle Glen had gone bowling with friends. Aunt June answered the phone, talked for a couple of minutes, then beckoned to me.

"Hi, baby. I was kind of hoping you'd be out having some fun on Friday night."

"There ain't much around here, Mom. So, uh, how are you feeling?"

"I'm OK. I'm sorry I couldn't call sooner. They don't let you use the phone for two weeks."

"I know." I heard her sniff and knew she was crying. I felt my insides twist. Please don't cry, Mom. You know I could never stand that.

She managed to say, "So how are you doing, baby?"

"I'm OK, Mom. I wish I could go home, but I'm OK."

"I want to go home too." She started crying hard. "It's not fair. We didn't do nothing so bad. It's just not fair."

A clawed hand was trying to tear through my stomach to reach my heart. I leaned forward, trying to breathe. "Please don't cry, Mom. Everything's going to be OK."

Her words came in a rush then, so hard and vehement that I think I actually stumbled backward. "You've got to help me, baby! The bastards are killing me. You've got to come and get me, baby. Please, baby, please."

Her words kept tumbling through the phone. I jerked the receiver from my ear and stood staring at it. Aunt June took it from me without a word. "Veronica, stop it! Stop it, or I'll hang up this instant!" Mom got some kind of grip on herself. Aunt June took a deep breath. "Now see here, Veronica. You can't do this to your boy. You're in the hospital under a court order, and he can't do a thing about that. Carl is fine here. He's not very happy, but he's fine. Now you have to get well so you can start being his mother again. But in the meantime, I won't allow you to call him with nonsense like this."

She listened to Mom for a moment. "Yes, I know it must be very difficult, and maybe it wasn't fair. But calling up here and getting Carl upset isn't going to make things any easier on anybody. I'm going to say good night now. We love you and we pray for you. You just do your best to get well. . . . Yes, I'll tell him. He loves you too. Now, good night."

She hung up and gave me a tight-lipped stare. "That wasn't your mother talking, Carl. That was her sickness. You're going to have to remember that. If she calls again in that condition, we're just not going to talk to her." She waited for me to reply, but all I could do was stare back at her. She sighed. "Well, why don't I make us some cocoa and then we can talk?" I shook my head.

"Carl, sooner or later, you're going to have to talk about this. The last few days, you've been trying to convince everybody that you're wearing some kind of impenetrable armor. But your uncle and I have raised four boys, and we don't get fooled by that kind of act. You're hurting, and you need to talk. And we're willing to listen and help in any way we can."

What did she expect from me? What did any of them expect from me? I finally found my voice. "Go to hell!" It was supposed to be a snarl, but it came out a bleat. I spun and took the stairs three at a time.

I lay facedown on my bed until long after I heard Bob and Uncle Glen come home. In the morning, a note lay on the rug inside my door: "Carl, I'm sorry if I pushed you too hard. By now, you already know that I am not as patient as I should be. I will do my best to wait until you can trust me. And when you're ready, I will listen and I will help. So will your uncle and your cousin. For years, we didn't behave much like we cared. But, Carl, we are family and you can depend on us. Love, Aunt June."

She'd underlined the last sentence twice. I read the note again, then crumpled it in my fist. How could I have made matters any worse? I'd blown it—bleated my pain and fear when I should have iced her with a cold "No, thank you." Now she'd be after me every minute to spill my guts. I spent a long time thinking before going downstairs. I'd apologize for telling her to go to hell. I might not like her, but she didn't deserve that kind of crap from me. Then I'd tell her very politely that I preferred to keep some things to myself. She might not give up right away, but I could be stubborn too.

I glanced at the wall clock in the kitchen, surprised to find it still very early. Aunt June looked up from her cup of coffee. "Feeling better after a good night's sleep?" I nodded. "Good. Ready for some flapjacks?"

"Uh, Aunt June, I'm sorry for what I said."

"I didn't notice that it caused me any permanent damage. You want to start with two or three?"

"Two, I guess." And the conversation ended there, leaving too damn much unsaid. My inner voice growled: You are a stinking coward, Staggers.

That afternoon, I turned down Bob's invitation to go with him to check beaver traps. Instead, I took a long walk across the fields. If any bears, wolves, or snipe were lying in wait, they were welcome to me. I was down—way, way down. Until Mom's phone call, I hadn't realized how much I'd counted on the treatment program making her better. But she wasn't going to get better. She wasn't even trying. She'd last out her time and then start drinking again. And I'd go back to Milwaukee to watch her finish destroying her life. And mine.

For the first time in years, I didn't seem able to keep anything balanced. The house of cards called the Plan had tumbled about me, and I couldn't even find the card that had Jennifer's face. The icy ol' professor was on the point of becoming a blubbering little kid. Even my cowboy-dad was silent—just when his advice might have done a little good.

Near dusk I paused on the end of the ridge nearest the Amundsens' farm. Signa came out of the house and trudged across the yard with her head down and her hands deep in her back pockets. For an instant, I had the crazy impulse to go down and talk to her. She swung the heavy barn door open and disappeared. For a minute longer, I hesitated, then turned away. I walked north along the ridge, putting as much distance between me and her as possible.

For the next two weeks, I let life go on around me. I went to school, but didn't bother to listen or study anymore. I avoided Signa—although she still seemed friendly enough. At least I was spared sitting near her on the school bus, since her father dropped her off and picked her up in the bulk milk truck he drove during the day.

Around the farm, I tried to hide how miserable I felt. I did the chores with Bob, but drew the line at helping him skin the animals he caught in his traps. At supper, I concentrated on my food and let the others do the talking. I spent the evenings in my room, supposedly studying, but most of the time I just lay on my bed, staring at the ceiling.

Mom called every Friday about the same time. Aunt June talked first, then I got on for a few minutes. Nothing much got said. The first time, Mom cried and I tried not to. The second time, she tried to sound cheerful and I tried—God, how I tried—to sound a little cheerful too. While we talked, Aunt June kept an eye on me from her chair in the living room. When I hung up, she'd put down her sewing or knitting and wait for me to start talking. I didn't, and she didn't push me. We had a truce of sorts. As long as I went to church on Sundays, she seemed willing to give me an inch or two of slack on the other stuff.

Aunt June sent Bob and me into town for groceries on the last Saturday in January. Bob handled the shopping like a pro, working out the prices per ounce or pound damn near as fast as I could. Dumb hillbilly, my ass. It was an act, and after nearly four weeks, it was really beginning to irritate me. We checked out and loaded the car. "Let's go down to the café," he said. "I want to see if Debbie's working."

"I forgot to buy smokes. I'll meet you there."

"Those things are going to kill you."

"Ya, Aunt June told me." He left, and I went back into the grocery store to buy my cigarettes.

As luck would have it, Ginger had just finished checking out. "Hidy, hidy," she said. "You've been avoiding me."

"Uh, not really."

"Here." She dumped a heavy bag in my arms. "You can help me get my stuff in the car. Cliff-a-roo was supposed to meet me here, but he's late as usual." She started pushing an overflowing shopping cart toward the exit.

I stood on the sidewalk next to her car, handing her bags. She complained nonstop about Cliff: "And, you know, he just doesn't get the hint sometimes. He thinks just because he's so big . . ."

For such a big ox, he moved damn quietly. Suddenly, a huge hand closed on my collar. My toes barely brushed the sidewalk as Cliff spun me around to face him. "What're you up to, scumbag?"

"Cliff! Uh, nothing. Just helping Ginger with her groceries."

"Clifford, you leave him alone! I've got a perfect right to talk to anyone I want to."

"You got nothing to say to this city slimeball." He gave me a shake that made my teeth rattle.

"Who says I don't? Now, you put him down."

He glowered at me. "Anything you say." He threw me like I was a sack of potatoes. I hit the sidewalk a good ten feet from him and slid into the wall of the grocery store, my head banging against the plate-glass window. I have to hand it to Ginger that she at least made a move to get between us. But Cliff pushed her aside. "I ain't done with him yet."

I caught sight of Bob. He was running as fast as he could on the icy sidewalk. Cliff saw him too, and pulled back a ham-sized fist. But Bob was much too slick for him. Three or four yards out of range, he threw up his arms to protect his face and hurled his body at Cliff's ankles. It was about the prettiest cross-body block I'd ever seen. Cliff went down like a redwood, gaining speed until he hit the sidewalk with a tremendous thud. Bob rolled on through and hopped up. "Come on, coz!" he yelled. "I'm not waiting around!" We ran like hell.

A sheriff's car swung around the corner, its lights flashing. "Oops," Bob said. "John Law." We stopped.

A middle-aged deputy sheriff with glasses got out and strode past us. "Hi, Bob," he said. "Stick around."

"Yes, sir."

"Cliff, you meathead, get your butt over by the car! You too, Ginger." The cop pointed the direction with his nightstick. Cliff shuffled over to stand by the squad car. Ginger touched the bruise on his forehead and made an Oh-but-that-must-hurt pout with her mouth.

"How the hell'd he get here so fast?" I whispered to Bob. My insides were knotting up; I wasn't sure if I was more afraid of Cliff or the cop.

Bob was watching the scene, a slight smile on his face. "He just lives up the block. Somebody in the store must have called him the second Cliff started on you. Don't worry, Jim's a good guy."

The deputy came back to us. "What happened, Bob?"

"I didn't see the start of it. This is my city cousin, Carl. Ginger's been trying to flirt with him for a month."

The deputy stuck out his hand. "Jim Halperin. How you doing?"

"I'll live."

"Well, tell me about it." I did. He shook his head angrily. "Damn, I get sick of those two. You want to press charges against Cliff?"

I shook my head. "Not if he promises not to kill me just for living."

"Fair enough." He turned and headed for Cliff and Ginger. I'd heard a couple of real tongue-lashings before, but nothing like this. On the main street of Blind River, the deputy screamed and yelled and threatened until Ginger started crying and I thought Cliff was about to. A small crowd enjoyed the hell out of it. Finally, the deputy brought Cliff over. "OK, now shake hands with these guys and tell them you're not going to give them any more crap." Cliff shook our hands, his hand like a big limp fish. "Say it," the deputy said.

"I won't give you guys any more crap."

"OK. Now, damn it, Cliff, I've just about had it with you. I'm going to call your dad and tell him that the next time you screw up I'm going to lock your stupid ass in the county jail. Got it?"

"Yes, sir."

The deputy addressed the small crowd. "OK, folks, the fun's over. Let's go on about our business. You too, Cliff." He turned to us again. "He gives you any crap, *any at all*, you call me, hear?" We nodded.

On the ride home, I asked Bob, "Why'd you do that? Cliff could have killed you if he'd kicked at the right time."

"Aw, he doesn't think that fast."

"But really, Bob. Why'd you get involved?"

He looked at me, his face puzzled. "Well, hell, you're my cousin. And my friend. What was I supposed to do?"

I shrugged. "Well, thanks."

"Besides, maybe this makes up a little bit for the day I hit you with the skunk."

I almost said, Ya, we're even, but then I looked at him and said, "Not a chance, you hick. It wasn't even a start." We laughed.

"I've got a deal for you boys," Uncle Glen said. We were driving north from Blind River midmorning on the Saturday following my brush with death. The ride had been silent up to this point, even Bob quiet in the shadow of the foul mood Uncle Glen had been carrying around for days. "I've had my eye on a pickup Johnny Benet's got for sale. If I can make a deal, you boys can have the Ford. That's if you turn to and help me get some things fixed around the farm. And you, Bob, have got to at least look like you study once in a while."

It didn't take Einstein to figure out what had led to this; Aunt June was doing some serious nagging. Bob glanced at me. I gave him a look that said, Hell, yes. "Sounds great to us, Pa."

"All right. But, damn it, if I have to ride you boys, I'll sell this car the same day. Understood?"

"Sure, Pa."

He went back to staring silently at the road ahead. Bob nudged me and I nudged back. A car. About damn time we got mobile.

The pickup wasn't close to new, but it must have been worth about twice as much as Johnny Benet's shack. Uncle Glen knocked on the warped door, waited, then knocked again. A voice called, "Ya, come in."

The place smelled only slightly better than the chicken coop. A small guy came out of a back room in greasy trousers and a dirty long-underwear top. He was

150

red-eyed and unshaven. "Hi, Glen. You caught me taking a nap. Had a long night." And a rough one, I thought. "Want some coffee?"

"No, thanks, Johnny. We'd like to give your pickup a look."

"Sure." He dug in his pocket. "Oh, the keys must be in it. Go take 'er for a spin."

I heard rustling from the back room. A huge fat woman stumbled to the door and stared blearily at us. "Who is it, Johnny?"

"It's Glen Staggers wanting to look at the pickup. Go back to bed."

Instead, she waddled into the room, a loose bathrobe barely hiding the gigantic mounds of her breasts. "I want some coffee. Or a beer. Ya, a beer."

Uncle Glen said, "Let's go, boys."

We took the pickup for a test run. Bob was laughing. "God, could you believe her? Who is she, Pa?"

"I don't know."

"I mean, can you imagine that little fart on top of her—" He couldn't finish, he was laughing so hard.

I was laughing too. "She's isn't a dog, she's a brontosaurus."

Bob cut in, "I mean, I knew Johnny Benet was low, but I never thought he—"

"You two, shut up!" We looked at Uncle Glen in surprise. "Let me tell you pups something. I don't care what he looks like or who he has in the sack. That's one of the best men you'll ever meet. I'd like to see the both of you keep up with him splitting wood or shoveling gravel or doing anything that takes more than a smart mouth. He'd work you into the ground. And he also happens to be my friend, so keep your wisecracks to yourselves!"

We were very quiet on the rest of the ride. Back at the

shack, Uncle Glen went in to dicker with Johnny. "I hope we didn't screw anything up," I said.

"Ya, it wasn't real smart running down Johnny. Pa and him go back a long way. And Johnny ain't a bad guy, really. He's just . . . well, you saw."

Ya, I'd seen. Thoughts of Mom came into my head. If she didn't kill herself first, maybe she'd end up in some shack with somebody like Johnny. I pushed the image away. Come on, Uncle Glen, buy that damn pickup.

Ten minutes later, he came back out. He tossed the keys to the Ford to Bob. "Allll righttt. Thanks, Pa." As we followed the pickup, he grinned at me. "Is this hog heaven, or what?"

"No, I think we just left it." We howled with laughter.

I reached for the knapsack. "You get the eggs tonight; I'll go for the milk." Bob raised his eyebrows and started to open his mouth. "Don't push your luck, Bob. And give me that rifle; I might feel like killing something."

"Like what, coz?"

"Like a skunk. Don't sleep with your mouth open."

As usual, Signa was milking on the line of cows nearest the door, while her father worked on the far side of the barn. "Well, howdy," she said. "What got you over here tonight?"

My courage was failing me fast. I shrugged. "Needed a change in the routine, I guess."

"Ya, gathering eggs is a bore. Almost as boring as milking. Just a sec, I'll get your milk."

She came back with the milk but made no move to load it in my knapsack. She stood smiling at me. I shifted uncomfortably. "I guess I really kind of came to see you."

Her smile broadened. "Well, here I am."

"Ya, I guess you are. . . . Look, Signa, could we just kind of go for a walk or something tomorrow? Dances and crowds are just more than I can handle right now."

"Hey, I'll take what I can get. Here, let me get rid of these bottles." She shoved them in the knapsack. I faced her. She reached out and straightened the shoulder straps. Her hands lingered a moment, and she bit her lip. "You know, I ain't really so scary. I'm just kind of big and loud. Remember that, huh? Hey, I gotta get back to these bossies." She turned away quickly.

"Ya, sure," I said to her back. "I'll meet you about one on the ridge, OK?"

"I'll be there."

Bob grinned at me across the supper table. "Find your way OK?"

"No problem. No problem at all."

Suddenly, he was serious. "You didn't see any funny tracks in the snow, did you? Kind of like someone was dragging a stick along?"

Uncle Glen looked up with his fork halfway to his mouth. "What are you talking about, Bob?"

"Well, I'm not sure, Pa, but I think maybe I saw some snow-snake tracks up by the chicken coop."

Uncle Glen shook his head. "Damn."

I glanced at Aunt June and thought I saw her hide a smile. "Now, just a second," I said. "Is there really such a thing as a snow snake, or are you just setting me up for another stupid joke?"

"You tell him, Pa."

"Well, they're pretty rare, but we've got a few around here. Trouble is, they're white and blend in with the snow. Makes 'em hard to spot."

"Poisonous?"

"No, but they're dangerous. You see, they travel in pairs. One lies across a path and trips you up and the other—"

Uncle Glen couldn't keep a straight face, and Bob had to choke out the punch line. "And the other pulls down your pants and crams snow up your ass."

The three of them howled with laughter. And, for once, I joined them.

I STAMPED MY FEET, HOPING THAT MY TOES wouldn't break off inside my freezing boots. Far below me, Signa scrambled nimbly over the fence at the lower end of the Amundsens' pasture and started the climb up the ridge. She waved, and I waved back, then shoved my hands deep in my pockets again. What the hell had I been thinking? It was February, not July, and hardly the season for a romantic stroll. I wiggled my toes, trying to count them.

It took her another five minutes to reach me. She was out of breath, her cheeks rosy and her forehead damp. "Whew, that climb warms you up. Been waiting long?"

"Well, a glacier or two zipped by, but I guess they come around pretty fast up here."

She laughed and took my arm. "You look cold. Come on, walking will warm you up." We started off along the ridge, the wind-packed snow rasping under our boots. "So," she said, "let's start over. Tell me about yourself. I hardly know anything about you, except that you're a brain and want to be some kind of engineer."

What the hell was I supposed to talk about? My drunken mother? My life of crime? "Well, there's not really a whole lot more to tell. . . . Hey, did I mention that Bob and I have a car now?" I told her about getting Uncle Glen's old Ford and then maneuvered the conversation onto her family.

Like Bob, Signa was the youngest. She had a grown brother and two grown sisters living elsewhere. "I miss them," she said. "It seems like everybody moves away from Blind River as soon as they get a chance. It's hard around here. There aren't many jobs, especially in the winter."

"How about working in the woods? That's what Bob always talks about."

"Ya, my brother used to talk like that too. But cutting pulp is a heck of a tough way to make a living. It's dirty and it's dangerous. Dad says a chain saw is the most dangerous tool in the world. Farming is tough too. We couldn't make it if Dad didn't drive a milk truck during the day."

I glanced at her, surprised to hear her talking seriously for a change. "Things are tough all over, I guess."

She laughed. "Oh, it's not all that bad. Tell me about life in the city."

It sucks most of the time, I thought, and was surprised at myself. "It's OK, I guess. Is that where you want to go after high school?"

"Maybe, but not right away. I hate to think of Mom and Dad running the farm without any help. Dad says he's going to sell out in a few years, so I'll probably stick around until then. I just hope I can get some kind of job in town. Someday I'd like to go to vocational school, and I'm going to have to save some money."

"What are you going to study?"

"Promise you won't laugh?"

"Sure."

"I want to be a veterinary technician. You know, kind of like an assistant to a veterinarian."

"Why should I laugh at that?"

"Oh, I don't know. You're a brain and you're going to be an engineer and I just figure you must be thinking: 'Yep, that'll suit her. Big ol' country girl stomping around in cowshit for the rest of her life.' I mean, that's what you've seen me doing about half the time."

She was hitting damn close to the impression I'd had

of her a few weeks before. Uncomfortably close. "Well, I don't know. I kind of admire you for being able to put up with it. I mean, how can you even stand the smell of that barn?"

She laughed. "Heck, you don't even notice it after a while. About the only thing that bothers me is having to wash my hair every morning so I don't go to school smelling like manure. But, hey, stop changing the subject. Tell me about you."

"Well, right now, I'm damn cold. Let's go see if Bob's back with the Ford. He's supposed to turn it over to me at three."

"Did you get him to wear a watch?" she asked.

"Well, no. I never thought of it."

"He'll be late, then. Bob doesn't believe in watches. He says he can tell time by the sun, just like an Indian. Your aunt was complaining to my mom about it the other day."

"Well, that's Bob, I guess. . . . Your mom and Aunt June are close, huh?"

"Oh, ya. They've been best friends since high school."

A nasty suspicion twitched in my guts. What had Aunt June been telling Signa's mom about my problems? I tried to push the worry away. "Well, let's head back anyway. We can get something hot to drink, while I count how many toes I've got left."

"How many pairs of socks do you have on?"

"About six."

"That's your problem. Air is better than socks. Wear a heavy pair over a light pair and you'll be fine."

Talking about cold weather got us back to Aunt June's kitchen and a cup of cocoa. Bob rolled in a few minutes later, and Signa and I went for a test run. If nothing else, the Ford had a decent radio, and I maneuvered the conversation onto music. After I dropped her off for the evening milking, I cruised for a few miles more. I felt good. It hadn't been much of a date, but at least I hadn't made a complete fool of myself. Maybe I'd bitched about the cold too much—just like a wimp—but she'd thought I was kidding half the time.

I turned the car around and headed back. And, like always, my good mood started breaking apart. What exactly was the deal here? Why did Signa want to go out with me of all people? God, she couldn't be that desperate. My inner voice had the answer: Because she doesn't know you, jerk. And you damn well better keep it that way, or bye-bye Signa.

I bit down on a piece of steak and winced. Aunt June glanced sharply at me. "When was the last time you saw a dentist?"

I shrugged. "I don't know. A while ago."

"Smile at me."

"I don't want to smile at you."

"Well, then show me your teeth." Uncle Glen shifted uncomfortably and asked Bob a question about the Ford. "Come on, show me," Aunt June ordered. I drew back my lips for a microsecond, then took another bite of steak. "Well, a good cleaning would get those tobacco stains off, anyway. I'm going to call for an appointment tomorrow. If you don't like the way I cut hair, you could go to the barber too."

I almost blew up. Since when do you run my life, lady? But in my anger I forgot to chew on the other side, and a sharp pain skewered my words. OK, OK, I should see a dentist. But why do you have to be so damn bossy about everything?

"So which of you boys are off courting tonight?" Uncle Glen asked.

"My turn tonight," Bob said. "Carl gets the car on Saturdays."

"I think it would be nice if you doubled," Aunt June said.

"I think that's their affair, Mother."

"That's just what I'm afraid of. Affairs." Aunt June stared at us.

"Oh, for God's sake," Bob said. He got up and stalked into the next room.

"Uh, Aunt June, Mom calls on Fridays," I said. "I gotta be here." Why was I getting into this? Bob could take care of himself.

She harrumphed but couldn't really argue with that. She glared after Bob, then started clearing the table. I finished my meal and joined Uncle Glen in the living room. He was trying to tune the TV. He whacked it smartly on the side, and the picture wobbled into focus, then went haywire again. He swore and gave the set another swat. "I think you've fixed it about as long as you're going to that way," I said.

"You got a better suggestion?"

"Yes, if you've got a screwdriver and a flashlight."

We turned the set around. I opened the back and started messing with the potentiometer in the high-voltage circuit. Uncle Glen stuck out an exploratory finger. "Don't!" I yelped. He pulled his hand back quickly. "That's a high-voltage capacitor, and it's got enough juice to blow you through that wall. Maybe twenty thousand volts."

His face went a little pale. "Maybe we shouldn't be fooling with this."

"Just give me a little light, and I'll be done in a minute." I heard Bob come down the stairs and leave.

Five minutes later, I had the set working almost like new. Uncle Glen sat back in his recliner with a satisfied grunt. He reached over and slapped me on the knee. "Thanks. Also, thanks for not letting me fry myself."

"No problem." I hesitated. Aunt June was in the basement, and it seemed the right time to ask. "Uncle Glen, would you mind if I asked you something?"

"Go ahead."

"I've been trying to get along with Aunt June, but it seems like the longer I'm here, the more she gets on me. I mean, she eased up for a while, but in the last few days, she's really been on my case. What the heck am I doing wrong?"

He sighed. "You're not doing anything wrong. You don't smile much, but I can understand that." He paused. "Your aunt is just feeling guilty. She can't do anything for my sis, so she's trying to straighten you out instead. As far as I'm concerned, I don't think you need much straightening. But she's got her ideas."

"Well, I don't really think it's her business. I'm—" I stopped and thought for a moment. "Wait a second, what do you mean she feels guilty?"

"Oh, she figures if we'd been more like family to you and my sis, maybe we would have seen the trouble coming. You know, been able to help before things got so bad."

"That's the dumbest thing I've ever heard," I blurted. "I've been trying to help her for years. If it's anybody's fault what's happened, it's mine."

He looked at me sharply. "You don't believe that."

What had I said? I ran it back through my head. "Well, not exactly my fault, but if anybody could have helped her, it would have been me."

He shook his head. "No, I don't think so. No offense, but you're still a kid. Kids can't be expected to handle that kind of load. I'm probably the one who should have known and done something. Your aunt's been telling me that. Not right out, but I can tell what she's thinking. But, hell, Ronnie and me are fourteen years apart. I left home when she was four, and we never saw much of each other after that. Maybe that wasn't right, but that's the way life worked out." He sat brooding for a long moment, then muttered, "Well, this show looks pretty stupid. Let's try another channel."

I was trying to process what he'd told me. Why the hell should Aunt June or Uncle Glen feel guilty about anything? Should Bob feel guilty? "Hey, coz, I really feel lousy that I let your old lady become a drunk and a hooker." What bullshit. I was the only one with any right to feel guilty. An alarm screamed inside my head. Wait a second, jerk. It isn't *your* fault. But deep down, I couldn't shake the feeling that somehow it was.

I was still arguing with that feeling when Mom called a half hour later. Aunt June got up from her sewing machine and answered. They talked for a minute or two longer than usual. To my surprise, Aunt June didn't call me, but hung up and came over to sit on the couch. My stomach tightened; something was the matter. "That was your mother, Carl. She was on her way to a meeting at the halfway house and couldn't take time to talk to you tonight. But she's fine. As a matter of fact, she sounded happier than I've heard her in a long time. She said she's 'graduating' to the halfway house next Wednesday. That's exactly how she put it. And she said she can have visitors there starting the Sunday after. I think we ought to go see her."

For an instant, I felt like all the air had been sucked out of the room. This soon? I wasn't ready. Not yet. Uncle Glen said, "Maybe we should drive down Saturday and come back Sunday afternoon. Milwaukee and back is too much driving for one day."

I felt Aunt June's gray eyes on me. "What do you think, Carl?"

I got my breath back. "I guess that'd be OK."

I took Signa to the movies the next night. From Blind River, we had to drive across forty miles of lonely country to Haycroft, the nearest town big enough to have a movie theater. I'd called it a howling wasteland when Bob and I had made the drive a couple of weeks before. And the idiot had rolled down his window, stuck his head out, and let go a howl. "You damn fool," I'd said. "Get back in here before you freeze your ears off."

But with Signa sitting warm and close beside me, the drive was almost too short. She played with the radio dial, trying different stations and talking about music. Our tastes weren't that different—easy rock, some oldies. I'd even begun to like a bit of country now and then—just as long as it wasn't the I-love-you-even-though-you're-a-drinking-bastard-who's-broken-my-heart-a-thousand-times sort of stuff.

The movie was a pretty good horror-comedy with enough thrills to keep the interest but not so much blood that you felt like blowing lunch. Signa sat with her knees on the back of the empty seat in front of her and munched popcorn happily. But when the first monster leaped out of the top of a grand piano—I'm not kidding—she jumped and reached for my hand. "Darn. I hate that kind of stuff."

Her hand was nearly as big as mine, and I could feel the calluses she'd gotten from working in the barn. Still, it was a nice hand. I relaxed and watched the picture. I don't react very much to movie monsters and paid for it a little later when a particularly nasty ghoul smashed through a door. Signa let out a yelp and damn near broke my hand with a hard squeeze. "Oops, sorry." She kissed my bruised knuckles. "Got to watch myself." After that I was careful not to let my hand relax.

Back in the cold, Signa said, "I've got to make some more taffy. I like taffy after popcorn."

"I thought you liked it anytime."

"That's true. Now you see, you know me real well, and I'm still in the dark about you. I really felt guilty last Sunday after you dropped me off. I mean, I'd done all the talking and never gave you a chance. And I was trying so hard not to be loud and pushy."

"You weren't. Besides, you've got more interesting stuff to say."

"Flattery, flattery. I'm just a country girl with a B-minus brain. You've got all the smarts and experience."

"Less than you think." I thought fast, trying to find a way to keep her off the personal stuff. "But I did keep my uncle from electrocuting himself yesterday." Saved again.

In the car, we had music to talk about, and we were almost back to Blind River before we hit another awkward pause. "Say," I said, "where's this river, anyway? I mean, I've been here over a month now, and I haven't seen any river nearby, blind or otherwise."

"It's south of town a few miles. You must have crossed it getting here from Milwaukee. It's not very wide, so maybe you didn't notice it. But it's pretty deep in some places, and I know a couple of pools where you can swim. Last summer, a couple of my girlfriends and I found this really nice spot. You want to see it?"

I said, "Sure," figuring she meant some time after it got warmer.

"OK, I'll get some hot dogs and stuff together, and we can cook lunch down there tomorrow."

"Tomorrow? It's kind of cold for a picnic, isn't it?"

"Oh, it's not so bad once you get a fire going. Just don't wear all those socks. Maybe we ought to ask Bob and Debbie."

"He's got to study for an English test. He's worried we'll lose the car if he doesn't get his grades up. I think maybe I'd better study too."

"Oh, come on. With your brains?"

"Well, it kind of helps to read the stuff." She looked at me, and for the first time in my life, I saw that I was about to disappoint a girl. "But I guess I'd have time to study tomorrow night." She grinned.

I stumbled through the brush with my arms wrapped around the bag of groceries. Why the hell hadn't we stopped at the wayside back where the highway crossed the river? I paused, breathing hard. Ahead of me, I could barely make out the blue of Signa's down coat. "Here it is," she yelled. Thank God, I thought. I pushed through the brush to her side. From what I'd seen so far on our expedition, the river could have easily been called a brook or a stream, but here it widened to maybe fifty feet. "We were so happy to find this spot," Signa said. "We'd been bicycling all morning and it was really hot and we were just dying. We couldn't wait to get our clothes off." She giggled. "Guess I didn't tell you we went skinny-dipping."

"Uh, no. Well, you had privacy, I guess. Is there charcoal in here for the fire?" I dug in the bag.

She looked at me hard. "You know, I can never tell when you're kidding. We're going to use sticks."

"Oh. I should have thought of that." Chalk up another one for the city boy.

I helped her gather a big pile of dead sticks, and she

started making a fire under the protection of the far bank. I spread one of the thick blankets and unpacked the groceries. "My God, you packed enough for an army."

"Well, I figured the walk would make us hungry. Besides, if there's a blizzard, we'll have to camp here for a few days."

"We wouldn't last long in the open."

"We'll make an igloo." She winked at me. "We could stay real warm in an igloo." I grunted.

I'd expected an afternoon of freezing my ass off—sort of a test to prove to her that I could take the outdoor crap. Instead, I found myself having about as good a time as I could remember. The fire kept us warm, and the hot dogs tasted wonderful, even the ones we had to fish out of the coals. After we'd stuffed ourselves, we piled on more wood and sat between the blankets. Signa snuggled close under my arm. "You know the old Indian saying: One Indian under a blanket freeze, two Indians stay nice and warm." She looked up at me and grinned. I kissed her for the first time then. And it was very nice in the cold afternoon with the smell of wood smoke and pine around us.

After a few minutes, she opened her eyes. "See any storm clouds?"

I looked at the sky. "No, but I'm hoping," I said.

When we paused the next time, she said, "You don't like talking about yourself, do you?"

"No. I guess maybe that'll take some time."

"I can wait," she said. "Even if it takes until we come back here next summer."

"On a real hot day?"

"Uh-huh. Come here, mystery man." She closed her eyes and brought my mouth down on hers.

I didn't tell her that afternoon that I'd be gone long

before the weather warmed enough to swim in Blind River.

I had to stay up half the night to get the reading done for the English test. Monday morning, I helped Bob review a little on the drive to school. "Don't tell me everything," he said. "I don't want to get an A. That'd really screw things up. Ma would start expecting A's all the time, and I'd really have to study."

I lit a cigarette. "Suit yourself."

Bob rolled down his window a crack. "God, I wish you'd quit those things. They stink. I know, I know, you don't need me to tell you what to do."

"Right again."

"So, how's that drafting project of yours coming? I haven't seen you working on it recently."

"I haven't done crap on anything in three weeks. I'm going to have to get caught up."

He grinned. "I must be having a good influence on you. Except that you're putting out too much in gym. I mean what got into you last Thursday in that basketball game? Maybe you can't shoot worth a damn, but you played some serious defense."

"I don't know. I just felt like blowing off some steam, I guess." I shrugged. "I've had some stuff on my mind. Things are better now."

"Ya, you looked pretty doggone happy when you got home last night. You and Signa had a good time, huh?"

"A lot better than I expected. Hey, we'd better review some more. I don't want you to bomb that test and lose this car for us."

"OK, shoot a question at me, professor."

I hesitated. "Uh, that's one nickname I really don't like."

"Oh, OK." We turned off the highway and drove up the main street to Hillbilly High.

I grabbed every chance to be with Signa. Maybe she was nearly as tall as I was and maybe she did have twice the muscles, but I didn't care. And I didn't care what other people thought, either. On Tuesday, we ran into Ginger and Cliff in the hall. Ginger put her nose in the air and marched by, but Cliff actually smiled at us and rumbled a "Hi, guys." Odd, but he didn't look a millimeter over eight feet tall. Howdy-Dowdy saw us together too, and I thought he looked at me more coldly than ever. Well, screw him.

I ate supper at the Amundsens' that night. It was the first time I'd said much more than hello to her parents, although I'd seen her father almost every time I'd come for the milk. I liked him. He never said much, but there always seemed a faint smile on his lean, leathery face and a sparkle in his blue eyes. Signa's mom more than made up for his quietness. She was big and hearty, always smiling, talking, and passing more food our way. Three times, I had to tell her thanks but I'd had enough dessert. Finally, Signa got firm with her. "Mom, we've had enough. It was great, but we can only eat so much." She turned to me. "Mom isn't happy until everybody's stretched out on the floor groaning and belching. I'd weigh three hundred pounds if she had her way."

"Fiddle," her mom said. "Your dad hasn't gained an ounce since I've known him. Well, we've got ice cream in the freezer for later. So, how's your mother doing, Carl? I hear she's going into some kind of halfway house."

That caught me off guard, way off guard. I thought I saw Mr. Amundsen give her a warning glance. Signa only looked at me curiously. "Uh, ya, she is. Tomorrow, as a matter of fact. I guess she's doing OK."

"How's that Ford running?" Mr. Amundsen asked. "I thought that monster was about ready for the scrap heap." I made some kind of answer, and he kept the subject on cars.

After dishes, Signa and I took a walk. The moon was high in a cold sky, and the northern lights flickered on the horizon. I lit a cigarette, not caring that Signa shared Bob and Aunt June's opinion of tobacco. "How much do you really know about my mom?" I asked.

"Nothing much. Bob told me she was sick but getting better. I thought of asking you about her, but . . . Well, you know I kinda promised not to ask you personal questions."

"Your mom and dad know something."

"Well, maybe your aunt said something to Mom. Hey, what are you so mad about?"

"I don't like people gossiping about Mom."

"Oh, nobody's gossiping. Mom doesn't spread around anything your aunt says."

I took a long drag and flipped the butt away. It landed on the hard snow and rolled away in the wind, scattering embers behind it. "And I suppose now you want to know all about my mom."

"Well, sure, I'm curious. Is she real sick or something? I mean, is that halfway house a place where they send people to . . . Well, you know, when there's no more hope?"

I snorted. "You mean, sort of a place halfway between this world and the next?"

"Something like that."

"No, you're way off." For a long moment, I watched the northern lights brightening and fading on the horizon. I felt Signa close to me, almost within reach. I took a deep breath of the night and let it out. "Mom's in a halfway house for alcoholics. It's supposed to teach her how to live in the world again, without drinking or getting in trouble. She's been in a lot of it. Drunken driving, disorderly conduct, and . . ." I shrugged. "Lots of other crap too. This last time they told her to get dried out in the hospital or go to jail. She chose the hospital. They sent me up here while she's trying to get straight." I turned my head to look at Signa and found her face completely untroubled. God, I'd just told her my darkest secret! Or almost my darkest, and it hadn't even fazed her. "Uh, that's about it."

"And it's working out OK?"

"Ya, I guess so."

She stepped closer and slipped her arm through mine. "Is that why you're always so worried?"

"I guess."

"So how long are you going to be around?"

"I'll know more after I see her this weekend, but probably a month or two."

She glanced back at the light in the kitchen window. "Then we don't have a lot of time to waste." She grinned. "Come on. Let's find some shadows and neck."

"Neck?"

"Ya, they still call it that in the city, don't they?"

"Well, sometimes, I guess. But—"

"Come on," she said, and pulled me toward the shadows.

I couldn't believe the sweetness of having my mouth on hers and her body snug against mine. The thought of such closeness had always scared me before, even when I'd wanted it most. I'd spent too many nights with my headphones turned loud to keep from hearing or imagining what Mom and one of her classy guys were doing upstairs. But this was different, so different that if

Signa hadn't had her arms tight around me, I might have floated into the night sky.

Later, I walked home by the light of the moon and the northern lights. At the top of the ridge, I rested, watching the shafts of red, green, and violet rippling on the horizon. My breathing slowed, fell to the inaudible, and then I heard the sound of the lights—a faint rustle like a breeze gently tearing the curtain from the window of a long-abandoned attic. And like that forgotten room, I felt open to the world after years of dust and silence— open at last to wind and rain and the flutter of wings. A voice deep inside me murmured: You're beginning to get it, son. So long, and take care of yourself. Ya, I thought, you too, Dad. I turned and started down the slope, the night around me luminescent with the charged ions of the aurora.

I was called to Dowdy's office the next afternoon. He ordered me to sit, then fixed me with a cold stare. What the hell was this all about? I glanced at Pankratz, who was sitting in a corner looking nervous. "Your chemistry teacher tells me you have an interest in electricity," Dowdy said.

"That's right."

"Have you been spending a lot of time in his lab during your free time?"

"No, hardly any."

"Were you in his lab after school in the last week or so?"

"Not that I recall. Can I ask what this is about?"

Dowdy studied me, and I didn't like his expression a damn bit. "It seems that he's missing a piece of electrical equipment. What did you call it, Mr. Pankratz?"

"A volt-ohmmeter."

Dowdy looked at me again. "You wouldn't know anything about that, would you?"

That ancient piece of crap? Hell, the one I'd bought at Christmas was a hundred times better. "No. I've seen it, but I never touched it."

"Well, Mr. Pankratz says he's searched his room and it's gone." Dowdy's stare hardened.

The son of a bitch was really trying to get me. My brain hit high gear. When had I seen that volt-ohm-meter last? "Maybe he ought to look under the sink where he put it on the day we took the electricity exam."

Pankratz said, "But I never store any—" Suddenly, his face went a little white. "Well, maybe . . ."

"Go check. We'll wait," Dowdy said. Pankratz left, and Dowdy leaned back, his cold blue eyes still on me. Don't try to make me sweat, you bastard, I thought. I reached down for one of the books at my feet, crossed my legs, and started to read. "Is he going to find it?"

I didn't look up. "If he hasn't moved it since I saw him put it there."

Dowdy sighed and started doing something with the papers on his desk. Pankratz came to the door. "Uh, Mr. Dowdy, it's there. Someone threw a couple of plastic pans on top of it. That's, uh, how come I missed it."

"Thank you, Mr. Pankratz." Pankratz bobbed his head and beat it. Dowdy went back to his paperwork. "Thank you, Carl. You can go." I gathered up my books. Missed again, you bastard. Must've disappointed the hell out of you.

Aunt June was marching up the hall. "What's going on?" she snapped.

"Nothing, Aunt June. Leave it alone."

"Like heck I will. Tell me." I gave her the outline, and she stormed into his office. I couldn't hear all the words, but there was no doubt Aunt June had the upper hand all the way. Near the end, she said plainly enough for me to hear: "If you have any more complaints with either of my boys, you come to me first." Dowdy's reply was muffled. "I mean it, Ed. You talk to me first, or I'll go straight to the school board." She came out, her face flushed but satisfaction in her eyes.

That night at supper, she replayed it for us, then laughed. "And I walked out feeling great."

And I'd felt damned uncomfortable. Later, I complained to Bob. "Why'd she do that? I mean, I appreciate her standing up for me, but I didn't need it. It was embarrassing."

Bob shrugged. "Ya, but they've been fighting for years. Don't worry, nobody's going to think you're a wimp just because she jumped in on your side."

Only after I went to bed did it finally hit me: "either of *my* boys." Since when? And did I like having that place in Aunt June's world?

From Thursday morning on there was talk of a big storm coming. Could I be so lucky? The thought of going to Milwaukee to see Mom scared the hell out of me. I just wasn't ready yet.

I left school at noon on Friday to drive to Haycroft for my dentist's appointment. I'd been dreading it nearly as much as the trip to Milwaukee, but the dentist found just the one cavity to fix, gave me only a short lecture on the evils of smoking, then let me go. I drove back through a light snow, searching the radio channels every few minutes for another weather report. Come on, storm.

And come it did. By the time I got to Blind River, I needed headlights to see the road ahead through a hard, swirling snow. Damn it, I hadn't wanted a blizzard this soon. Signa and I had planned to double with Bob and Debbie, but the storm would screw up that idea.

But good ol' Bob was resourceful. "Debbie's going to stay over at Signa's tonight. We'll go over there and play some cards, eat popcorn, and make out after Signa's parents go to bed."

"Bob!" Aunt June glared at him.

"Oops. Sorry, Ma. You weren't supposed to hear that." He winked at me. "Come on. Let's go pick up Debbie before it gets any worse out there."

Of course, Signa didn't miss the chance of putting three extra pairs of hands to work on a batch of taffy. And, weird as it sounds, I enjoyed it. At one point, I looked up from working a rope of taffy and caught her watching me. She blew a kiss at me and mouthed, "Wanta neck?"

The blizzard didn't let up until late Saturday afternoon. Aunt June called Mom after supper and told her that we couldn't come because of the roads. Then I got on the phone for a few minutes. "I'm sorry, Mom. I was looking forward to seeing you." (Well, hell, what was I supposed to say?)

She sighed. "I know, baby. Me too."

"You doing OK, Mom?"

There was a long pause. "Yes, I am, baby. I've been thinking. I mean, really thinking this time. Maybe what they've been saying is true." She took a deep breath. "That maybe I shouldn't drink anymore. You know, like I've got this allergy with liquor and that my life would be a whole lot better if I didn't drink. Would that make you happy, baby?"

I suddenly felt very cold. Hey, don't lay this decision on me, lady. "I'll go along with whatever makes you happy, Mom."

"Well, maybe I'd be a better mother to you. I

mean . . ." She started crying. "I mean, I think of all I've put you through, and I just feel so darn guilty."

"Please don't cry, Mom. I do OK."

"I know, baby. I know. I just should have done better." She sniffed a couple of times, trying to get control of herself.

My insides were knotting up. "Just try to be happy, Mom. That's all I ask. . . ." I searched for a lie. "Uh, Mom, I've got to go now. Uncle Glen wants me to get in some wood. We'll see you next weekend."

We said good-bye and hung up. Quit drinking. Ya, I'd believe that when I saw it. Was she also going to stop bringing home her classy guys? Golly gee, maybe I could even move my bed out of the basement. Sorry, lady, I gave up believing in miracles a long time ago.

Bob came bouncing down the stairs and reached for the phone. "You done? I'm going to call Debbie and see if she can stay at Signa's another night. We can get over there on snowshoes."

Uncle Glen called from the next room, "Don't make any big plans, boys. We've got a lot of snow to plow."

"Aw, Pa."

"Aw, Pa, nothing. You know the routine. You guys get dressed; I'm going out to start the tractor."

Bob called Signa's just in case we could still work something out, but Debbie's dad had already rescued her by snowmobile, and Signa was busy moving snow. We bundled up and headed out to start clearing the drive.

About nine-thirty, we were nearly finished when I heard the clanking of tire chains. Signa drove into the yard in the Amundsens' battered Jeep pickup. She dropped the plow blade and made a half dozen expert passes. Uncle Glen waved and, with Bob hanging on the

174

side, piloted the tractor toward the machine shed. I hopped into the Jeep. "Hi, I didn't know you could drive this."

"Oh, a farm girl can drive anything. Especially when she's got a guy waiting." She did a U-turn and drove down the drive until we were hidden from the house. She parked and switched on the dome light. "Want some cocoa and a sandwich?"

"I'd rather neck."

She gave me a quick kiss, then pushed me back. "I smell too bad to get close."

"I don't care." I slid my arms inside her coat and pulled her to me, my hands on the moist back of her sweatshirt. After a couple of minutes, I tried to investigate some other places. She caught my hands. "Hey, not just now, huh? I've been clearing snow since milking, and I haven't had a shower. This is my cowshit and sweat perfume you're smelling, chum. And it doesn't make me feel real feminine." I leaned back, looking put out, but she caught my chin in her hand. "But this stinky country girl does love you, guy." She kissed me, then turned away quickly. "Where the heck are those sandwiches? Here we are." She dragged a paper bag from under the seat.

For some reason, it was tough to say it. "Uh, this city guy loves you, too."

She was in my arms then, her body tight against mine. We stayed that way until the idling motor of the Jeep started to cough. "Oops." She pulled away and revved the engine. "There." She looked at me, her blue eyes moist. Then she giggled and held up a crushed sandwich that had been caught between us in our long embrace. We both started laughing.

Most of the sandwiches were only slightly flattened.

We ate them and drank the cocoa. She wiped her fingers on the bag and glanced at her watch. "Jeez, it's getting late. I've got to get home."

I put a hand on her shoulder. "Oh, feel feminine for a few minutes."

She gave me a long, serious look. "You know, you really make me feel that way. And I have trouble handling that sometimes." She turned away and stared out at the night. In the reflection on the windshield, I saw her wipe away a couple of tears.

"Signa, I don't know what I said wrong, but—"

"You didn't say anything wrong." She looked down at her hands. "It's just me. I was thinking about you while I was plowing snow, thinking about how happy you've made me the last couple of weeks. Then I remembered that you're not going to be here very long. And when you're gone, you'll be gone for good. I know you won't come to see me or write to me. You'll get somebody else, somebody pretty like Ginger. And, heck, you'll be embarrassed even to remember going out with a bulldozer like me."

"Hey, stop that. Just . . ." I fumbled; I didn't have the vaguest idea how to deal with this. "Look, I meant what I said. I love you. I don't have any answers about the future. I don't know what's going to happen with Mom, or me, or my life. But I do know you're the best thing that's happened to me in a hell of a long time. Maybe ever. Embarrassed? Hell, you're the one who ought—"

Her lips cut off my words. She reached back, feeling for the switch of the dome light, and then we were together in the warm darkness. Beneath her sweatshirt, her skin was soft and smooth and, for a while, I didn't care if I ever went back to Milwaukee or made any of my other dreams come true.

Finally, she pulled away, squeezing my hands tight in

hers. "If we go any further, we're likely to spend the night here."

"I'm willing."

"Do you think my dad or your aunt would get us first?" She kissed me hard, making a low growl in her throat. "OK, hands off the driver! Here we go." She slammed the Jeep into gear, and we jolted up the drive in reverse. I thought we were going to crash surer than hell, but she surprised me again.

Overnight, the wind blew parts of the drive shut. We started clearing it right after breakfast, but Uncle Glen and Bob didn't seem in any hurry. At first, I thought they might be as stiff as I was from all the shoveling of the night before. Then I caught on—a little more delay and we'd have to miss church. Well, that was OK by me.

Bob had plans. "We haven't had a good sledding party all winter. I'm going to start calling kids as soon as we're done. Sound good?"

"Sounds like just another way to freeze your ass off to me."

"Aw, you city kids don't know what a good time is. Just wait."

By two in the afternoon, a crowd of kids were trooping up the ridge to join Signa, Debbie, Bob, and me around a bonfire. Signa yelled down to them, "We need wood! Nobody slides until they bring wood!" Obediently, the kids dispersed into the trees and came back with armfuls of sticks to load on the toboggans.

Cliff heaved a huge chunk of tree trunk on his shoulder and lumbered up to us. "This big enough, Signa?"

"That twig? Come on, Cliff. You can do better than

that." Cliff grinned and headed back for the woods, but Ginger went over to stand shivering by the fire. Some kids stumbled up the opposite slope after breaking a trail for the toboggans. Bob yelled to us. "Come on, let's try a run."

The four of us piled on. I took the last place and looked skeptically over Signa's shoulder at the precipice below. God, it was steep. "Do I have to do anything?" I asked.

She looked over her shoulder at me. "Haven't you ever been on a toboggan before?"

"Well, no. You don't get much chance for this in the city. Or at least I didn't."

"Well, don't worry. Just hang on tight and lean the way I do. Hey, somebody give us a push!"

I'd seen bobsled races on television, but those suckers were slow compared to us. We rocketed down the slope. Halfway down, we hit a hummock, and terra firma disappeared under us. Bob let out a whoop, the girls screamed, and I heard a voice very much like my own scream, "Holy shiiittt!" *Thaawopp.* We hit the ground going twice the speed. I was going to die. We were all going to die. A second hummock sent us airborne again. *Thaawopp!* I don't know if I closed my eyes then or if my sight just blurred over with the rush of speed and fear. Something like an eternity later, we were down and coasting to a stop.

We tumbled off the toboggan. Signa lay laughing in the snow. "Oh, God, that was great." She reached for the front of my coat and pulled me on top of her. "What'd you think, chum? Wasn't that great? You sure were laughing hard."

"That was hysteria. Why didn't you tell me we were going to fly most of the way?" She laughed and hugged me.

"You two going to grope each other until you get run over?" Bob yelled. "Let's go." We trudged up the slope. Another toboggan came whizzing by, the kids screaming all the way. Bob looked back at us, then said loudly to Debbie, "God, those two are just like a couple of mink. I mean, every time you look around they're pawing each other. It's disgusting."

She pinched his ass. "You should talk."

Signa looked at me. "You want to go again?"

"Sure." And I did. I'd been scared shitless, but it had definitely been one hell of a thrill.

For another hour and a half, kids labored through the snow to the top, only to go howling down in a few seconds. I think we got the record for runs. Finally, almost everyone collapsed by the fire. I put an arm around Signa. She grinned at me and snuggled close. "Almost as much fun as plowing snow, huh?"

"Just about."

"I'm glad you didn't go to Milwaukee this weekend."

"So am I." But her mentioning it brought back thoughts of Mom. She'd be feeling like hell today— probably just sitting around the halfway house trying not to think about having a drink with some classy guy. Or even some bastard. And here I was having a good ol' time.

"What'd I say?" Signa asked, her face suddenly worried.

"Huh? Oh, nothing. I was just thinking for a second."

She touched my cheek. "Hey, don't find any dark lining in this cloud. You're so good at that it scares me. Let's just have fun, huh?"

"Who's for a snipe hunt?" Bob shouted. "They oughta really be out now." There was a good deal of discussion. Like me, some of the kids didn't know a thing about snipe. It turned out that snipe were these six-inch-tall birds with white and gray feathers. "They're hard to spot because they blend in real good with the snow," Bob explained. "And usually they're real quick to fly if they see somebody. But they've got real bad eyesight, so when the shadows get long, they get kind of confused and just run around on the snow. If you move up real quiet, you can throw a coat over 'em. That's snipe hunting."

"I caught one in a stocking cap once," Cliff rumbled.

"Oh, Cliff, you did not," Ginger said. "I watched, and you missed by a mile."

"That was another time."

Some of the other kids started telling snipe-hunting stories. I looked at Signa. "Am I supposed to believe any of this?"

"Sure. Why not?"

"Just wondering."

"OK, everybody, shut up a minute," Bob said. "Shall we try teams or have a drive?"

"Let's do a drive," Cliff said. "If we catch enough, we can cook 'em right here on sticks." He looked my way. "They taste like chicken, only better."

"That OK with everybody else?" Bob asked. "OK, we'll do a drive. You guys who haven't caught 'em before can do the driving. The rest of us will wait along the ridge and catch 'em when they run out of the woods. But we need one experienced person to lead the drive."

Signa waved a hand. "I'll do it."

Bob grinned. "Good. Signa's in charge of the drive. OK, catchers over here with me, drivers go with Signa."

Eight or nine other kids joined Signa and me. We started for the woods. "I don't know about this," I said. "I ain't got nothing against snipe."

"Oh, we probably won't catch enough to eat. OK, you guys, listen up. I'm going to put you in a line maybe twenty or thirty feet apart. Make lots of noise. That'll stir 'em up. But you can't go around the brush. They'll just hide in there and wait for you to go by. You've gotta scare 'em out."

She got us in a long line a quarter of a mile from the ridge. She put me in the middle. "I'll see you in a while, chum. Just head straight for the ridge and make a lot of noise." A few minutes later, I heard her holler, "OK, drivers, go!" We started off. It was heavy going, the snow deep and the brush thick. The line straggled, and I caught only an occasional glimpse of the kids on either side of me. The brush got thicker. A branch grabbed my stocking cap and zinged it twenty feet behind me. I stumbled back to get it, then hurried to catch up. Another hundred feet on, I stumbled on a log hidden by the snow and fell headfirst, my left knee banging hard on something under the snow. I lay there for a minute cursing, then got up and wallowed on. I hadn't seen a snipe yet, and I sure as hell didn't care.

Finally, I heard shouts coming from the ridge. "There's one! Get it! . . . There's another. . . . Watch out, Cliff. One just got by you. . . . God, look at 'em all. I ain't never seen so many." I moved a little faster and, at last, I was standing at the foot of the ridge. Three or four other drivers had already made it out of the woods and were climbing toward the kids sitting or lying around the bonfire. "There's one now," Bob yelled. "Jeez, it's a big one. Looks kinda like my city coz." More laughter. I spotted Signa lying on her elbow near him, toasting her toes and grinning.

Another kid stumbled panting from the brush. He stared up at the group on the ridge. "Oh, hell," he said. "I should have known." Shaking his head, he started the climb. I followed, my anger already seething. I sat down a few feet from Signa and smoked a cigarette, then another. Below us, the last of the drivers finally made it out of the woods to whoops and cheers from the crowd around the fire.

The party began breaking up. I started for the house. Signa caught up with me. "What's the matter?"

"Figure it out for yourself."

She hesitated. "I guess you don't like practical jokes."

"Very perceptive of you. Public humiliation's never been a favorite of mine."

"Oh, pooh. A whole bunch of kids got fooled. Next time you can wait on the ridge."

"No, thanks. You guys can keep your country rituals."

"God, you are really mad."

"No shit."

We walked for a while without speaking. "You know, I bet there are some city jokes you could play on Bob or me."

"Probably, but that doesn't mean I would."

She took my arm and leaned against me before I could pull away. "I'm sorry, chum. It's just an old joke. I should have told you."

"It's kind of difficult to walk with you hanging on me."

She took her arm away. "Sorry."

She didn't say anything more until we got to the house. "Could we take the car and go somewhere?" I started to say no, but she reached for my hand. "Please?"

I gazed at her, then shrugged. "Oh, I guess." Bob and Debbie came up, dragging the toboggan. Bob smiled a little sheepishly at me. "Let me have the keys," I said. "Debbie can get a ride home with somebody else." They exchanged glances, then Bob reached in his pocket for the keys.

We parked at the wayside where the road south

crossed Blind River. I lit a cigarette and gazed at the point where the frozen river disappeared in the bare trees to the southeast. "Well," Signa said, "at least you seemed to have fun sliding."

"It was OK. I'm not in any hurry to do it again."

"Why not?"

"I'm not into risking a broken neck for a few cheap thrills."

"But you had fun."

"I could have had fun doing something worthwhile."

"You're still mad, aren't you?"

I rubbed my eyes. God, I was exhausted. I should just stop this whole damn conversation and take her home. "This country stuff just isn't for me. I ought to be back home working in my shop. I've got things to do."

"What's so important?"

Well, fixing about two hundred stolen stereos, for one. "Earning money for college. Keeping my grades up. Starting to think about choosing the right engineering program and lining up the financial aid. Just a few little things like that."

"But it's over two years before you go to college. What's the rush with all that stuff?"

And for some reason, the dam broke, sending a torrent of shit rushing downstream. "That's what gets me about you guys up here! Nobody's in any hurry. Nobody's worried about getting anywhere! Like Bob. If he was any more laid back, he'd be a vegetable. He's a bright guy, but all he wants to do is drive a damn pulp truck. What's with you people? Do you really think life is like Aunt June's cheap Christmas cards? You got one, right? All the cute little deer, staring into that cozy little house, where good ol' Santa Claus is putting nice little presents under the tree for all the good little girls and boys? Well, bullshit! Life isn't like that. It's tough. Half the people you meet are bastards. And it's you or them. So you gotta take what you want, because nobody's going to give you anything except shit and humiliation."

Signa tried to say something, but I'd completely lost control. "No, you listen! For years, all I did was take shit. But not anymore. And I don't care what it takes to get what I want. I even moved to the basement so I didn't have to see Mom coming in drunk with another of her classy guys. And I sleep with headphones on so I don't have to hear the partying or the screwing upstairs. But sometimes the headphones don't really do it. You see, her bed's got a loose frame, and sometimes when she and some guy really get going, the headboard starts hitting the wall." I slapped my hands together. "A-wham, a-wham, a-wham. And I can't help but hear it getting faster and faster. But I don't care anymore. I don't care because I know it's not me getting screwed anymore. It's Mom getting it a-wham, a-wham, a-wham—"

Signa grabbed my hands. "Stop it!" Tears were running down her cheeks. She leaned forward, holding my hands against her face. "Please stop it," she sobbed.

My God, what had I been telling her? For several minutes, we sat in a numbed silence. Outside, the light faded to gray. Finally, I went on quietly. "So, I've got this plan. The plan that's going to get me out. I'm going to be valedictorian of my class and land the biggest scholarship around. Then I'm going to get an engineering degree and find a life I can stand. Because I can't stand the one I've had. I'm sorry my mother's a drunken whore, but it ain't my problem. I'm going to get what I want. And I really don't care if I have to run over people and rules to get it."

I felt Signa's tears on the back of my hands. "You know what I see?" she whispered. "I see a guy—a really good, kind guy—running around banging his head against walls." She looked up at me, her eyes red. "God, that must hurt. And it could kill you someday. You've gotta have a little fun and not feel guilty about it. You can't take everything so seriously all the time. Heck, that snipe hunt was just a stupid joke. You've just got to learn how to have some fun. . . . Maybe even to laugh at yourself a little." She let go of my hands slowly and turned away to dig in her purse for a tissue.

"I'm sorry. I guess I'm not built that way." I reached for the ignition key.

She reached out a hand to stop me. "Just a couple more minutes." I leaned back and lit another cigarette. I felt cold and empty. Well, better now than later. Let her go on with her life, and I'd go on with mine. Alone again—but I was best alone. Howdy, professor. Welcome back to stay. "Let's go for a walk," she said. She didn't wait for me to reply, but swung her door open and got out.

Oh, hell, one more time. I joined her, and we walked slowly along the riverbank in the last of the light. I almost jumped when she took my hand. "Well, you're a challenge, chum." She leaned her head on my shoulder. "But I'm going to teach you how to have fun. You can count on it."

Hadn't she figured it out yet? "No, you don't. It ain't gonna work, and I don't want to waste your time or mine. Let's just forget it." Then she was crying again and hanging on to me. "Come on, Signa. There just isn't any point to this. It's just not—"

"I don't want to lose you! I don't want to lose you just because of some stupid snipe hunt."

The snipe hunt? Hell, I'd almost forgotten about the snipe hunt. "It's not that. It's because of what I am. What I told you."

"I love you better for what you told me."

I was speechless. I hesitated a long moment, then put my arms around her. This was crazy. Absolute madness. And, God, I loved her for it.

We drove into Blind River. Signa called home and got permission to miss milking so we could eat supper in town. There weren't many people at the café, and we had a quiet corner to ourselves. We didn't talk for a long time. Finally, I said, "I've got to know one thing. Why?"

"Why what?"

"Why do you want to bother? What makes you think I'm worth it?"

She concentrated on wiping up potato-chip crumbs with a finger. "Just because."

"That's no answer."

She pushed a strand of hair back over an ear, then leaned on folded arms, still not looking at me. "Because I want you for my guy. I wanted you the first day I met you. You were sitting there in the cafeteria with Bob, looking so cool and confident, like nothing could ever really bother you. Then when you guys came for the milk, you gave everything—including me—that same cool stare, like you'd already figured out all the surface stuff and were starting to look deeper. And that kind of scared me, but I said to myself, 'That's the kind of guy I need. Somebody to teach me how to be confident and understand things. Besides, he's good-looking and taller than me and . . .' Well, I just knew that you were the guy I wanted."

"You read it all wrong. I was nervous as hell in school, and I felt like throwing up from the smell in that barn. . . . And, by the way, you scared the hell out of me."

She stared at me. "God, why?"

186

I shrugged. "Because you were tall and strong and so sure of yourself."

"But I've never felt sure of myself! And I don't like being built like a darn bulldozer. That night we made taffy, I went to bed thinking how much easier it'd be to get you if I looked more like Ginger or Debbie. But I figured if I got Bob to work on you that maybe I could get a date with you anyway. And, boy, was I going to impress you then." Suddenly, she was on the point of crying again, but she tried to laugh. "And then I really screwed it up. I was so nervous, I started getting loud and, you know, kind of bossy. And I could tell that turned you off. You didn't like dancing with me, and I didn't know what to say to you. God, I was trying so hard that I just started acting stupid. I gave you that little dig in the ribs, and you almost took my head off. I just about started crying right then."

"Signa—"

"No, I want to finish this!" She brushed away a couple of tears. "And, by the end of the dance, you were just sitting in the bleachers, staring at us like you were thinking, 'God, what a stupid bunch of hicks, and that horse Signa is the worst.' And I wanted so bad to change your mind, but I couldn't think of a darn thing to do. I cried for two hours after you guys dropped me off. I told myself just to forget it, that I'd been dumb even to think I'd had a chance with you. But, darn it, I wanted one. For once, I didn't want to cry myself to sleep just because things never seemed to work out for me. Big ol' Signa—everybody's buddy but never anybody's girl. I was sick of that, and I was sick of laughing through every party just to go home feeling rotten because no guy ever asked me for a date. So, I got up and took a hot shower while I thought everything through again. And I made up my mind that, for once in my life, I wasn't giving up. And I didn't. I never missed a chance to get near you all that time you didn't even want to look at me. And I told Bob that he just had to keep bringing up my name. I mean, I threatened him with everything I could think of. . . . And, well, it sort of worked. Until this afternoon, anyway." She bit her lip, then looked at me. "Are you sorry I didn't give up?"

I started laughing. "God, no! I mean, this is all twisted. Just completely turned around. I couldn't get you out of my head from that first night, when you saved me from spending the rest of my life stuck in a blob of taffy. And you've got the dance thing all wrong too. I was the one who screwed it up. I couldn't figure out what to say, or how to act, or anything. Hell, I went to bed that night thinking that I'd never have a chance with you or maybe anybody else ever again."

I could have said a lot more—tried to trace the whole twisted course of what had happened—but my voice just drifted off. Everything was just too weird to explain—and too wonderful to be believed. We gazed at each other. Suddenly, she grinned. "I know what I want to do now."

"Me too. Let's get out of here."

It was late when Bob tapped on my open door. I looked up from the history text. "Are you still pissed at me?" he asked.

"A little, not a lot."

He shuffled. "Hey, I'm really sorry about the snipe hunt. I guess kids up here just expect some crap like that. I didn't think you'd take it so personal."

I shrugged. "Ya, well, it just hit me at the wrong time. I'm sorry."

"So, we're still friends?"

"Sure."

"Maybe you could think of it as kind of an initiation. I mean, I didn't think of it that way at the time, but . . . Well, now you're kind of one of us."

I hesitated. "Well, I guess there are worse things to be."

I THINK THE NEXT THREE DAYS WERE THE happiest of my life. I was riding a crazy high with no thought that I was ever going to fall off. In school, I stole every second I could with Signa. After school, I'd rush through the chores, inhale supper, and get over to her house as fast as I could. I must have been making an absolute fool of myself, but I was in too much of a hurry to care. I had to be with Signa.

Wednesday evening, I'd just hit the bottom of the stairs and was making for the door when the phone rang. "Hi, baby. How you doing?"

"Fine, Mom. Just fine."

"Do you have a few minutes to talk?"

"Uh, sure." I glanced at my watch. "How are things going?"

"Just great, baby. I'm really happy here." She started babbling about the halfway house and all the new friends she'd made. God, I'd never heard her so happy. ". . . And we talk out a lot of things in the group-therapy sessions. It was really tough at first, but it gets easier. We cry sometimes, but we laugh a lot too. I mean, it's just really great to get all that junk out in the open."

"It sounds like you're really enjoying yourself."

"I am, baby. I really am. Life just seems a lot clearer, a lot simpler now. I mean, all I've got to do to make everything come out OK is just stop drinking. That was real hard to face at first, but now I know I've got this allergy with booze and, well, it's just not so tough to think about not drinking." She paused, and then her voice got very serious. "I'm getting better, baby. I really am. I'm sorry it took me so long to figure out how sick I was. But I'm really going to beat it this time. Please believe that, baby. I believe it. I really do."

"I believe you, Mom. That's, uh, really great." I hesitated. What more was I supposed to say? "You can tell me all about it when we come down next Sunday."

"Well, that's what I wanted to talk to you about, baby. You see, I'm kind of running the entertainment committee now, and I had this chance to get free tickets to the circus at the arena. I mean, it sounds kind of dumb for a bunch of adults to go to the circus, but most of us haven't been since we were kids. Anyway, the tickets are for Sunday afternoon, and, well, it just doesn't seem right for me not to be there after I made the plans. So, I was wondering if maybe we could put off the visit another week. I mean, I could stay home and see you guys, but if it's OK—"

"I think it'll be OK, Mom."

"I mean, it's not that I don't want to see you, baby. I want to see you very much, but—"

"It's OK, Mom. Really. Go and have a good time."

For a moment, she seemed at a loss for words. "Hey, do you know what? I'm letting my hair grow out. You know, getting rid of the blonde-floozy look. It looks funny now, but pretty soon it'll be all brown again. You probably don't even remember when I had brown hair."

"Not really."

"Well, it's the same color as yours, baby. That real nice, shiny brown. I don't know why I ever bleached it to begin with. You'll like it."

"I'm sure I will, Mom."

There was another pause. Neither of us seemed to have anything more to say. Finally, she went on. "Well, maybe I'd better hang up before we run up too big a bill. Thanks for being so understanding, baby. I'll see you a week from Sunday. That's not very long, and soon we'll have lots of time together. My counselor thinks I'll be strong enough to make it on my own by the middle of April. Then we'll have lots of time to talk and have fun. Good, clean fun. Does that sound good, baby?"

"Sure, Mom. I'll see you soon."

"I love you."

"I love you too, Mom." I hung up, grabbed my coat, and headed for the door, the cold, and Signa.

Halfway up the ridge, it hit me. The middle of April, she'd said. In six or seven weeks, I'd be going home. *But I didn't want to go home.* The realization staggered me like a physical blow. I felt my boots fight for traction, then suddenly I was running toward the top of the ridge and the sky beyond. I reached the crest in a sobbing lunge and collapsed on the snow.

For a long time, I lay there, looking down on the farm standing small and lonely in the winter dusk. I forced myself to really see it, to really feel the loneliness and the cold of the country. I must be out of my mind. I didn't belong here. Blind River had no place for me, no future. Signa couldn't change that. None of them could. I belonged in the city, trying to make the Plan and Jennifer and all my crazy dreams come true. And most of all, I belonged with Mom. Maybe after all the failures, she'd finally found her way. Maybe, if I could just love her a little more this time . . .

The ol' professor spoke in my head. Oh, bullshit. When did you start believing in miracles, jerk? It'll be the same old crap all over again. But so what? It's not like you've got any choice about staying or going. They sent you up country and they'll bring you back.

The first gust of the night wind blew across the ridge, spinning eddies of snow ahead of it. I closed my eyes against the sting of ice crystals on my face. The ol' professor spoke almost gently: But, remember, all that really matters is the Plan.

And Mom, I added. I waited another long minute with my eyes closed and the icy wind in my face. Then I wiped my eyes, climbed to my feet, and started down the far side of the ridge.

I tried to bounce back, tried to tell myself that I still had lots of time to let the good times roll. But they ended when the call came a week later. I took the phone from Aunt June and heard Steve's voice over the sound of heavy traffic. "They got us, professor! Everything and all the names. Stand by to take some heat."

"*What*? How?"

"It was that damn Bill Hoyt, man. I thought he'd given up, but he must've gotten better at it. He was following us tonight for sure."

"Followed you where? My God, what did he see?"

"Charlie and me were stashing some stereos in your basement. I went home to get the last of 'em. And when I got back, Hoyt's there with the cops. Charlie's already in cuffs, and I can see he's talkin' like crazy. I just kept driving."

"But you said you got the stuff out of my basement!"

"No, man. I told you everything was cool. Hell, I didn't have any safer place, so we just kept piling the stuff in there. I figured you'd understand when you got back here. Last time I counted, we had seventy-two units waiting for you to fix."

I slumped on a chair. "Oh, my God." I thought desperately. "Look, Charlie doesn't know about my connection. Maybe—"

"He knows everything, man, and he'll talk. He'll save

his ass if he can. Hey, I gotta go, man. They're going to be looking for my car. I'm going to ditch it and buy another fast. Then I'm gone. History."

"Wait a second. Come pick me up. Let me think a second, and I'll tell you where."

"No, man. It's everybody for himself now. This is the best I can do for you."

"Steve, damn it. You owe me."

"Na, I don't owe you shit, man."

"Steve!" I was talking to the dial tone.

I looked around. Uncle Glen and Bob were laughing at something on TV. Aunt June was humming while she cleaned up the kitchen. My God, it was about to start raining shit, and everything was just going on as usual. Seventy-two units! The memory of my hiding place behind the furnace came to me. Oh God, don't let them find that. But they would, and no prayers were going to change that. I had to move, had to get upstairs and pack. I'd take the car as far as Haycroft and leave it at the bus station. Give me a ticket anywhere, man, just as long as it's far far away.

But I couldn't move. I just sat on that chair. The ol' professor's voice was screaming inside my head: Move, damn it! Run. If you don't, you're going to be staring at prison walls. I couldn't. After a long time, I got up, hesitated, then went into the living room and sat on the couch next to Bob. It never occurred to me to say anything about the shit storm coming. I just watched TV until it hit.

The phone rang again an hour later. Uncle Glen had just come out of the bathroom, and he picked it up. He didn't say much, only listened. He hung up and turned to give me a bewildered look. "What is it, Glen?" Aunt June asked.

"That was Jim Halperin from the sheriff's office. He wants to come over and talk to Carl."

"Why?" I could feel all three of them staring at me. "Did something happen while you were driving the car, Carl?" she asked.

I didn't look at her. "No, it's about some stuff I did back in Milwaukee."

"What?"

"I think you'd better wait for him to tell you."

I sat staring at the carpet. Aunt June and Uncle Glen had a whispered conversation in the kitchen. Aunt June beckoned Bob, and he joined them. I heard him say, "I don't know. He never said anything to me."

Fifteen minutes later, headlights flashed in the window for a second, then slid off as the squad car rolled past the house to park in the back. Uncle Glen opened the kitchen door, and I heard Halperin's muffled voice. I remembered him from the day he'd chewed out Cliff on the main street in town. Tough dude. I gathered my feet under me and stood. I had no plan, no face to put on. The ol' professor was as good as dead. And so was the sunny, giddy Carl of the last couple of weeks. No different faces left, just my own.

Halperin was cleaning the condensation from his glasses. "Hi, Carl. Sit down. We need to do some talking." He looked at the others. "Glen, June, you can sit in, but you're going to have to be quiet. Any interruptions, and I'll have to take him out to the squad." They nodded.

We sat at the table. Halperin adjusted his glasses and glanced at some notes on a clipboard. "We got a call from the Milwaukee police this evening. It seems that they broke a theft ring, and Carl is implicated. I'm supposed to ask some questions about his involvement.

Now, Carl, I'm going to read you your rights. Listen carefully." He read them just like they do on the TV cop shows. "Do you understand?"

I nodded. "Then sign here. Now, do you want to answer questions?" I shrugged. "I need a yes or a no. From what they told us, they've got some pretty good evidence. So, it may be in your best interests to cooperate. But you do have the right to refuse, and that can't be held against you."

"I'll answer questions."

"All right." He began. I dodged a few at first, but after a while, it didn't seem worth the trouble. It was obvious that Charlie had known almost everything about my role, and he'd told it all. The cops had found the hiding place behind the furnace where I kept the accounts book, my savings book, the checkbook, and the fake serial-number stickers. In all, they had enough evidence to lock me away for a long time. I ended up telling Halperin the whole story. Aunt June and Uncle Glen watched in numbed silence. Through the door to the dining room, I could see Bob listening, his face lax with confusion.

Halperin asked questions for nearly an hour. Halfway through, the phone rang and Bob answered. "He can't talk right now, Signa. Something's, uh, going on. I'll tell you about it later. . . . Ya, sure. Talk to you soon."

Signa. Ya, I remembered her. She'd been a girl I'd known for a little while a long time ago—a girl who'd thought she'd loved me, but had never known what I really was. Halperin looked up at me. "Sorry," I said. "Can you repeat that?"

Finally, it was over. Halperin glanced through his notes. "Well, you guys were pretty busy. My guess is that you'll be charged with being a party to a crime of theft, conspiracy to commit felony theft, and accepting and concealing stolen property. None of that's good." He sighed. "Well, give me a couple of minutes to write out a statement for you to sign." He worked while we all watched in silence. He finished and shoved a sheet across to me. "Can you read?" I stared at him, anger for the first time penetrating my gloom. "I have to ask," he said. "It's part of the procedure."

"Ya, I can read."

"Good. Now read that carefully, then sign if you think it accurately summarizes what you told me."

I read it. In the back of my head a voice bleated: Don't sign anything, jerk. There's still a way out. There's just got to be. I signed my confession and slid it back across the table to Halperin.

He studied the signature, added his own, then snapped the sheet onto his clipboard. "You'll have to appear in court to answer the charges. They'll let you know the date." He studied me for a moment, his eyes oddly sympathetic. "And stay out of trouble. You've got more than enough already." He stood. "That pretty much does it. I'll call Milwaukee and tell them what I've found out. It'll be their decision what happens after that. Anybody have any questions?"

What? No handcuffs? No ride to the county jail? No fingerprints or mug shots? "Uh, do you mean I get to stay here for now?"

He nodded. "They may want you down in Milwaukee next week, but my guess is that'll be more like two or three weeks. They might even decide to handle everything in Haycroft. You'll have to wait and see."

Uncle Glen said, "I'll walk you to the car, Jim."

I sat staring at the tabletop, half wishing he'd taken me with him. How could I face my aunt and uncle? Or Bob and Signa? When I heard Uncle Glen come back in, I got up, walked past Bob, and trudged up the stairs.

Behind me, I heard Aunt June say, "We've got to call Veronica. It's better she heard this from us than somebody else."

Uncle Glen sighed. "Ya. Give me a chance to think for a minute first."

I lay in the dark, so overwhelmed that all the electricity in my brain slowed to a snail's pace. My God, it was all over. Everything I'd ever planned and dreamed. I heard voices below, but I no longer cared what was being said about me. It just didn't matter anymore.

I heard a car pull in about ten. Signa? God, I hoped not; I couldn't handle that now. Bob came to my door. "Jim Halperin's back. He wants to see you downstairs."

Halperin sat at the table, blowing on a mug of coffee. "Carl, is there anything you didn't tell me?"

"Not really. Why?"

His eyes were colder than before. He took a long sip of the coffee, his stare never leaving my face. "Did you guys ever hurt anybody? You know, get surprised and beat somebody up?"

"No! I mean, not that I know of."

"How about your buddy Steve Sheridan?"

"He never told me anything about that sort of thing."

"Know where he is? Or where he's headed?"

"I told you I didn't. All I got was that one phone call, and I repeated everything he said."

Halperin grunted. "Well, the Milwaukee police are very interested in talking to him. And to you. They want you down there tomorrow. Friday at the latest." He turned to Uncle Glen. "They can send somebody to get him, or you can take him down. I think it'd be better if you did the driving."

Uncle Glen nodded. "I'll take him."

"Some social worker called up and left his number.

198

Maybe you'd better call him." Halperin glanced at his clipboard. "A Richard Mullan. His number is . . ."

Mullan, I thought. Oh, crap. Why does it have to be that s.o.b.?

I was packing when I heard them on the stairs. I started to close the door, then let my hand drop. Hell, they'd force their way in if they had to. Aunt June came to the door, Uncle Glen looming behind her and Bob a step or two behind him. "Carl," Aunt June said, "we just want you to know that whatever happens, we're going to stand by you. We are *family*, Carl. Just remember that." And, by God, that tough, bossy woman started crying. She turned away quickly and made for the stairs.

Uncle Glen looked after her, then cleared his throat. "I, uh, called your mother. I didn't tell her everything, just kind of the outline. It didn't seem smart to lay too much on her right away."

"How'd she take it?"

He shrugged. "Well, I guess about as you'd expect. She's upset, but she thinks they won't do much to you because of your age. I kind of let her think it was minor stuff. You know, just a few stereos. I guess you'll have to give her the full picture when you see her. I told her we'd come by the halfway house in the next couple of days."

I lowered my eyes. "I don't think I can handle that."

"Well, we'll see. . . . Anyway, your aunt's going to talk to Dowdy in the morning. While you're checking out of school, I'll call that Mullan fellow. We'll try to get on the road by nine-thirty or ten."

I nodded. Checking out of school. Well, I'd done that before. In a day or two, I'd probably be checking in at

Lincoln Hills School where, as Mullan said, things got "very heavy."

Later, I heard Bob moving around in his room. I went to his door. "Bob, will you do me a favor? Tell Signa good-bye for me. And tell her I had a really great time these last few weeks." He met my eyes for a second, then looked down and nodded. "And tell her I'm sorry, Bob. That I wasn't worth the, uh . . ." I couldn't say the word *love*. "That I just wasn't worth it." He nodded, still not looking at me. "Thanks," I said, and went back to my room. I knew I'd hurt Bob too, but there wasn't anything I could do about that. He'd get over it. They all would.

When I came out of the house in the morning, Bob had the Ford turned around and pointed down the drive. I thought of asking him if I could pilot our crate one last time, but I couldn't spare any energy on sentiment. Somehow I had to clear my head and start concentrating on what lay ahead.

We were halfway to school when he asked, "Do you suppose you'll be coming back?"

"I don't think so, Bob. I'll probably get sent to the juvenile prison."

"But why? You haven't done anything before, have you?"

"Nothing I got caught for. But this is heavy, Bob. We made a lot of money."

"Maybe they'll put you on probation or something, and you can come back up here."

I sighed. I didn't need this. Things were going to get real tough real quick, and I had to get my act together. Ever since I'd gotten up, I'd been trying to kick-start the ol' professor. No luck, so far. "Look, Bob, you don't get it. I was the brains of that gang. I was the one who came up with the ideas that kept us in business this long. They're going to nail me, Bob. So just forget about me coming back. But, what the hell, I was leaving soon anyway. Now I hope I never see this place again."

"Why?" He gave me a hurt look.

"Because, damn it, I never fit in. I'm city, man. I do not like this country crap. And maybe you haven't noticed, but I also happen to be a nerd. While you've been waltzing around building your biceps strangling grizzlies, I've been hiding in a basement fixing stolen stereos. I'm a city boy, a nerd, and a thief. You don't want me around here."

"Bull," he said. "You're no nerd. Hell, I know what a nerd is, and you ain't. You fit in here right from the start. I couldn't have done that in Milwaukee."

I lifted a hand and let it fall. "Bob, look—"

"No, listen for a second. I mean, I know it was tough on you at first. I used to feel sorry for you. You weren't used to the cold or the work, but you did it anyway. And so what if you didn't like trapping or skinning animals? I didn't mind. I like to trap, you like to fix stereos. So what?"

"Most of those stereos were stolen, Bob."

That slowed him down. For a couple of minutes, he drove without speaking. "Look," he said. "Nobody ever thought you were a nerd. Ma's been impressed. She'd never say so, but I can tell. And Pa's been real impressed, especially when you kept him from frying his ass on that high-voltage dingus in the TV. And Signa sure doesn't—"

"Just don't bring her up, Bob. I just can't handle that." I lit another cigarette and watched the woods and fields slide by. "Bob, I fooled some people for a while, but now everybody's going to know what I really am.

And I'm sorry if I let anybody down, but I'm leaving for good—and I'm glad."

He was silent until we were almost to Hillbilly High. Then he said quietly, "You know what Ma said about standing by you? Well, that goes double for me."

"Thanks, but you're wasting your time."

I left my folders in our locker and carried my books down the stairs to the first floor. Come on, professor. Wake up. I need you. No answer.

Aunt June glanced at her watch when I came into the office. "I've got to get ready to feed some kids, Carl. I've talked to Mr. Dowdy, and he knows what's going on. He'll help you get checked out. Your uncle will be here soon, and you can get started for Milwaukee." She patted me on the shoulder. "I'll try to get up here to see you off. Just go right on in now."

I knocked lightly on the door. Dowdy looked up. "Put your books on the desk and have a chair, son." I did, and he started checking off the books. Well, you son of a bitch, I thought, I hope you enjoy the hell out of this. You suspected something on the first day, and now you've got the proof. "Do you have any library fines or lab fees?" he asked. I shook my head. "Well, that should just about do it, then." He leaned back, studying me. "Would you find it strange if I said I'm sorry to see you leave?"

I started in surprise. "Hell, yes!"

He gave me a rueful smile. "I imagine you would. It's not my habit to apologize for how I do my job—I don't think there's need very often—but I'm sorry that I didn't get to know you a little better. Your aunt told me some things this morning that I wish I'd known before."

What the hell was going on? "Like what?"

"Well, I wish I'd known that you came from a background where alcohol abuse was a major factor."

I bristled. "That's pretty personal, Mr. Dowdy. If I'm finished here—"

He held up a palm. "Yes, it's very personal. But I come from that kind of background too. We have something in common. However, you've got an advantage. It took me until I was forty years old and an alcoholic myself before I figured out what had been bugging me all those years. You've got a chance to get your life together a lot earlier."

"Mom didn't screw up my life, I did."

He fixed me with a long look. "You may think so, but I doubt it. I want to tell you one thing straight out. And, believe me, I say it as one who's been there. You don't understand what's happened to you growing up in an alcoholic home. It warps a person's outlook. Right now, you don't understand the real reasons for what's happened to you. But there are books that can help you, there are organizations that can help you, and there are people who can help you. I hope you find them."

We stared at each other for a long moment. "Am I all checked out now?" I asked.

"You're free to go." He stuck out a hand. "Good luck."

I took it, but let it go before he could do any warm-squeeze number. At the door, I turned. "Mr. Dowdy, just lay off Aunt June, huh? She doesn't need your harassment. She's a darn good person."

He looked at me in surprise, then he laughed. "Well, I know that. We've been friends for fifteen years. Sure, we have our differences and get on each other's nerves now and then. But it's never anything serious. Heck, you've got to have something to do around a small school or you'd go nuts. Believe me, your aunt and I are good friends."

I stared at him. My God, he wasn't kidding. I mumbled, "I guess I didn't understand that."

"Don't take everything so seriously. Now, good luck. We'll look forward to seeing you again." He was still chuckling when I left the office.

Uncle Glen was waiting by the outside doors. "Hi. All set?"

"Ya," I said. "Let's get out of here."

He glanced down the hall. "June said she'd be here to say good-bye."

"I already said good-bye to her, Uncle Glen. Doing it again isn't going to make things any easier." He shrugged, and we headed for the parking lot.

In Aunt June's little Chevy, he said, "Well, it looks like we'll have clear roads, anyway."

I nodded. He got the car started and pulled out of the lot. As we passed the school, I looked up at the windows of the third floor. First period was over, and the halls were crowded. Suddenly, the door on the ground floor crashed open and a big girl, who carried her books like a boy, burst through to look up and down the street. Signa saw us and waved frantically. I looked away, as if I hadn't seen her. In the side mirror, I saw her slowly lower her hand. She hugged her books to her chest and stood looking after us. I watched until her image faded into the shadows of the building, then turned my eyes to the road ahead, lying chill and hard in the cold morning light.

We pulled up in front of the Bergstrom foster home in midafternoon. Mullan's beat-up Volvo stood in the driveway—the praying mantis was already waiting for the fly. Mrs. Bergstrom opened the door and gave me a big smile. "Hello, Carl. Nice to see you again." She extended a hand to Uncle Glen. "I'm Marjory Bergstrom, the foster mother."

Inside, Mullan was seated at the kitchen table with a kid maybe twelve. The kid's eyes were red from crying. "Hi, champ," Mullan said. "Be with you in a minute." We stood in the alcove while Mullan talked to the kid in a low voice. The kid nodded a couple of times. Mullan stood, slapped him on the shoulder, and came to introduce himself to Uncle Glen. The kid disappeared into the next room.

We sat at the table. As usual, Mrs. Bergstrom got busy making coffee. "So," Mullan said, "how was life in the north woods?"

"OK," I said, then added, "I had a good time."

"Good." He opened a folder. "Well, now you're back, and we've got some new problems." He pursed his lips. "Quite a few new problems. I talked to a detective this afternoon. Let's see, where's his name? Milshevski. He wants to see you in the morning. You'll probably stay here through the weekend. Maybe longer. They're still trying to find your friend Sheridan, and until they do, they're going to want you close by." He looked at Uncle Glen. "How long are you going to be staying, sir?"

"Uh, I don't know. I have to work on Monday."

I broke in. "Go back as soon as you can, Uncle Glen. You can't do any good here."

I think that was a relief to him. "Well, I should see my sister, but after that, I might leave if there's no point in staying. You can always call me, and I'll come down."

Mullan nodded. "I'd suggest that you two visit the halfway house tonight. I think it would be appropriate for Carl to talk to his mother before he has any more interviews with the police. I can take Carl to the station tomorrow if you want to get going in good season."

Uncle Glen shifted uncomfortably. "If that's OK with Carl."

"It's OK with me," I said.

Mullan dug a form from his folder. "OK, Carl, I want to be sure you understand your rights. Listen carefully."

"I know them by heart."

"Good, but you still have to listen." Again, I had to sign the form saying I'd been given my rights. He arranged papers, then fixed me with a long gaze. "Now, I need to know just one thing. And it could make a lot of difference. Did you or your buddies ever hurt anybody physically?"

"No. I mean, not that I know of. I never went out on the jobs; I just fixed the stuff and got it ready to sell."

"And none of the others ever mentioned anything violent to you?"

"No. Steve was the only one I ever talked to, and he never said anything about that sort of thing."

"Would he have told you?"

"I think so." I hesitated. "On second thought, maybe not. But I don't think Steve's really the violent type. He talks tough, but I think he'd rather run than fight."

"And the others?"

"I really don't know them. But I think they'd run too. Uh, what's going on?"

"I can't tell you that right now. You'll probably find out when the detective talks to you in the morning."

"But—"

"Nope. Sorry, but that's the way it's gotta be. I'll see you in the morning."

———

Before we left for the halfway house, Mrs. Bergstrom told Uncle Glen that he could stay the night, since she only had one other foster kid at the moment and lots of room. She grinned at me. "You keep missing the fun crowd—all those punks with purple and orange hair, spiked bracelets, and safety pins through their noses." I wasn't in the mood for her humor and just nodded stiffly. That didn't faze her, of course.

None of the questions about something violent made any sense. What the hell had happened? During the drive to the halfway house, I must have come up with a half dozen different theories, but none of them worked. After a while, I couldn't keep my mind on it. Suddenly, I heard myself ask, "Uncle Glen, what do you think of Dowdy?"

He laughed. "What brings him to mind?"

"Just something he said."

"Well, I don't know. Ed's OK, I guess. He's not the brightest bear in the woods, but I think he does a pretty good job."

"And he and Aunt June don't hate each other?"

He laughed again. "No, nothing like that. They just irritate each other now and then. Sometimes I think they do it for fun."

"Well, Bob seems to think—"

"Oh, Bob just likes to be dramatic. You've got to take what he says with a grain of salt. Better help me out here; I think I'm about to get lost."

I gave him directions, then went back to trying to figure out why I'd been so paranoid about Dowdy. All along, I'd been positive the bastard was out to get me. But when I replayed everything he'd ever said to me, I couldn't find anything very threatening. My God, I was losing my grip on reality. If Dowdy wasn't a bad guy, then who was and who wasn't?

Mom hugged me, her eyes teary. "Baby, you look great. You've put on some weight." She turned to hug Uncle Glen. "Thanks for coming, Glen."

"Sure, sis. How you feeling?"

"Good. Real good." She wiped her cheeks and tried to laugh. "How do you like my two-tone hair?" She ran her fingers through it.

He grinned. "It's different. You'll probably set a new style."

She looked at me. "Do you like it short, baby?"

"It's nice, Mom. It suits you."

"Well, sit down. I'll get us some Cokes." She disappeared.

We sat on folding chairs at a card table. Uncle Glen reached over and slapped my knee. "Hang in there," he said.

Mom brought the pop, then rattled on for ten minutes about the halfway house, her new friends, and how good the therapy sessions made her feel. Finally, I had to break in or go crazy. "Mom, I'm in a lot of trouble."

She reached for my hand, her eyes filling again. "I know you are, baby. And it's all my fault."

"Don't talk like that, Mom! It's not your fault, it's mine." I took a deep breath. "Look, I've got to give you the whole picture." That took me fifteen minutes. She cried some, but I was surprised how well she held together. I finished by telling her the questions Mullan had asked. "Believe me, Mom, I don't know what they're talking about. I never did anything violent. And if the other guys did, no one ever told me."

"I believe you, baby. I know you never could. You're not like me."

"Mom, just stop that!" With an effort, I got my voice under control. "Look, just don't go on some guilt trip that's going to get you drinking again. I can't be responsible for that."

"That's not going to happen, baby. I'm done with drinking. I've hurt too many people already." We sat in silence for a long minute. Finally, she said quietly, "It'll be all right, baby. You're cooperating with the police, and it's your first time. They'll let you off easy. And I'll be out of here soon. We'll make a new start."

I nodded, not looking at her. Ya, when I get out of prison. Uncle Glen cleared his throat. "Well, sis, I think we'd better get going. We need to eat and get straightened out at that foster home."

"Are you going to the police station with my baby in the morning?"

He hesitated. "Ya, sure. I'll do that."

We stopped at a McDonald's on the way back, neither of us saying much while we ate. When we got back to the foster home, Mrs. Bergstrom said, "A girl called for you, Carl. She wants you to call collect."

Signa. "I don't want to talk to her. If she calls again, just tell her I can't talk to anybody."

"Nope. I don't do brush-offs. You'll have to tell her yourself." I glared at her. She grinned. "Things haven't changed a bit around here."

I waited a half hour, then called Signa. She answered on the first ring. "Hi, chum. Hey, I've heard of some strange ways to dump a girl, but you found a new one."

"Come on, give me a break, Signa. I—"

"I'll break your head if you ever try it again."

I sighed. "Bob talked to you, right?"

"Ya, he told me you've got your tail in hot water over

some stuff you did down there. But that doesn't make any difference to him, and it doesn't make any difference to me."

How could I make her see? "Look, Signa, I was the brains of a gang that stole thousands of dollars' worth—"

Her voice broke, and she started crying. "I don't care what you did! You're my guy, and I'm going to keep you!"

"Signa, for God's sake, stop it. It's not worth it. I'm not worth it."

"Yes, you are!"

I leaned against the counter, blinking back tears and trying to get control of my voice. "It's not going to work, Signa. You're just dreaming."

"Then that's your fault! You taught me how to believe in dreams. And I don't give them up anymore. I'm going to stick with you whether you like it or not!"

I couldn't keep the tears back anymore. "Why, Signa?"

"Because I love you, stupid."

After that, there was a pause. I wiped my eyes. God, how could I handle her? I'd never been able to handle her. Finally, I said, "Signa, I'm sorry, but I've got to hang up now. They've got this rule—"

"Not until you say you love me! And if you don't say it, I'm going to come down there and sit on you until you do."

I took a deep breath. "I love you."

"Just don't forget that, chum. Or that I love you. Call me tomorrow."

"OK."

"Promise?"

"I promise."

———

The Blaupunkt! The detective watched me. I'd expected a beefy cop who'd put me on a stool under a spotlight and hurl questions in a rasping voice. But this guy was young and slender with an easy voice and a face that looked as if it could smile. "That rings a bell, huh?"

I felt Mullan and Uncle Glen watching me. "Ya. Ya, it does. The guys got it from some hippie van back before Christmas. I asked Steve about it, and he said, 'Why? Is it something special?' And I lied, just told him I'd never seen the brand before. I mean, I knew what it was, and I knew we'd never sell it for what it was worth. So I stuck it under my bench. I was going to put it in my own car when I got one."

"So you knew it didn't come out of a van?"

"Oh, I believed him. He wouldn't have hit a BMW or a Mercedes; most of them have alarm systems. He just didn't know what he'd gotten by accident, and I wasn't about to tell him."

The cop leaned back and stared at me for a long moment. "You never hit luxury models, then?"

"Sometimes Steve would get carried away and go after a Cadillac or a Lincoln. But even he wasn't stupid enough to try the German ones. That's just asking for it."

"Can you describe the van?"

"All Steve said was that it was painted up weird. Rainbows and stuff. And I remember he said he'd spent a couple minutes looking around for stray dope but didn't find any."

The cop made a couple of notes, then started trying to punch holes in my story. At last, he seemed satisfied. I had to ask: "Uh, can you tell me what this is all about?"

He considered that. "I suppose so. That Blaupunkt was stolen from a BMW last November. The owner tried to interfere and was seriously beaten. Very seriously. He'll probably never recover completely."

"It must have been the guy who owned the van."

"Maybe. Or maybe it was your colleague, Mr. Sheridan."

"No, I'm sure Steve wouldn't have hit a BMW. He didn't know anything about Blaupunkt stereos, but he knew BMWs were poison."

"It'd be very helpful if we could talk to Mr. Sheridan. You haven't got any new ideas on where we might find him, do you?"

"Believe me, I wish I did."

The detective gazed at me for another long moment, then looked past my shoulder at Mullan. Mullan must have given him some kind of nod of agreement or something. The cop said, "All right, that's it for today. I'll be in touch."

I said good-bye to Uncle Glen outside the station. He looked very relieved. "Well, the mystery's solved. Once they catch that Sheridan kid, I think you'll be out of the woods."

If they caught him, and if they believed us. "Part of the way, I guess."

Uncle Glen stuck out his hand. "Well, it's almost noon, and I should be on the road. Call every night or two. We'll come down anytime."

"Thanks, Uncle Glen." I felt my eyes start to mist, and I didn't want him to see that. "Thanks for everything."

He grinned and gave my hand a last squeeze. "Our pleasure. Just hang in there. We'll see you soon."

Not likely, I thought, as I started across the parking lot to where Mullan was waiting in his old Volvo.

———————

I could see the footprints left by the police in the un-shoveled snow at the back of our house. The door stuck for a second, and inside, the house smelled stale and empty. Mullan sat at the kitchen table and leaned back. "I'll only be a few minutes," I told him.

"Take your time."

I took a deep breath and started down the basement steps. I was hoping that the cops had left my equipment alone, but not a screwdriver remained on my work-bench. They'd emptied my dresser drawers on the bed and pawed through all my clothes and junk. They'd even overturned my box of old toys and left them in a jumbled pile in the middle of the floor.

For a few minutes, I sat on my stool, looking at what was left of my cave. I'd found safety here once, but the basement seemed smaller, damper, and darker now. And even with the law about to smash me, I wasn't sure I'd turn back the clock. Might-have-beens began slither-ing through my brain. Damn, I had to get out of here. I rummaged through the heap of clothes on my bed, took a couple of shirts, and headed for the stairs.

Mullan opened his eyes and stretched. "That all you're taking?"

"I couldn't find much; they got everything worth a damn." Mullan didn't reply, just sat watching me with his hands behind his head. I sat. "You don't seem very surprised to see me in all this shit."

"Not really. I figured you were hiding something. So did one of the school counselors I talked to before you went north. Naiman, I think his name was. At first, I thought it was drugs, but your high-school record seemed too good for a doper's. Still, I had a hunch you were into something."

"Why?"

He shrugged. "Experience, champ. Kids from screwed-up homes are usually screwed up in one way or another."

For a second, I had the irrational urge to snap: Who says this home was screwed up? Instead, I just nodded. For a long minute, we sat in silence. The back legs of Mullan's chair made a soft squeak as he rocked back and forth. "I thought I could beat it," I said. "I thought I could make it out of here and have a life of my own."

"You still can."

"Like hell. I won't get my scholarship or go to college now. I was going to be an engineer. Now I'll end up being just another loser."

He raised his eyebrows and let them drop. "Sounds like a cliché, champ, but if you want to win bad enough, you'll win. Want to lose, and you'll lose."

"Oh, come on. How can I beat this thing? The cops are going to nail me to a wall."

"Oh, I don't think you can beat it. You're going to have to pay. Maybe you'll spend some time at Lincoln Hills, or maybe they'll let you off with court supervision and restitution." He let the front legs of the chair fall to the floor, and his eyes suddenly lost their lazy look. "But that's not the big deal here, champ. What's important is getting your head straight. You're screwed up. Haven't you figured that out yet?"

The sudden intensity in his eyes threw me off. I fumbled. "Hey, I didn't ask—"

"Well, let me spell it out for you, champ. There was never a doubt you were going to get nailed for this crap. I've seen a lot of amateur crime, but this was really amateur. Really dumb. You may think you're a bright guy, and maybe you are in a lot of ways, but this . . ." He shook his head. "This was crap from the word go. Just

214

crap. Sooner or later you were going to get caught. Period."

I felt myself redden. "Wait a second! Don't give me some shit about wanting to get caught. I won't buy that."

"Oh, I'm not saying you wanted to get caught. I'm saying you really didn't give a damn one way or the other. Deep down, you never believed in those fancy plans of yours. You figured that sooner or later everything was going to go to hell on you, so you stopped caring what happened."

"Well, what the hell was I supposed to think? You try living with—" I stopped, the rest of the sentence frozen on my lips.

Mullan leaned back. After a pause, he said quietly, "Well, that might be the question, champ: What are you supposed to think? You're screwed up. Right now, you don't know what to think or even how to think. You're going to have to get your head straight. Then maybe, just maybe, you can start making those plans of yours more than a bunch of crap you told yourself to keep from going crazy."

I looked down at the floor, and my voice sounded like a little kid's. "I don't think I like this."

"Probably not. But once you know life's gotten you screwed up, you can do something about it. And, by the way, you ain't the Lone Ranger. Other people have been there too."

"Like you?"

"Maybe. Maybe not. It doesn't make a lot of difference, does it? It's you who's got the head problem right now."

I stared at the floor for maybe five minutes, listening to Mullan slowly rocking. Finally, I straightened. "I don't know. Maybe you're right."

"It's been known to happen. You think about it, and we'll talk on Monday." He unfolded his long frame from the chair. "Sure you got all you want here?"

I fought the whole idea. Dowdy had said much the same thing, but what the hell did that dumb bastard know? But hearing it from Mullan shook me. He was one tough son of a bitch who'd seen a lot. And if he was right, if I was really that screwed up, what the hell could I do about it?

There weren't any easy answers. I wanted to stew by myself until some things boiled to the top. But brooding wasn't on the schedule in Mrs. Bergstrom's house. I wasn't back ten minutes when she announced it would be a "stimulating activity" for me to help Jeff, the other foster kid, with his math homework. Friday night, she led another assault on the grocery store. Jeff, her kids, and I pounded along in her wake, aware that any second she might heave a can, box, or bottle back to us.

The phone was ringing when we stumbled in under a load of heavy bags. Mrs. Bergstrom picked it up. "For you," she said. "Young and female. Remember, only five minutes; I let you off easy last night."

I couldn't conduct much of a conversation with Signa while everybody was unpacking groceries around me. At the end of my five minutes, I turned my back on them and whispered, "I love you." I hung up and found Mrs. Bergstrom grinning at me. I reddened. She winked. "Don't step on that box of spaghetti."

It snowed late that night. At breakfast, Mrs. Bergstrom looked at me and Jeff. "See that white stuff out there? That's called an opportunity. Do my sidewalk and driveway first. Flat fee of five bucks. Then go see what you can extort from the neighbors." I glanced at Jeff. He gave me a helpless shrug.

He was a good kid and worked hard. Between us we made thirty bucks that morning. It was, I reflected, the first honest money I'd made in a long time.

The cops got Steve in Madison on Saturday night for a traffic violation. Mullan told me about it on the drive to the police station on Monday morning. The cops weren't much interested in me anymore. Apparently, Steve was telling the same story about the Blaupunkt, and they were now more interested in trying to find the van than talking about our theft ring.

By ten-thirty, I was sitting with Mullan in a booth at a greasy spoon. Mullan added cream to his second cup of coffee. "So, that's how it stands, champ. In a week or ten days, the court will send you a copy of that petition for determination of status. Two or three weeks after that, you'll have to appear in juvenile court. What happens then will depend on the police report, my recommendations, and how the judge is feeling that morning. Any questions?"

"Uh, what are you going to recommend?"

"I'm going to need some time to think about that." His tired blue eyes searched my face for a moment. "So, what do you want to do until the big day, champ?"

"I've got a choice?"

"Yep. You can stay in a foster home or you can go back up north."

I hesitated. I wasn't good at choices anymore. Maybe I never had been. "Mrs. Bergstrom's foster home?"

"I could probably swing that. Is that what you want to do?"

God, I just didn't know what I wanted anymore. "I guess if it's OK with everybody, I'd like to go back up north for a while."

"I checked it out this morning. Nobody's got any objections." He took a sip of coffee. "So, did you do any thinking over the weekend?"

"A little."

"And?"

"I've got to do some more. There are some people up north I can talk to."

"That sounds good. Let me know how it goes." He handed me a notecard. "I wrote down the titles of a few books on being the child of an alcoholic. You may think you're already an expert, champ, but you ain't. It'd be a real smart idea to do a little research."

I glanced at the card, then stuck it in my pocket. "Thanks. . . . So, uh, when does the bus leave for the boonies?"

He glanced at his watch. "An hour and a half. Just time to get your bag."

ONCE AGAIN I WAS RIDING A BUS UP COUNTRY. I did a lot of thinking on the trip, none of it worth much. At one point, I took out Mullan's scrawled list of books and read it carefully. Maybe he was right—maybe I really didn't understand shit about being the son of an alcoholic.

I'd seen Mom again on Sunday afternoon, when Mrs. Bergström had dropped me at the halfway house for a couple of hours. Mom had seemed happy enough, real happy as a matter of fact. She was an old hand by now, and she spent a lot of time trying to jolly up some of the newer residents. Five minutes after I got there, she dragged me over to this gray-faced skinny guy who chain-smoked cigarettes and looked as if he'd give anything for a drink. "Talk to Phil for a few minutes, while I make more coffee and fill the cookie plates. Phil, this is my baby, Carl." I shook his bony hand.

Phil seemed glad to talk. After I mentioned I'd been living in Blind River for a couple of months, he got going on the times he'd spent hunting and fishing up north. "I fished that Blind River a few times. Good trout stream, but all overgrown with tag alders and full of slippery rocks. And it's got so many twists you don't know where the hell you are half the time. No wonder they called it Blind." He paused. "It's kind of like life that way." He grinned sheepishly and looked down.

"I suppose," I said.

"But, boy, there are some fish. Once I caught a sixteen-inch brown on a . . ."

He rattled on about fishing until Mom dragged me off to meet more of her friends. In the whole two hours, we never did get a chance to talk alone. Maybe that was the way she wanted it. I don't know, but I was just as glad it worked out that way.

I put the card covered with Mullan's scrawl back into my pocket and watched the snowy fields along the interstate. Ya, maybe the s.o.b. was right, but I didn't want to read those books. That was asking too damn much. A voice inside me said, You're chickenshit, that's the problem. Well, maybe so, but I still wasn't going to read them. I closed my eyes and tried to think of something else. But they'd taken all my dreams. They'd even taken my bench equipment and my interest in electronics. Once upon a time, I'd thought of little else. Now it seemed like just one more thing I'd lost.

The bus company was having equipment problems, and I had to sit for hours in Green Bay. It was evening before I could board a bus running northwest toward Blind River. We stopped at every dreary town and crossroad, sometimes dropping off a person or a package, often just waiting for passengers who never appeared out of the March night. My anxiety level was approaching overload proportions. My God, why was I doing this to myself? The break had been clean, final. Now things could never be the same with Signa or Bob or in the home of my aunt and uncle. Soon I'd have to say goodbye again. Say good-bye, and start paying some very heavy dues for all the stupid crap I'd done.

But another part of me couldn't wait to get back. A line from a long poem we'd read in my freshman English class kept bouncing around in my head. Something about home being the place where they had to take you in. I'd been given a little time to call Blind River home again—maybe just time enough to get strong again, to get ready to face Lincoln Hills or returning to life with Mom. And I had no idea which fate I feared more.

Finally, we crossed the river, turned back east, and bumped the last few miles to the Blind River Texaco station, where I'd once had to wake Uncle Glen and Bob. The lights of the Ford flashed on and off as the bus pulled in. Signa hopped out of the passenger side. She nearly knocked me over with a running bear hug. "Hi, chum! 'Bout darn time you got back!"

She gave me a lip-bruising kiss, and I felt my rib cage give under her hug. "Ouch. God, take it easy, Signa. I missed you too."

"Sir, do you have anything under the bus?" I turned to see the bus driver hiding a smile. A couple of faces in the bus windows wore big grins.

"Uh, no. I only had the one bag."

"Good enough. Thanks for riding Greyhound."

The interruption gave Bob a chance to reach around Signa to shake my hand. "Howdy, coz. Welcome back."

God, they were good friends, the best—maybe the only—friends I'd ever had. But after the greeting, things got awkward. On the drive back, they tried to keep a conversation going on the local gossip. But there wasn't much—my arrest was probably the biggest news in six months. After the third or fourth clumsy silence, I told them what they wanted to know. And, of course, they had to get all the details. Hell, to these kids, big-time crime was Jim Halperin busting a guy for making a U-turn on the main street of Blind River. They asked questions for ten minutes after Bob had the Ford parked in our yard.

I saw Aunt June come to the window a couple of times. I looked at Signa. "They're staying up late for me. I think I'd better go in and talk to them."

"Sure, chum." She hugged me. "I'll see you in school."

Bob drove her home, and I took my bag to the house. Aunt June and Uncle Glen were all smiles, almost as if I'd returned from receiving some kind of award. We sat down, and I told them everything.

"Glen, how about a lawyer?" Aunt June said. "Maybe we ought to go to Haycroft and talk to Joe Bartlett."

"No, Aunt June," I said. "I don't want you spending a lot of money on a lawyer. Mullan says the public defender's office will give me one."

"When will you see him?"

"About half an hour before I go to court." She looked unhappy. "Look, Aunt June, they've got me cold. I'm going to plead guilty. It's that or pleading insanity, and I don't think they'll buy that." I took a deep breath and delivered the lines I'd been practicing. "I don't want you to worry. Just let me stay here for the next few weeks until I have to go again. After that, there won't be much you can do for me." Suddenly, my face scrunched up and my voice went all haywire. I almost sobbed. "Except maybe write now and then."

I was trying very hard not to bawl. Aunt June put her arms around me, and I felt Uncle Glen's big hand on my shoulder. Aunt June said, "Carl, we are going to stand by you. You and your mother. We told you that, and we mean it."

We sat like that until the Ford rumbled into the yard. Aunt June patted my back a final time. "You need some sleep. Go to bed before Bob comes in, or he'll ask you questions until midnight." I rubbed away the tears I'd tried to hide and headed for the stairs. Behind me, Aunt June said, "Oh, Glen, what are we going to do?"

The next morning, I returned to the wonderful world of Hillbilly High. When I picked up my books from the main office, a note from Dowdy lay on top of them. "Welcome back. I'm available anytime you want to talk. ESD." No thanks. Maybe he wasn't the bad guy I'd once thought, but it would be a cold day in hell before I poured out my troubles to Howdy-Dowdy. At the door to the halls, I took a deep breath. OK, here goes. Just ice the bastards.

But nobody treated me like a leper. The kids who'd said hi before still greeted me in the halls. I felt their renewed curiosity, but no one seemed inclined to throw rocks. Between English and history, Cliff damn near knocked me over with a slap on the back. "Hey, good to see you again, man."

"Uh, thanks, Cliff." I looked after him. Strange, but he was only seven feet tall these days.

Like before, Signa found me every chance she could. She linked her arm in mine, called me "chum," and walked by my side without seeming to care a bit that everybody knew I was a criminal.

After drafting, I waited for Bob at our locker. As usual, I had a book open in my hands, but I wasn't reading. Oh, hell, I might as well have a look at them. I scrawled a note: "Bob, I'm in the library."

Hillbilly High's library wasn't exactly one of the world's great research facilities, but I guess Dowdy had made sure that it contained quite a bit on alcoholism and drug abuse. I found two of the books on Mullan's list and checked them out, hoping the library aide wouldn't spread it around that I had a drunk for a parent. That's paranoia, I told myself. And even if she does, so what? Half the rest of the world knows.

I stumbled out the back door and stood shivering in the darkness. My God, that son of a bitch Mullan had been right! And Dowdy too. I didn't know shit! I lit a cigarette with shaking fingers and held it in a cupped hand against the wind. I'd met my own ghost, and he'd scared the hell out of me.

I'd started reading in the early evening, curious but not expecting to find much I didn't already know. Wrong. Dead wrong. With mounting panic, and finally horror, I began recognizing myself on damn near every page. I didn't act as an individual, I did things because I'd been programmed by the alcoholism of my parent. Hell, I wasn't an individual at all; I was a robot! And stamped in big letters on my chest were the initials C.A.—Child of an Alcoholic. They'd made millions of us.

What had finally sent me stumbling from my room was the checklist of C.A. behavior near the end of one of the books. Children of alcoholics: guess at what normal behavior is; feel different; judge themselves harshly; have difficulty having fun; take themselves seriously; lie to themselves and others; have difficulty with authority . . . On and on the list ran, and I dropped neatly into damn near every slot. I'd been programmed for every role I'd ever played. There wasn't any real me anymore; there never had been.

The coal dropped from my cigarette, burning my fingers on its way to the snow. I got another going and hunched in a corner out of the wind. I knew what I had to do. And, God, it was going to be tough—tougher than anything I'd ever imagined. But there was no turning back.

It took me ten days. I read and reread everything in the school library on alcoholism, then went to the county library in Haycroft for more. I outlined the handbooks, lined up all the neat theories, then tore off the covers and went looking for the flaws in the wiring. Maybe I'd done a lot of stupid shit in my life, but I was still one hell of a smart bastard and I was going to learn the guts of this C.A. stuff if it killed me.

All the while I hardly said a damn thing to anyone— even Signa. But inside, I was howling with rage—at Mom, at that jerk who'd been my real dad, at the law, at life, and most of all at myself for being such an ignorant bastard all these years.

It was a Friday afternoon, and I'd been hell to live with for a week and a half. Bob was behind the wheel of the Ford, babbling as usual. I rode, smoking cigarettes and staring at the landscape. I knew everybody was being patient with me, but that only pissed me off. I didn't want their patience and understanding. I wanted to be able to deal with things myself—to be the self-reliant ol' professor again. But all the stuff in those books had killed him for good.

"This is the first really good thaw," Bob said. "Look at all those dark hollows on the fields. We'll be seeing grass before you know it." I grunted and lit another cigarette. "I've got to mark today on my calendar. Did I ever tell you that I keep track of stuff like that? You know, the first thaw, the first robin, the first flock of geese, the first snow—"

"Bob, give me a break, huh? Just shut up."

He shrugged. "OK. Just talking." He started fiddling with the radio dial.

"I mean, come on, Bob. Don't you get bored up here? I mean, keeping track of the weather and the birds, for God's sake. I'd go nuts if that was all I had to think about."

Bob found a radio station he liked. "Well, there's always rock and roll."

"Don't you mean rrrrock an' rolllll? Hey, lay a little of that hillbilly talk on me."

He gave a short laugh. "Shurre 'nough, son. Aaanything you want."

"Don't humor me, Bob." He smiled slightly.

We didn't say anything more until we got home. I stopped him on the way to the back door. "Hey, Bob, I'm sorry. I didn't mean that crap. I'm just kind of nerved up right now. You know, waiting to get my court date and all."

"No problem, coz. Us hillbillies have got thick skins." He hesitated. "You want me to see if anything came today?" I nodded and leaned against the hood of the car, my stomach tight with anxiety. I dug for a cigarette, then let my hand drop without finding one. God, please give me a little more time.

Bob came out the back door, a thick envelope held away from his body. Aunt June hesitated in the doorway, then stepped through and sat down on the steps. I took the envelope from Bob. He stepped back, almost as if he expected it to explode. I ran a shaking finger under the flap and unfolded the stiff pages. "Petition for Determination of Status—Alleged Delinquent Child. Whereas, Carl W. Staggers of . . ." I scanned the text, then looked at them. "I've got to go to court in two weeks. On April first." The absurdity hit me. April Fool's Day! I began laughing so hard I had to turn away from them. I heard Aunt June start toward me. "No, I'm OK, Aunt June." I choked back my giggles and handed the papers to Bob. "Here, you guys read it. I've got to go for a walk."

They watched me as I started for the fields. "Carl," Aunt June said, "put on your boots first."

Friday-night routine: eat supper, see Bob off on his date with Debbie, wait for Mom's call, then go over to Signa's to watch TV. Mom called at the usual time and, as usual, I braced myself. Aunt June talked for a couple of minutes, but instead of calling me, she hung up. My stomach flipped over. Something had gone wrong. God, what was it this time? But Aunt June was beaming. "She's got a job, Carl. She's running a cash register at a K Mart and said she could only talk for a couple of minutes on her break. She's going to call you tomorrow morning and tell you all about it." She sat down on the couch and smiled at Uncle Glen. "That's about the best news I've heard in weeks. That means she won't be hanging around that darn bar anymore."

Uncle Glen grunted. "Ya, I was worried about that."

They both looked at me. I nodded. "That's great news," I said.

I sat stiffly in front of Signa's TV, making a show of watching the movie. As usual, she leaned back with her feet on the coffee table, her right hand wrapped around a can of pop and her left hand playing idly in the hair on the back of my head. I shook her fingers away. She gave a small sigh and took a drink from the can. "Mom's got a job," I said.

"Oh? Hey, that's good. . . . I mean, that is good, isn't it?"

"Ya, it is. Real good—except that everybody seems to be getting their shit together except me." I stared at the TV.

She let out a small noise, almost of pain. She put an arm around me. "Oh, baby, you will. You've just got to give it time."

"Please don't call me that," I said. "That's what Mom

calls me all the time, and I hate it. I hate it so goddamn much—"

"Sure, chum, sure." She pulled me against her. "Come on, give your ol' country girl a hug."

I said against the side of her neck, "I've got two weeks to get it together. The petition came today." She tightened her arms around me.

On Sunday afternoon, I was finally ready to talk to somebody. Signa and I sat with our backs against the warm face of a huge boulder on the far edge of the field that Aunt June's grandfather had cleared with horses and dynamite. The snow had melted in a circle around the boulder, and we sat half hidden in the ring of brown grass between the immovable stone and the snowdrifts still beyond its warmth.

When I started talking, she turned on her side and lay with her body just touching mine and her big blue eyes watching my face. Ever since my return, she'd waited for me to tell her things. In a way, maybe she'd waited since the first day we'd met. But I no longer had much to say. Carl Staggers—once known as the ol' professor— felt as hollow as a Chinese kite adrift in a spring gale. Paper dragon, paper tiger, paper monkey—just painted paper about to tear apart and flutter away, leaving all that had ever been inside as invisible as the wind itself.

"We've got a name," I said. "All the stupid bastards like me are called C.A.'s—children of alcoholics. We've been studied, tested, and had books written about us. I read some of those books, and it was like somebody started hitting me between the eyes with a hammer: Hey, you, stupid! Wake up! Your life's been just a bunch of bullshit dreams. This here is reality, boy. A-wham, a-wham, a-wham. Just like when that headboard on

Mom's bed used to hit the wall. Hey, stupid, listen to reality. You can't hide from it beneath headphones. This is it, so listen good."

I felt her fingers curl around mine. I took a deep breath. "I didn't tell you everything about that headboard. You see, when I was twelve or thirteen, I heard that wham-a-wham-a-wham one afternoon when I'd just gotten home from school. I was too stupid to know what was going on, so I looked in." Signa winced, the shudder traveling all the way down her body. "Mom was on the bed with this big sweaty blob of a guy on top of her. And they—"

Signa squeezed my hand so hard it hurt. "Don't," she said. "Just don't try to remember all the details."

I sat for a long moment with my eyes closed, then went on—my voice odd and distant. "When I closed that door, it was kind of like I was closing it on reality. I just wandered off into a dreamworld. I moved to the basement and started getting really heavy into electronics. It's hard to explain, but it got so electricity was all that really mattered to me. It was efficient, clean, and impersonal. I didn't have to worry about emotions or love or anything human when I dealt with it. I built this big dream around electronics. I called it the Plan, and it was going to make me happy. I was going to become an electrical engineer. Big companies were going to chase me, offering these gigabuck salaries. I was going to drive a BMW and live in this beautiful house in the suburbs. I even invented this dream girl to go along with everything else. Her name was Jennifer, and someday I was going to find her and marry her. Then we'd live happily ever after as the stars of the local country club. God, what a joke.

"But to make the Plan work, I was going to need a scholarship, and I was going to need money. The scholarship was no problem. Hell, I was already on my way to becoming class valedictorian. But money was different; money was going to be one very serious problem." I shrugged my shoulders. "So, when I got the chance, I became a crook. It seemed like a hell of a good idea at the time. I didn't give a damn about the law, and I figured I was too smart to get caught. But I was bullshitting myself. And you can't do that forever. Sooner or later, reality hits you between the eyes and you've got to wake up."

I paused, trying to get everything straight in my head. "I guess it's been trying to wake me up for a long time, but even getting busted didn't really do it. It was reading those damn books. That's how I learned that all my dreams were bullshit. And now I've got nothing left. Hell, I don't even know who I am anymore. I'm not sure I ever knew. The last couple of years, I've been really schizoid. Half the time I've thought of myself as a nerd, just this gray slug hiding in a basement. But the other half of the time, I've been the ol' professor, this super intellect with a stainless-steel heart and frozen methane for blood. The ol' professor didn't need friendship or love or any of that emotional crap. He was different, so different that he didn't have to play by anybody's rules but his own.

"But those books say I'm just another stupid C.A. I follow a pattern. My mother's screwed up, so I'm screwed up. I'm programmed to fail, because failure's all I've ever seen. Mullan told me that I never really believed in my dreams—that they were just crap I told myself to keep from going crazy while I waited for life to go to hell. I didn't want to believe him, but he was right. Now I look back at that crap Steve and I did, and I can't believe how dumb I was. I really didn't give a damn if I got caught or not."

I paused for a long moment, staring at the high blue of the sky. "Why?" she asked softly. "Why did you stop giving a damn?"

I sighed. "I don't know. It's all tied up with Mom, I guess. For years, I thought if I could just love her enough, she'd stop drinking. But it never worked. No matter how hard I tried, she just never stopped. And I knew that drinking was going to kill her. Maybe she'd pick up the wrong guy, and he'd cut her throat. Or maybe she'd wrap the car around a telephone pole. Or maybe her liver would just give out. But, sooner or later, she was going to end up dead. And if I was such a worthless bastard that I couldn't save my own mother, why should I bother to give a damn about anything, including myself?"

Her hand tightened on mine. "Do you give a damn now?"

I had to swallow a lump in my throat. "Ya, I do. But it's too late. If I'd read those books a year ago, I might have realized what was happening. Maybe I could have gotten out of the theft ring in time. Maybe I could have saved something of the Plan. At least, maybe I could have saved a little bit of myself. Something that I could build on. But now, I'm screwed. I'll go to Lincoln Hills or home to Mom. Either way, I'll never make it to college."

I paused. I had to say this, had to try one last time to make her see. "Signa, I'm a loser. That's what happens to C.A.'s who don't figure things out in time. They become losers like their parents. I'm going to be a loser all my life. Hell, I've even got a loser name. Staggers. I'm going to stagger through my life. I'll probably end up just another drunk like Mom. It's a pattern, a program, and it's too late for me to break it."

Neither of us spoke for maybe five minutes. The sun

beat on the boulder. The ring of snow receded a few more microns. "Are you finished?" she asked.

"I haven't got another damn thing to say."

She pushed herself up. "Good." She dug in my breast pocket for a cigarette and stuck it between my lips.

"What's this? You never let me—"

"I thought you'd like a last one." She struck a match and held it to the cigarette. "Enjoy." She got up, kicked a hole in the snowbank, and started pounding handfuls of snow into hard, lethal snowballs.

"Signa, what are—"

"Just shut up and smoke that cigarette. And write down the address of that Jennifer bimbo. After I'm done with you, I'm—"

"Hey, she was just make-believe. Just a—"

"Oh, sure. You thought you could two-time this ol' country girl." She turned and fired a snowball that splattered inches from my head. "That one was just for practice! Smoke fast, sucker. About ten more seconds and—"

I jumped up. "Signa, I just told you my deepest—" A snowball zinged by my ear and I ran.

"And another thing," she yelled, "what's this crap about being a nerd? Do I look like the kind of girl who'd go out with a nerd?" She was firing snowballs like a machine gun, and I was jumping and dodging, unable to get in a single sane word. "You're no nerd, you're a two-timing louse!"

She ran out of snowballs and charged. And, boy, could she run fast. I dodged her a couple of times, but then she got a hand on my collar, jumped on my back, and rode me headlong into the snow. She pinned me with her knees, one hand shaking me by the collar, the other trying to wash my face with snow. "Are you going to give her up?" she yelled. "Promise never to see her or phone her or write her or even think of her again?

Huh? Are you going to do that, boy? Because if you don't, you're going to die right here."

"I'll give her up. I'll give her up. I promise." I was laughing so hard I couldn't catch my breath.

Signa let me roll over but kept her weight squarely on my chest. I'd never seen her eyes so blue, so fierce. She pulled my head up and kissed me hard. "And one last thing, chum. You ever call yourself a loser again, and I will kill you. That's a promise. Signa Amundsen doesn't go out with losers, so you can't be one. Period. Now say, I am not a loser."

"I am not a loser."

"Make it sincere."

"I am *not* a loser."

"That's better." She let go of my collar and came down into my arms. "I'm going to love you, chum. And you can't be a loser if I love you."

I didn't say anything, but held her close and stared at the sky—a sky dark blue as evening came on. A blue like her eyes. Signa, if love could just do it, I thought. But it doesn't. It's never quite enough. I'm sorry, but reality gets you in the end. You'll learn that soon.

On the walk back, she pulled me close to her side. "Don't get me wrong, chum. I know you said a lot of important things. Real deep things. I know you believe you've got everything figured out. But I think it's going to take more time. Like your plan. I don't think it was all bullshit. You can save some of it, but it's going to take time for you to get things worked out."

"Time is the one thing I don't have."

She didn't say anything for a minute. "Chum, maybe they won't send you to that Lincoln Hills place. Or at least not for very long." She hesitated. "Then you could come back up here, instead of living with your mother."

I shook my head. "No, I couldn't do that."

"Why not?"

I sighed. "Because she's my mother. No matter what she's done, she's still my mother. And this time, she's really trying to get well. I can't just say, 'Hey, Mom, I've got this girl up north, so I'm going back to live with Aunt June and Uncle Glen.' No, I owe her more than that."

We walked on across the field, the thawing snow wet under our boots. "I didn't mean to sound selfish, chum. I think you ought to come back here for yourself. Because you need some time."

I hugged her. "I know you're not selfish. But I couldn't come back. Not even if they gave me the chance."

But, God, it was tough. Every day I spent in Blind River, every day I had with Signa and the rest of them made it tougher. The closer I got to going, the more I began seeing how much I was going to lose. I held tight to each day, trying to make it last forever, but time just rolled by faster and the pain just got worse, until I was almost looking forward to putting the going behind me.

I had only a week left in Blind River when I came in from school the next Thursday. Aunt June was getting supper ready. "Your social worker wants you to call."

I got through the social-services switchboard, and Mullan's lazy voice came on the line. "Hi, champ. How're things going up there?"

"OK," I said. "I read a couple of those books you recommended."

"Help any?"

I shifted uncomfortably. "I guess I understand some

things a little better." I hesitated. "Anyway, I'm working on it. So, uh, do you have good news or bad?"

He sighed; he'd wanted more. They all wanted more than I could give. "Well, a little of both. I've finished investigating your case, and I'm going to recommend against sending you to Lincoln Hills. Instead, I'm going to ask the court to put you under supervision and require you to pay restitution. Now that's not the final word, champ. I've known judges to overrule social-services recommendations, but the chances are good you won't do any time. That's the good news. The bad news is that you and your buddies are going to have a whopper of a restitution bill, three thousand bucks apiece. That you didn't do any of the actual stealing doesn't make any difference under the law. You're going to get hit just as hard as the others. Harder, if you consider that you're also going to lose that nifty little bank account of yours and all your electronics equipment."

I took a breath. "I bought most of that equipment before I got involved. I collected a hell of a lot of cans to get the money."

"Doesn't make any difference, champ. That equipment was used in the commission of a crime. They're going to sell it and put the money into the restitution account. And none of the money they make at the sheriff's sale will knock a dime off the three thousand you owe. You're out of the electronics business, honest or dishonest. Better start thinking about getting back into collecting cans." He waited. "Well, how you taking this, champ? Still there?"

"Ya, I'm still here."

His voice softened. "Now, look. I said that you were going to have to pay. Now you know how much. But getting your head straight is still the most important thing. Agree?"

"I guess."

"OK, let's assume the judge goes along with my rec-ommendations. Where do you want to go afterward?"

My future stared me in the face. I took a deep breath. "Back to my mother's."

"Sure about that, champ? Things could get pretty rough back here. You'll have to make a new start in school. You'll have to get a job to pay off that three thousand. And you'll have your mother's problems to worry about. It's going to be a little tough to get your head straight with all that going on. Seems to me it might be smarter to stay up north for a while, where you've got some people who can help you out a little."

Don't do this to me, Mullan, I thought. God, this hurts enough already. "Ya, I've thought about all that stuff. But I've still got to go home. Mom needs me."

"Now, look, champ. She's—"

"Mr. Mullan, I really don't have any choice. I've got to help her if I can."

He sighed, sounding very tired. "OK, I'll recommend that the court release you into your mother's custody. I talked to her counselor yesterday, and he said she'll probably be ready to leave the halfway house in about three weeks. That means you'll have two weeks between your court date and her release. Where do you want to spend them?"

I hesitated. "Could I go to Mrs. Bergstrom's?"

"No problem. But why not go back to your aunt and uncle's?"

"I can't keep going through these good-byes. They just hurt too damn much. I've got to get out of here for good."

"Okeydoke. Mrs. Bergstrom's it is. I'll talk to the counselor at the halfway house and arrange to get you

236

into some of the family-counseling sessions. I'm also going to recommend to the court that you be required to attend Alateen or some other form of group therapy during your supervision period."

"Do I have a choice on that?"

"Well, champ, I understand that Lincoln Hills has a pretty good program. Other than that, I can't think of one."

"I get the picture."

"Good for you. Well, I'll see you in court a week from tomorrow. Let me speak to your aunt for a second if she's around."

"Sure," I said.

Well, I wasn't going to Lincoln Hills, but somehow any feeling of elation escaped me.

I had a pretty good guess what Mullan and Aunt June talked about. After supper, Aunt June and Uncle Glen sat me down for a talk. "Carl," Aunt June said, "are you sure you want to live with your mother? I mean, I know you've got a lot of loyalty and love for her, but—"

"I'm sure, Aunt June."

"Carl, she's going through some difficult times of her own. Maybe it'd be better if you came back here."

I looked down and shook my head. Uncle Glen tried. "Son, we think—"

"That's the problem! I'm not your son." I glared at them, not sure if I wanted to cry or get mad. "Look, I really appreciate all you've done for me, but I can't stay here. Maybe Mom and I have gotten our lives pretty screwed up, but we're a team. Maybe a lousy team, but still a team. I can't leave her now! Not when she's got a chance to get off the booze for good."

"Carl," Aunt June said, "when you first came up here, you were mad as the dickens at her. You could hardly stand to talk to her on the phone."

"I know, I know. I was wrong about that. I was wrong about a lot of things. She was sick, and I really didn't understand that. But now she's trying to get better. If she'd had a heart attack or something, I'd stick with her. This isn't any different." I searched their faces—they weren't convinced. "Can't you see? Until I came up here, she was the only family I'd ever had. I can't walk out on her now." I got up and started for the next room. "I'm sorry, there's just nothing more to say."

Aunt June caught my hand. "Remember," she said, "you've always got a home here."

"Thanks," I said. "Thanks for everything." I passed by Bob, who was standing in the shadows beyond the door. "You need to grow bigger ears, Bob. All this eavesdropping must be a strain."

He felt his ears. "They're getting bigger already! Ma! Carl's making my ears grow."

The idiot. God, I'd miss him.

Nobody took my decision well, and they all tried to open the subject again in the next few days. Finally, I had to get a little nasty about it. Both Signa and Bob went away hurt. But I had to start getting tough again, and they'd live. I talked on the phone with Mom a couple of times—short, almost meaningless conversations: we'd have a lot of time to talk soon; we'd have some good clean fun; we'd work everything out; somehow we'd get our lives in shape.

———————

On the last Wednesday, I handed in my books at the main office of Hillbilly High. Back at the farm, Bob and I did the chores in silence. I waited until after supper to go for the milk. I'd tell Signa I could only stay a minute because Aunt June needed the milk right away. I'd promise to write, say I'd come for a visit, then walk away without looking back. Hell, she'd have a new boyfriend by summer, and I'd be long forgotten.

The eaves of the outbuildings dripped, and brown grass poked through the melting snow along the path to the top of the ridge. I shifted the twenty-two to my other hand and started the climb. For weeks now, I'd been carrying the rifle every time I went for the milk. At first, I'd taken it because of my lingering fear of bears, wolves, and crazed snipe. Later, I'd begun to toy with the idea that I might actually try to shoot a rabbit. But I'd never seen one standing still long enough until that night.

He was a big snowshoe, his white winter coat mottled with brown. He crouched maybe fifteen yards from the path, his tiny rabbit brain fixed on the idea that I would pass by without seeing him. I steadied the rifle, the sight lining up with the narrow space between the dark, unblinking eyes. They seemed to shine, to throw back the light of the rising moon. My finger tightened on the trigger, then I jerked the barrel to the side and sent the bullet snapping into the snow a foot from his head. The snowshoe leaped six feet in a bound, and his powerful hind legs sent him careening across the snow. "Run, you bastard," I yelled. "Outrun everything." I sent a second shot high over him and stood gasping for breath as the rabbit disappeared into the shadows cast by the moon on the ridge.

———

Signa set the milk bottles on the front step beside the rifle and the knapsack. "So this is it," she said.

I'd already told her all I'd planned to say. "Ya, I guess so."

"Chum, are you sure—"

"Just don't start on it, Signa. It can't do any good."

She brushed a couple of tears from her cheeks. "You promise to write and to come and see me?"

"Ya, I promise," I lied.

For a long minute we stood there, the spring night around us. Suddenly, she grinned. "Have you ever necked in a hayloft?"

"Uh, no. But Aunt June needs—"

"Come on. If this experience doesn't make you want to come back, nothing will."

Bob's voice was a mixture of whine and anger. "Ma, I've got a right to come! He's my cousin, and he's my friend. I can miss a couple of days of school for him."

"Bob! You know somebody's got to gather the eggs and keep the fire going so the pipes don't freeze."

He grumped. "Oh, hell. Well, OK. Debbie and I can manage, I guess. But I still think you ought to let me come."

Slick, Bob. Damn slick. I closed the porch door quietly behind me. Aunt June hesitated. "I don't think you ought to have her over here with nobody else around."

"Ma, we'll be so busy gathering the eggs and keeping the fire—"

She let out an exasperated sigh. "Glen, do you think the Amundsens would come over and do the chores while we're gone?"

"I told you they would." Uncle Glen was trying hard

not to laugh. I stamped my feet on the rug by the kitchen door and went in to the warmth.

Mom and I sat on one side of the table in a tiny cubicle a few yards from the courtroom. The public defender paged through a folder labeled "Staggers, Carl W. (juv. off.)." He asked me a question every now and then, but mostly he just read. Finally, he turned back to the social-services report. "They're going to play hardball on the restitution. But none of this is carved in stone; we can always try to get a reduction."

Mom looked at me. She wore a modest dress, only a little makeup, and her hair was a short, even brown. My mother, the drunken floozy, now looked like a middle-class housewife whose kid had somehow wandered into bad company. "What do you think, baby?"

"Could we win?" I asked.

The public defender shifted his pudgy body on the hard wooden chair. "I never tell anybody they can't win. But—" He shrugged his shoulders. "From the look of things, I'd say this is about as good a deal as you're going to get. This judge is pretty tough on juvenile offenders, and I'm not sure I'd want to push him any."

I nodded. "Well, let's just see if he'll take Mullan's recommendations."

"OK." He glanced at his watch. "Let's go."

The public defender showed me to a seat at a table in the front of the courtroom. "Sit tight. It'll be a couple of minutes." He went over to talk to the assistant district attorney, who was standing near the court reporter and a couple of other middle-aged fat men. They all smiled and joked—just a bunch of good old boys going through the daily routine. Mullan, who'd been sitting in the front row with his eyes closed, levered himself up and joined them.

I glanced back to where Mom sat with Aunt June and Uncle Glen. Mom gave me a small wave and what I guess was supposed to be an encouraging smile. Hell, she'd been in court before; it wasn't so bad. Aunt June and Uncle Glen looked uncomfortable but tried to put on smiles. Suddenly, I wished very much that Bob had been allowed to stay. He would have made some kind of face to break the tension. But the bailiff hadn't even let him sit down. Probably Bob and Mom's friend from the halfway house had their ears plastered to the tall doors at the rear of the courtroom.

We were in maybe the smallest courtroom in the building, but those doors seemed a mile away, their height distorted by the distance. My mind started to wobble. Nothing around me was real anymore. I wasn't real anymore. Professor, where are you? Can't you help me just this one last time? No answer. I sat alone with all the fear and sadness about to shatter me into a billion tiny pieces.

The door to the left of the judge's bench opened. "All rise," the clerk called loudly. "This session of . . ."

The public defender scurried back to my side while the judge, a big black guy well past sixty, made his way slowly up the steps to the bench. He surveyed us, stopping to fix me with a probing gaze. Then he rapped the gavel and boomed, "Be seated." He began to shuffle through the papers before him.

The assistant D.A. started, "Your Honor, the state is presenting a petition for determination of status for an alleged delinquent child, Carl William Staggers. . . ." He went on for a couple of minutes, stating what everybody already knew, then sat down.

My lawyer stood. "Your Honor, we have no defense to

present to the charges. However, we would ask that the defendant's clean record and good character be considered. His mother, aunt, and uncle are present and can testify to his character if you deem necessary."

The judge harrumphed, obviously unimpressed. "Swear Master Staggers." I stood before the witness chair with my hand shaking violently as the clerk swore me in. I sat, and the judge looked down at me. He was huge, as big as a mountain. "Do you understand why you're here?"

"Yes, sir."

"You admit to the charges?"

"Yes, sir."

"Why did you do these things?"

I hesitated. Because of my mother. . . . Because I never had a dad except this fantasy cowboy. . . . Because I had this plan. . . . Because there was this girl named Jennifer waiting for me somewhere. . . . "I don't know. I must have been crazy." I looked at the floor. That wasn't enough, not nearly enough. "I, uh, wish I hadn't. I'm . . . I'm not going to do any of it again."

He gazed at me for a long moment, his huge eyes boring into me, then he turned away and slowly paged through a file. "According to the social-services report, you have an exceptional academic record. By any chance, did you think that made you too smart for the rules?"

"No. . . . Uh, well, I guess it did for a while."

He went on as if he hadn't heard me. "You wouldn't be the first bright youngster who came here with that idea. Some of them come several times before they learn different. I hope you are not one of those slow learners." He turned his gigantic head to look at me again. "Because eventually this court will teach you otherwise. Today you have a choice to make, young man. Follow society's rules, and you have a promising future ahead of you. Break those rules, and you'll come before this court to pay for that decision. And the price, Master Staggers, will be painfully high. Do you understand me?"

"Yes, sir," I squeaked.

"Am I going to see you here again?" I could only shake my head. "Very well. Today, I'll accept your assurance of that." He held up the social-services report so I could see it. "Has your attorney discussed the social-services recommendations with you?" I bobbed my head. "Do you have any problems with them?"

My pulse rate shot over the two hundred barrier and went howling off the top the chart. Goddamn it, say something, jerk! Tell him you can't— I swallowed the giant lump in my throat. "No, sir."

"Very well. You may step down."

Somehow I made it back to my seat. Mom gave me another smile: You did OK, baby. The judge leaned forward, making a couple of notes on a pad. "I can't do it," I croaked.

The public defender leaned toward me. "What?"

"I can't do it. I can't go back to live with Mom. I just—"

"Is there a problem, counselor?" The judge stared at us.

"Uh, if you'll just give us a moment, Your Honor." He leaned close, his voice a hiss. "Now what is this? We've got a court in session here, for God's sake. Now you—"

"Change your mind on something, champ?" Mullan looked down on us—tall, thin, and calm, his voice as lazy as ever.

I started whispering frantically. "Mr. Mullan, you've got to do something. I can't go back to her. I just can't risk everything on her. She might start drinking, and I can't live through that again. I couldn't stand waiting for some cop to come to tell me she's dead or—" I fought back the tears. In a second I'd start blubbering like a little kid right in front of everyone. "I just can't risk going crazy again!"

Mullan put a hand on my shoulder. "Steady, champ. Everything's going to be all right." He looked at the public defender. "Ask for a five-minute recess. I'll take it from there."

The public defender nodded and rose to ask the judge. The judge stared at the clock on the wall. "All right, five minutes. We'll make it informal. Tom—" He beckoned to the clerk. "Let's look at the schedule for the afternoon." Mullan patted me on the shoulder and went to talk to the assistant D.A.

Five minutes later, Mullan addressed the judge. "Your Honor, I would like to make a change in the social-services recommendations. Carl thinks that it would be better if he returned to his aunt and uncle's home in Blind River. I concur with that decision. I don't anticipate any difficulty in obtaining courtesy supervision of Carl from the Haycroft County Department of Social Services."

The judge looked at the assistant D.A. "Does the district attorney's office have any objection to this change?"

"No, Your Honor."

"Mrs. Staggers, do you have any objections?"

Mom looked at me, her eyes flooding with tears. She started to speak, then stopped and got to her feet. "No, Your Honor. I think it'd be better for him." She turned to look at me again.

"Very well. You may sit down, Mrs. Staggers." The judge shuffled papers a final time, then leaned forward slightly. His voice dropped to an even deeper rumble. It was the voice of the Law, and it must of scared the hell out of a lot of kids before me. "I have considered the evidence pertaining to the petition for determination of status presented by the district attorney's office and find the child Carl William Staggers delinquent. With the change noted in the record, the department of social services recommendations are adjudged reasonable, and I so order. Court will reconvene at one o'clock." He rapped the gavel and everyone stood. He was about to descend the stairs when he turned. "And good luck, young man. When you don't know what to do with yourself, go fishing. The fishing's good up there."

I tried to find something to say. Thanks or something. But he was gone before I could get control of my voice, his black robe billowing behind him as he disappeared through the door to his office.

Mullan came over and slapped me on the shoulder. "Way to go, champ. I'll be in touch. Good luck." He headed for the hall.

"Mr. Mullan." He turned. "Will you tell Mrs. Bergstrom thanks for me? Uh, tell her to watch out for those punks with the purple and orange hair and, you know, the spiked bracelets."

He grinned. "I'll do that."

The public defender shook my hand. "Good luck. You'll be getting a couple of things in the mail. Just file them." He left.

I stood alone by the table. Aunt June had taken Uncle Glen's arm, and they were nearly to the rear doors, now thrown wide by the bailiff. Mom's friend from the halfway house poked her head in. Mom called, "Just a minute, Gerri." She turned back to gaze at me.

"I'm sorry, Mom. I just couldn't—I just couldn't face it." We both moved then and met halfway, our arms around each other. "I found out some stuff, Mom. I don't understand most of it yet. But I'll never understand it if I come back to the city." I started crying.

"I know, baby. I know. I've learned a lot too." She

kissed my cheek. "I need some time too. We'll work it all out. I know we'll make it." She pulled back, holding me by the forearms and trying to look brave. "But try to have some fun, baby. You were never any good at that. Just have the right kind of fun, and everything will work out."

"You try too, Mom."

She hugged me again. "I will, baby. Don't worry about me for a while. . . . When I get straightened out, I'll come and see you guys."

"Mom, I'm never coming back."

I could feel her tears on my neck, and she hugged me tighter. "I know, baby. I know." We stood that way for a couple of minutes, then she wiped her eyes and tried to smile. "It's time to go, baby. You've got family waiting."

I SLIPPED OUT THE BACK DOOR INTO THE dawn. Down in the swamp, the birds had just begun to sing—a noise I usually found a good excuse to turn over and pull the pillow over my head. This is probably, I told myself, the craziest thing you've ever done.

I still had a few minutes to spare, so I wandered over to the woodpile to inspect yesterday's progress. Not bad, not bad at all. In another week, we'd have to order another twenty pulp cords. For a moment, I rested my hand on the splitter. It had a reassuring feel—solid and powerful. It lacked the finesse of electronic equipment, but it didn't lie to me either. A pull of the cord, and the engine would pound to life. Pressure on the control handle and the hydraulic ram would slide along the rail to push a chunk of hardwood against the welded steel blade at the far end. And, as Bob would sometimes sing out over the roar of the engine, "Snap! Crackle! POP! Rice Krispies." The idiot.

Bob had laid out the idea of going into the wood-splitting business on the ride north from Milwaukee. "First, we'll have to sell the Ford and buy a pickup."

My ears and brain were still ringing from the whoop Signa had let go when I'd told her the news over the pay phone at the courthouse. I looked at Bob. "Huh?"

"I said, 'We'll have to sell the Ford.'" And he told me his plan to pay off my restitution. He had the whole thing worked out from buying the hardwood in pulp cords to selling the split wood through the weekly newspaper. "Only one problem—we could really use another guy. Somebody who could really heave wood around. A real moose." Our eyes met, and we said it at the same time: "Cliff."

So Cliff—who was only six-four or six-five these days—came in with us. Bob ran the chain saw, I ran the splitter, and Cliff humped wood, heaving the big round chunks into a pile next to the splitter, then tossing the split wood into the pickup. Firewood Fiends Ltd.— blame that one on Bob—delivered and stacked its product in the late afternoons, after supper, and often on weekends. The days were long and hard, but Bob knew how to dicker, and we were making a decent buck by the end of June.

Every Friday, Bob divided the week's profits. Cliff pocketed his share with a satisfied grunt and an adoring look at Bob. Bob and I would take a ten or a twenty apiece for spending money, then I'd take the rest to the bank. I told Bob half a dozen times that he didn't have to put the rest of his share toward paying my restitution. But he always said, "Aw, you can pay me back someday when you're making the big bucks. Don't worry; I'm keeping track, coz." And the hillbilly probably knew how to calculate compound interest, too.

So day in and day out, we made wood. I'd never imagined growing to love bull work. But I did. I loved the rhythm of it—bend, grip the chunk, deep breath, lift, drop it clank on the rail, reach for the hydraulic control, bring the ram forward, snap-crackle-pop, ram back, throw the split wood on Cliff's pile, then bend again. . . . Within the heat, sweat, and noise I found the solitude I needed. I didn't really think much, but I knew that deep within the rhythm of the work, my mind was busy sorting, making connections, and finding smoother, easier paths.

I unscrewed the cap on the gas tank and glanced in. Enough for Cliff to get started. Firewood Fiends would be a fiend short today, while I took care of some un-finished business. I put the cap back on and started for the top of the ridge.

Signa scrambled nimbly over the fence, waved to me, and started the climb up her side of the ridge. I sat down on the grass to wait for her.

"Hi, chum. Hungry?"

"Ya, and I've got a wet ass. Why didn't you warn me about the dew?"

"Complain, complain. Here, peel these eggs while I get out the rest of the stuff." She started unpacking a breakfast that would have fed five. "How'd your meeting go last night?"

"Good. You ought to come sometime. I don't think any of the ol' Haycroft Alateens would mind. Really, they're a pretty mellow bunch."

"I'll think about it. Is there a place where we could sneak off and neck?"

"You've got sex on the brain, you know that?"

She grinned. "Only when I think of you, chum. Have a sweet roll baked by yours truly."

I ate an orange, two eggs, and three sweet rolls, then lay back on the grass in the early-morning sun. "God, I don't think I can move."

She stretched out beside me, propping her head on her hand. "So what do you think of my idea now? Breakfast on the ridge at dawn. Pretty neat, huh?"

"I can't believe I really got up this early. I need a nap."

She lifted one of my eyelids with a thumb. "Na, you're all right." She kissed me, then sat up and started gather-ing paper plates and eggshells. "Well, I guess it's about that time, chum. I've got bossies to milk, and you've got some miles to cover."

"I guess so." I stretched and sat up to help her.

Her face was serious when we said good-bye. "Well, you drive careful and stay out of trouble."

I laughed. "Everybody's acting like I'm going to Milwaukee for a month, and that I'm going to knock off a couple of banks while I'm there. Come on, I'm just going down to help Mom move and to get the rest of my stuff. Stop worrying. I'll see you tomorrow."

She glanced over her shoulder before kissing me good-bye. "Dad keeps a rifle just inside the barn. He could probably wing you even at this distance."

"I'll take my chances."

I stopped at the chicken house to gather the eggs on my way back. The rooster glared at me, and I glared back. "I warned you. Try it again and it's fried-chicken time." As usual, verbal threats did no good, so I sent him scurrying with a stamp of my foot and set about rifling the nests.

Aunt June wanted to feed me another breakfast. I told her no, thanks, and picked up my bag. "You're sure you've got everything?"

"Aunt June, I'm going to Milwaukee overnight, not on an expedition to the Amazon."

"Well, I just want to be sure."

"I've got all I need."

Outside, Uncle Glen was checking the oil in his pickup, and Bob was standing around hoping I'd change my mind and ask him to come along. Uncle Glen slammed the hood. "I think you'll be OK. Keep an eye on the temperature gauge; it's going to be a hot day."

"Uncle Glen, if you'd rather, I can take our pickup."

"No, I wouldn't trust that heap from here to town."

"Pa!" Bob yelped. "That pickup is the same age as I am, and you know that was a very good year."

"For pickups maybe." Uncle Glen winked at me and stuck out a hand. "Well, give our best to my sis. Tell her to come anytime."

"I'll do that." I shook his hand, then Bob's.

"Take it easy, coz," Bob said.

I made good time and got to our old house by eleven. Mom and her friend Gerri were already hard at the packing. Mom gave me a hug and a kiss. "Hi, baby. You're looking great. You've been in the sun a lot."

"You're looking good too, Mom. How are you feeling?"

"Real good, baby. I thought maybe this packing would be kind of sad, but I'm enjoying it. Getting rid of a lot of old trash. We're going to sell everything that doesn't fit in the apartment or into the new way of life."

Gerri called from the kitchen: "Hey, Ronnie, do you want to keep these pans or put them in the garage sale?"

"We've got enough pots and pans already. Sell 'em." Mom looked at me again. "Better grab anything you want, baby, because the rest ain't going to be around long."

I started carrying boxes to the pickup. By midafternoon, we'd moved all Mom wanted to keep. We got back to the house to find three guys from the used-furniture store wrestling the last of the furniture and appliances into a truck. The boss handed Mom a check. "Thank you, ma'am. I think we got everything that wasn't nailed down."

He left, and Mom turned to me. "You should have part of this, baby. You know, to help pay that restitution."

"You keep it, Mom. I want to handle that myself." She looked a little hurt. "But if I need help, I'll let you know."

"Ronnie, you got any more Ajax?" Gerri called.

"Just a second," Mom called. "I'd better go help her, baby. Gerri doesn't rest until she's got something licked. She used to drink a fifth a day, and she says working keeps her mind off wanting to drink again."

"Whatever works, I guess."

To my surprise, Mom actually grinned. "You bet."

I wandered through the empty rooms. A glint in the corner of the living room caught my eye. I went closer. A shard of the quartz paperweight that Mom had hurled at the tall cop lay shining in the afternoon sun. I picked it up and held it for a long moment in my palm. Maybe I should keep it—a souvenir to remind me of the past. Oh, horsecrap. I tossed it in a box of trash and went looking for some empty boxes for my stuff.

Mom came down to the basement just as I was finishing packing the last box. She started glancing into the boxes I'd marked for the garage sale. "Don't you want to keep some of this stuff?" She picked up a toy truck, hesitated, then dropped it back in the box.

"No, Mom. Just send me whatever it brings."

"I think you should keep your baseball glove. I remember the Christmas I gave it to you—"

"You're right." I took it from her and stuck it in with the last of my clothes.

She sighed and perched on my stool. "They took all your electronic stuff, huh?"

"All except the repair manuals. I guess they didn't want to mess with those."

"You're taking them?"

I nodded. "Ya, I'll get back in the business someday. The straight part of it, that is."

"Baby, I'm so sorry things didn't work out better. I know I'm responsible for all that went wrong."

I hesitated. "Mom, I'm not looking for anybody to blame anymore. My counselor is always saying, 'Take it easy.' You know, don't worry about things you can't change. I lost a bunch of test equipment, but I've still got my brain and I've still got the knack. And they'll be there when it's time for me to get back into electronics. I'm going to be OK, Mom." She sat staring at the gray concrete floor. I hesitated. "How about you, Mom? Are you going to be OK?"

She laughed a little sadly. "Oh, ya. I'll be OK. Gerri and I were just joking about how good a beer would taste right now. But I know we don't really want one." She looked up. "I guess you probably think of me as real old, but I'm not even forty yet. I've got a lot of life ahead of me." She winked at me. "I might even meet some classy guy who doesn't drink and goes to church twice on Sundays. How would you like that?"

I laughed. "How about one who doesn't drink and saves his Sunday afternoons for football or baseball games?"

"Maybe that'd be better." She got up. "Want to take the stool with you?"

"No, sell it with the rest. Let's get this junk upstairs."

I'd planned to stay overnight, but we were finished by late afternoon. "Mom," I said, "I think I'll get on the road. I can be at the farm by dark and get in a full day of work tomorrow."

She hid disappointment. "Sure, baby. All we're going to be doing is scrubbing up the place. You just drive careful, baby."

"Uh, Mom. Could we kind of give the 'baby' thing a rest? I think I've kind of outgrown that."

She smiled. "Sure. But don't expect too much too soon. Habits ain't easy to break."

"Ya, I know." I put out my arms to her. "Come see us soon, huh?"

For a while on the road, my mind wanted to crawl back into the past. But I stopped it. Not now. Take it easy.

The sun was dipping into the trees by the time I reached the wayside where the road north crossed Blind River. I stopped, used the rest room, got a drink from the hand pump, then sat down to smoke a cigarette on the riverbank. One of these days, I'd have to quit the damn things, or Bob, Signa, and Aunt June would get serious about their threats.

A station wagon pulling a tent camper came down the road from the north, swung in, and parked. Car doors opened and closed, and I heard the high voices of little kids and the deeper voice of a man. The rest-room doors banged open and shut. The man gave a tired sigh and started working the handle on the pump. The kids exploded from the rest rooms and charged over to get drinks.

I sensed someone on the bank above me and turned. Jennifer stood there in the twilight, looking at the river with a faint smile on her lips. Her husband trudged up the bank. "Well, the kids are bathroomed and watered," he said. "I looked at the map, and we've only got another thirty miles to go. Let's get the kids in the car and try to make it by dark." She leaned against him for a moment, still smiling, her gaze still on the river. He sighed and put an arm around her shoulders. They stood there together for a long minute, before turning away to call the kids.

I waited until they left before going back to the pickup. Of course, it hadn't really been Jennifer, but a slender dark-haired woman with kids. Still, I let myself think it anyway: I'm glad you're happy, Jenny. He looked like a good man.

I backed the pickup around and pointed it up country. Five miles beyond the river, the road from the south ended at a T. I turned right and, with the setting sun warm on my back, drove the last few miles home.